PETTY CRIMES and VINDICTIVE CRIMINALS

Shane Simmons

ISBN: 978-1-988954-15-8

Published by Eyestrain Productions
eyestrainproductions.com

Table of Contents

Ashes to Ashes

THE GROUNDSKEEPER THREW the last few shovelfuls of dirt onto plot eight, row thirty-nine. There was no marker at the head of the grave. The man inside the simple box six feet underfoot was an unknown, listed as "John Doe." He was one of many in the vast family Doe that consumed much space and little thought in the pauper's cemetery. Each was duly accounted for on the detailed chart which mapped out the contents of every plot in every row—just in case it ever mattered. It never did.

There was no priest or other holy man to administer the last rites. That was done weekly, en masse, back at the morgue before the accumulated collection of floaters, drug ODs, and frozen transients—unclaimed all—were put to rest in holes hollowed out by the long-tooth arm of a municipal backhoe. Total cost per client: fifty-three dollars, charged to the city's taxpayers. It was fifty-three dollars more than the government had spent on any of them when they were alive, and most of it went to pay the groundskeeper's hourly wage for filling in the holes in a neat and orderly fashion so their occupants, in death at least, would never again be an eyesore.

Besides the groundskeeper, no one ever attended the simple ceremony that saw the plain pine boxes lowered into the pre-dug pits and covered over quickly and quietly. A pair of exceptions had recently sprung up, however.

They were a young couple, urban, successful, and thirty. They came to a pauper's burial once every week or two, stood silent vigil over one of the graves as it was filled, and left a single red rose each. They both wore black, for style rather than grief, as though they planned to hit a few trendy clubs once they roared off in their dark European sports car parked down by the gate.

It was on their fifth visit to yet another anonymous grave that the groundskeeper had to ask, "You knew him?"

"Can any of us really know someone?" said the man solemnly.

"It's hard, I'll give you that," agreed the groundskeeper. "Especially when it's some heroin junkie no one bothered to claim."

"Someone's son," said the woman.

"Maybe someone's father," said the man.

"I'm sure the family would have appreciated us being here."

"I'm sure *he* would have appreciated it."

The groundskeeper couldn't quite place the tone of the couple's eulogy. He just knew it made his skin crawl. A few pats with the flat of his shovel settled the earth, and he was off on his break a moment later without pursuing further conversation.

The couple climbed back into their sleek two-seater and consulted the page of obituaries that lay folded on the dashboard. The day's highlights were all circled in red.

"That cleansed the palate," said the man. "I like these little no-name ceremonies. They lack the circus atmosphere of the priest and the family and the crying, but it's nice for a quiet change."

The woman took an inventory of their dozen fresh roses. They were now less four.

"If we wait around an hour, we can catch those two homeless people they picked out of a dumpster," suggested the man.

"No," she answered. "Let's go where the action is."

•   •   •

The funeral parlour was filled with unfamiliar faces, strangers all, including the guest of honour in the box. The couple stepped into the room and was greeted by an elderly woman hovering over a memorial album, fishing for signatures. She offered her hand, which was eagerly accepted.

"Thank you," said the old lady, "I'm glad you could make it."

The man took a pen in hand and signed the album for himself and his wife, saying, "We wouldn't have missed it for the world."

The couple's faces didn't ring any bells with the old lady. Awkwardly, she asked, "I'm sorry, I didn't know all of Edie's friends. You are...?"

The woman, still holding her hand gently, consolingly, told her, "Mr. and Mrs. Ashley Carter. And you?"

"Please, call me Louise. Ah..."

The old lady waited for a first name from the woman.

"Ashley," was the response.

"I'm sorry, you're both named...?"

"Ashley. Ashley Carter."

"That's quite unusual."

"Well, I thought I'd adopt my husband's name since I already had half of it. It makes co-signing things so much easier."

"It's very romantic," said the old lady, unsure.

"We're very close," Mrs. Carter said, as her husband took her arm and led her down the aisle to the casket.

The coffin was open as the Carters had guessed it would be. They tried to restrain their nervous anticipation as they waited impatiently in line for those seeking to pay their final respects to disperse. The queue moved at a fairly brisk pace as each person filtered past the coffin in turn, but the Carters brought traffic to a grinding halt as they lingered over the body and examined the handiwork of the funeral directors at length.

"She looked quite young," said Mr. Carter, as he laid eyes on the dead woman for the first time.

"Cancer is an ageless disease," said Mrs. Carter.

"They say she was sick a long time."

"Not a bad job, puffing her up again for show."

"Makeup job is a bit pedestrian."

"I wonder if the wig was her choice or theirs."

"I would have gone with a more summery dress."

"I wish they opened the bottom half, too," said Mrs. Carter, lamenting her favourite pet peeve, "I want to see her shoes."

● ● ●

The Carters were the very last to leave the parlour. Even the body of Ms. Edie Whoever was gone, packed into the back of a hearse for a final spin that would deliver her to the crematorium. There, the embalmer's fine work would be burned to cinders, and the bones of the deceased would be pulverized into tiny shards. Once it was all over, and Edie was safely in her urn, there would be hardly enough left of her to pot a plant.

The Carters soaked up the post-funeral ambiance, enjoying the calm silence after the storm of tears. The recorded organ music had been shut off until the next body and batch of mourners arrived.

Mrs. Carter absently checked her watch, then hissed, annoyed, "Dammit, we missed the Farkas do."

"Yes, but we're still in time for the will reading," said her husband.

"I don't know, Ashley. Will readings don't play as well for me without the eulogy and a bunch of loved ones pretending to sob before the loot is divvied up. It's like skipping dinner and going straight for dessert."

"What about your sweet tooth?"

Mrs. Carter didn't take long to give in.

"All right. We'll make an appearance. But we want to leave in time for that suicide at one."

• • •

The Carters sat together on a bench at the back of the lawyer's office. Fewer people than they had anticipated had shown up for the will reading, so they wanted to be near the door in case a hasty exit was called for. No one had questioned their presence so far, but it remained a possibility. A quick route out always helped minimize embarrassment in the event of unwelcome questions or an unexpected confrontation.

The lawyer was well into the reading, droning the details of Mr. Andrew Farkas's final wishes in as unemotional a tone as he could muster. The few friends and relations present each nodded in turn as their names were matched with a modest amount of estate plunder specified by the dead man. If anyone was happy or displeased with their inheritance, it was impossible to tell.

The reading continued like clockwork and the Carters began to fidget in their seat, bored by the lack of high drama. The only one there who offered any visible signs of emotion was a woman in her mid-forties who maintained a brave front even as a stream of tears ran down her cheeks at a steady pace. Her head tilted up slightly when her name was finally mentioned.

"To my daughter, Elaine," read the lawyer, "I leave all proceeds from the sale of the house and its contents. This is subject to the condition that all these items are put on the block and liquidated immediately upon my death."

Elaine let out a long, sad sigh that broke into quivering convulsions towards the end. It was drama to be sure, but the offering was too little too late for the Carters. Mrs. Carter leaned over to her husband and suggested, "Let's go."

"All right," he whispered, "It seems to be wrapping up. Let's make a discreet exit."

The Carters rose slowly and shuffled silently to the door. Everyone else in the room, with the exception of the lawyer at his desk, had their backs to the couple and didn't notice them leaving. Then the lawyer read the words, "To my dear friends, Mr. and Mrs. Ashley Carter..."

The whole room turned in their seats to look at the Carters. Mr. and Mrs. Carter froze in place, uncertain whether they should start apologizing or fleeing. Before they could make a firm decision one way or the other, the lawyer continued.

"To them I entrust my mortal remains. I have always found you to be a couple of exceptional taste, and believe no one is better suited to arrange for their disposal in a discriminating manner."

With this final legal decree from the dearly departed, the lawyer reached into a desk drawer and retrieved a simple plain cardboard box, fresh from the crematorium. As he placed it on the edge of his desk, the room fell silent enough to hear the soft rustling of ash inside the box. There lay the last of Andrew Farkas, waiting for the Carters to step forward and claim him.

The number of tears running down Elaine's face doubled.

• • •

The Carters' condominium was clean, modern, and manageably mortgaged. The walls were white and antiseptic, the furniture black and sparse. What personal possessions had been left on display were precisely arranged. Most were *objets d'art* from a kaleidoscope of world cultures, carefully selected so as not to draw undo attention from casual visitors. Yet each and every one pertained in some way to burial rituals and funereal practices lost and forgotten by all but the most specialized anthropologists. On the rare occasions when someone made a comment or asked which gallery they found a particular piece in, the Carters would simply exchange the smile of a couple who shared a private joke.

Today Mr. Carter added Andrew Farkas's simple box of ashes to the collection, giving it a place of honour in the centre of the mantle that overlooked their living room and dining area.

Mrs. Carter was in the bathroom, filling the tub with the cold water tap on full. She called to her husband over the sound of splashing.

"I think it was a lovely gesture just the same."

Her husband answered from the other room, "I can't argue with that. But the man was a total stranger. I mean, don't you find it odd? We never knew he existed until we read his name in the morning's obituaries."

Mrs. Carter had a champagne bucket of ice on hand, minus the champagne. Once the tub was full, she shut off the water and dumped the contents of the bucket into her bath.

"It's obvious he knew us somehow," she said.

"But from where? We don't know any old people. None living at least."

Mrs. Carter hung her robe on a peg behind the bathroom door, tucked her hair under a shower cap, and stepped into the tub. She took a deep breath as the frigid water touched her toes, but routine had prepared her for the shock. She relaxed for a moment as she stood shin-deep, then lowered herself into the water.

"He must have been keeping an eye on us somehow—from a distance—to know so much," said Mrs. Carter.

She took another deep breath and laid down in the tub, letting the iced water flow over her. Shifting to one side, making sure no ice cubes were trapped under her back, she settled to the bottom, leaving only enough of her face above the waterline to breathe.

"He knew our names," said Mr. Carter, "That's all."

"He knew we would be at the will reading. Even before we did. And he knew we had impeccable taste."

"He didn't say 'impeccable,' he said 'exceptional.' That doesn't necessarily mean good."

After only a few minutes, Mrs. Carter was out of the tub again, towelling herself off. Removing the shower cap, she began to pat her body down with baby powder from head to toe, turning her skin white.

Mr. Carter paced around the living room idly. He stopped to sprinkle a few flakes of tropical-fish food into the twenty-gallon tank that stood against a blank white wall. The fish didn't touch it. They were all dead, floating at the water's surface, or twirling around among the plastic plants at the bottom, caught in the filter's swirling current. After a few minutes, the flakes soaked up enough water to begin their slow autumn-leaf drift to the bottom where they would remain untouched. Mr. Carter noted his tetras were looking a touch threadbare. Soon he would return to the pet shop for some fresher specimens that had expired on their way to market. Even the rarest and most colourful fish in the sea could be had at a huge discount once their lifelong swim had come to an end. Mr. Carter found their beauty easier to appreciate once they were stiff and still.

There hadn't been another word from his wife for ten minutes now. Impatient, Mr. Carter called out, "You ready?"

There was no response.

Mr. Carter walked into the bedroom and found his wife lying stalk still on their plush bed, her hands folded across her chest. Mrs. Carter wore a period dress that was white, lacy, and virginal. Two Victorian pennies, double the size of their modern counterparts, rested on her closed eyelids, and her body was perfectly framed by several dozen red roses spread atop the sheets. The tableau was shrouded by a thin veil of white silk strung over the high framework of the bed, allowing only a ghostly view inside.

Pulling aside the drapes, Mr. Carter gently sat down on the edge of the bed. His fingers brushed his wife's pale cold flesh sensuously, but provoked no reaction. Reaching for a small mirror on the end table, Mr. Carter held it under his wife's nose and waited for nearly a full minute. It never fogged.

The illusion complete, Mr. Carter began to unfasten the elaborate clasps on his wife's dress and remove his own clothing.

• • •

The next day, Mr. Carter came up from the condo's lobby with the morning's mail. He leafed through it: bill, bill, bill, funeral director's trade journal, bill.

The postman had made his rounds an hour earlier, which meant it was about time for the couriers to start arriving. The Carters' building had no less than eight lawyers, seven accountants, and six senior blue-chip executives all living under the same roof, so overnight packages came daily by the dozen. It was unusual, but not unheard of, for the Carters to have a surprise package arrive from a friend, relative, or business associate at this time of day. The knock on the door by a young man in a smart red uniform announced that this would be one of those days.

Mr. Carter signed for the package—a simple square box that was neither very heavy nor very light. He looked for a return address, but the street and house number meant nothing to him. The name was another matter, however.

"Who's that from?" asked Mrs. Carter, as she came out of the bedroom sporting the day's new all-black ensemble.

"Him," was the answer she got.

"Who?"

"Him," repeated Mr. Carter, this time nodding towards the box of cremains on the mantle.

Mr. Carter tore off the strip of packing tape that fastened the box-top flaps together. Inside, among the Styrofoam chips, was an urn. Tastefully painted, with smooth sloping edges, the urn was a flawlessly fired porcelain receptacle standing a little over a foot tall. Mr. Carter held it up and looked at it skeptically. It clashed with the ultramodern flat where everything was either black or white with straight edges and sharp corners.

"Not quite what I would have chosen for my final resting place," he concluded.

"They're not *your* ashes," said Mrs. Carter. "Besides, I think it suits him."

"How do you know it suits him? We don't know a thing about the man."

Mr. Carter went to fetch Andrew Farkas's cremains from the mantle as Mrs. Carter wiped down the urn with a dish towel in the kitchen.

"On the contrary," she said, "I think we're learning more about him by the minute."

"Hold it steady," said Mr. Carter, as he removed the lid of the urn and began to carefully shake the contents of the cardboard box into their new home.

Grey ash and tiny fragments of bone that hadn't been incinerated by the intense heat of the crematorium oven poured into the urn with the sound of sifting sand. Halfway through the transfer, a metallic clink against the porcelain caught the Carters' attention.

"What was that?"

"Something that wasn't a part of Mr. Farkas," concluded Mrs. Carter.

The couple looked into the urn, but could see nothing in the collection of grey soot that used to be Andrew Farkas.

Mr. Carter opened a drawer of cutlery under the kitchen counter and produced a pair of hand-crafted chopsticks usually reserved for the arrival of Asian takeout. He reached into the urn and began fishing around in the ashes. Striking something solid, he carefully took hold of it with the tips of his chopsticks and pulled it free. Blowing the dust off, Mr. Carter dropped a plain ring into his wife's hand. Another few moments of searching through the cremains produced the ring's twin.

The Carters examined the simple bands. They weren't gold, but some duller more durable element.

"They look like wedding bands," concluded Mrs. Carter.

"How'd they get in there?"

The Carters both knew that all jewellery was routinely removed from bodies before cremation. Had Mr. Farkas been wearing them, they would have certainly been noted by the funeral home, marked down on an inventory, and returned to the family after the service.

Mrs. Carter ran through the possible explanations, but only one seemed feasible.

"He swallowed them," she said. "Before he died. In the hospital."

"Why would he do that?"

Mrs. Carter shrugged, "Hospitals are full of thieves. Especially during visiting hours. No one could get their hands on them this way."

"They must have meant a lot to him," said Mr. Carter, taking them both in hand and looking closely at their inner edges for any markings. He found what he was looking for, worn by age and heat and encrusted with ash, but still legible. There were two inscriptions, one in each ring—a short series of numerals.

Mr. Carter read the first to his wife, "One, four, comma."

This was followed by, "Eight, seven, three."

"It's hardly a declaration of undying love," he decided.

Mrs. Carter took one of the bands and slipped it onto her husband's ring finger.

"I thought we didn't do jewellery," he said.

Nevertheless, Mr. Carter followed his wife's lead and placed the other on her finger.

"These are too charmingly macabre not to wear. I let you get away with skipping the whole engagement-ring routine, so you can indulge me now."

"The price is right," smiled Mr. Carter.

"I want to know a great deal more about Mr. Farkas. How about you?"

"Where do we start?"

"Where better than the end?"

• • •

A few phone calls was all it took to determine which hospital Andrew Farkas had expired in. Claiming to represent a major insurance-company franchise was usually enough to guarantee the full cooperation of the receptionists at any medical facility. They were only too willing to transfer the Carters to the ap-propriate department, and these departments were, in turn, pleased to offer up whatever information the Carters wanted once they realized they weren't going to be badgered with the usual series of questions insurance companies were dreaded for.

It turned out the Carters were regulars at Andrew Farkas's hospital of choice, and had been going there since their third date—a magical, perfect evening of multiple code blues culmi-nating in a genuine flatline that was pronounced within earshot of the young couple. A short car ride later and they were riding the elevator down to the damp concrete corridors of the sub-basement. Loud, bustling emergency rooms or tense, dramatic surgical theatres held little fascination for them. The basement was where the real action in any hospital was. No one questioned the Carters as they made their way to the end of the hall. There wasn't a soul between the elevator and the solid metal door to stop them. What few staffers ever came down here weren't paid enough to question the presence of a well-dressed couple who looked like they knew where they were going.

Three sharp knocks on the door echoed through the corridors and fell only on deaf ears. After a lengthy wait, a series a locks and latches were heard being worked, and at last the steel-plated barrier swung in, opening a narrow crack that let some of the cold air on the other side whistle out.

Calling the scruffy man who looked through the gap a coroner would be generous to an extreme. He was an attendant—part janitor, part petty bureaucrat, in charge of light cleaning duties and the shuffling of much paperwork. He resided over his one-room empire with an unquestioned authority that can only come with the security of a seniority job, and the knowledge that there was not one other person in the entire hospital with an eye on his unenvied position.

The man said nothing, though he instantly recognized the Carters. Mr. Carter produced a fresh pack of cigarettes with a modest wad of twenties stuffed down one side and held it out for the man. The man accepted it greedily, paused long enough to inhale the pleasing scent of money and tobacco mixed, and then opened the door the rest of the way.

"Ten minutes," the man announced, telling the Carters how much privacy they had bought. He then left the pair alone together in the vast hospital morgue, shutting the door behind him as he took his legislated coffee break outside.

The Carters enjoyed the nervous thrill of anticipation they always felt when they stepped into an uncomfortably low room temperature. It was chilly enough to keep the recent arrivals fresh as they waited to be redirected to the appropriate funeral home, medical examiner, or teaching hospital, but the thermostat stopped just short of allowing the live guests to see their own breath.

"What have they got for us today?" wondered Mrs. Carter aloud, as she strolled down the wall of body drawers like a window shopper at Christmastime.

Mr. Carter snatched a clipboard that hung on a nail and read the latest. "Couple car wrecks. A floater."

Mrs. Carter stopped at a newly occupied drawer and Mr. Carter compared its number to the clipboard list.

"That's a Jane Doe. The verdict isn't in."

Grasping the handle with both hands, Mrs. Carter gave the drawer a sharp pull, opening it as far as it would go. She unzipped the body bag inside and stared down into the dead face of a young woman who had never made it out of her teens. Probably a runaway, almost certainly a prostitute, her skin was grey and clammy. The autopsy scars up and across her chest had been artlessly stitched back together in a rough manner that enticed Mrs. Carter. She ran her finger along the assembly-line cut-and-paste job some indifferent civil servant had made as required by law. The impersonal desecration to determine a cause of death no one cared to hear sent shivers through her.

"Nice," she said. "I bet he couldn't keep his hands off this one."

Mr. Carter rifled through an "out" box on the lone desk at the head of the room and pulled one of the files.

"Farkas, Andrew," he said, holding it up.

As Mrs. Carter caressed the dead woman's stitchwork, Mr. Carter scanned the file for highlights.

"He was here all right. Died just a few days ago. The body was claimed almost immediately."

"Cause of death?" asked Mrs. Carter, cutting to the chase.

"Admitted after complaining of diarrhea, severe stomach cramps. Pronounced dead six hours later."

"Sounds like the flu."

Mr. Carter looked at an additional test result clipped to the bulk of the paperwork.

"Sounds like a lot of things. They didn't narrow it down until this morning."

"What's so special about this morning?"

"The blood tests came back. Someone was paying attention and ordered a toxicology."

"And?"

"Positive for arsenic."

"An oldie but a goodie. I don't suppose the police have been tipped off."

Mr. Carter returned the file to its box and began to unbutton his shirt.

"I'm sure they'll want the body back for a full autopsy."

"That may be difficult," Mrs. Carter smirked.

Reluctantly she drew herself away from the body in the drawer—more beautiful in death than it ever could have been in life—and zipped up the bag again.

As Mr. Carter dropped his pants, his wife checked the clock on the wall.

"How are we for time?" she asked.

"Better make this quick."

"I won't be long."

Mrs. Carter shoved the body drawer back in place. By the time she turned around, Mr. Carter was lying naked and still on one of the empty stainless-steel gurneys.

Mrs. Carter approached the slab. She took a blank toe tag from a box full of them and snapped the elastic string around her husband's big toe. He didn't flinch.

Mrs. Carter pulled up her dress and climbed onto the gurney to mount her husband. In short order, she was riding him hard, the toe tag jiggling with each thrust. Her passion built steadily, but she remained distracted, talking through their concocted scene.

"It's obvious he was in the funeral club—one of the other casket chasers we always see lined up to pay their last respects to people they've never met. I've been picturing their faces all day, trying to guess which one might have been him."

Mrs. Carter ran over her mental list of these silent acquaintances she and her husband had seen at dozens of other funerals. Some they'd even become familiar enough with to exchange a look of recognition, but never a verbal greeting of any kind. That was simply not done in this antisocial circle of enthusiasts.

"There's the young woman in the old hat, the old woman with the orthopedic shoes, and the lady who's missing a joint of one of her fingers. Obviously not any of them. The men I'm not as clear on. There's that young guy who looks like he's about ready to be fitted for a box himself. There's the one who goes just to hit on widows. And the man who's probably a funeral director himself and wants to check out the competition."

There was no response from her husband, but Mrs. Carter didn't expect one while he was in character. Suddenly she had a brainstorm.

"Ah, yes! There *was* an old man. I nearly forgot, it's been so long. He liked outdoor, graveside services. He got around on a cane, but he was always alone. We haven't seen him since the weather turned cold."

Mr. Carter spoke, but kept his eyes shut.

"I remember."

"Shut up," she told him, "You're dead."

• • •

Returning to his station following his break, the attendant flicked the ash off the end of his two-thirds-smoked cigarette and pocketed it for later. Opening the door to the morgue, he found the Carters buttoning up their final articles of clothing. Mr. Carter offered the man a polite nod as he pulled on a sock.

"Call us if you get anything really messy," Mrs. Carter told him, as she slipped out into the corridor.

"I have something else you might be interested in."

The Carters stopped in the hall, interrupting their discreet departure.

"Something messy?" inquired Mr. Carter eagerly.

"Only the handwriting," said the man, and pulled out an interoffice envelope he had rolled up in the pocket of his lab coat.

On the back, at the end of a long list of staff names that had been written and scratched out over the course of the envelope's life, was the name "Ashley Carter" etched in uneven print.

"What is it?" said Mrs. Carter.

The attendant explained, "It bounced around the hospital all day yesterday until it came through here. I was the only one who recognized the name, so I held onto it. Interested?"

The couple stared at the large brown envelope and silently came to the same conclusion without needing to consult with each other.

"How much?" asked Mr. Carter, and started counting his cash-on-hand.

"A hundred," said the attendant, but quickly thought better of it when he saw how eager the Carters were to cough up a finder's fee.

"...and fifty," he added.

Mr. Carter paused for a moment, annoyed with himself for having walked straight into another fifty dollars-worth of extortion. His wife stood next to him, dying in anticipation of getting her hands on the contents of the envelope. She was more than willing to pay double or triple the asking price to find what new message had been left for them by the late Andrew Farkas. Still, Mr. Carter hated being played for a sucker, even if his wife had no appreciation for the art of negotiation. He stared down the attendant, telling him with his eyes, "Don't push it."

The money and envelope were exchanged. As the man closed the heavy door behind the Carters, he broke into a protracted smoker's cough that didn't speak well for a prognosis.

"See you soon," suggested Mr. Carter ominously through the narrowing gap, and flashed the attendant a smile that gave him chills and made him latch the door as soon as it was shut.

●　●　●

A green space behind the hospital had been meticulously designed with paths and bushes and trees for convalescing patients to enjoy as soon as they were up and about, or before they were forced to settle indoors as a permanent fixture of a death bed. Nurses wheeled the less mobile around so they could smell the flowers and hear the birds sing. Benches had been spaced along the path for family visits in a fresh-air environment, away from the smorgasbord of germs and viruses that floated around the hospital halls, waiting to rack up some fresh customers for the ear-nose-and-throat men inside. It was on one of these benches that the Carters sat to open their mail—a single sheet of gift-shop stationery covered with handwriting.

Mr. Carter looked over his wife's shoulder, and together they read the correspondence which ran, "If you've received this letter, I know I've chosen wisely. You remind me so much of my Emma and me when we were your age and newly married. We were the only ones who could understand each other's fascination with the state of death and the act of dying. You're wearing the rings, aren't you? I knew you'd appreciate them as we did when we obtained them from a private collector who claimed they'd been on the fingers of Tsar Nicholas and his wife when they were executed by the Bolsheviks. The tale is doubtless apocryphal, but I know you'll understand why we chose them as our wedding bands. Forgive me for dwelling on the past. It's a terrible habit I've been trying to break myself of. Perhaps you can help me."

The writing trailed off at the end of the letter abruptly, perhaps prematurely.

"That's it?" asked Mr. Carter, disappointed with the vagueness the note closed on.

Mrs. Carter flipped the page over and confirmed, "That's it."

"A man—a total stranger—at the end of his life. And he spends his last moments writing us a letter," pondered Mr. Carter, trying to understand the significance.

"It's sweet," concluded Mrs. Carter, "Cryptic but sweet. I wish we could send him a get-well card."

Down the path, a geriatric patient strolled along in his hospital gown and slippers, using an IV pole as a walker. Halting in mid-step, he silently began a slow-motion collapse to the gravel base underfoot. In quick succession, the nurses and interns in the green space saw the man go down and rushed over to assist. One of them began artificial respiration on the unconscious patient while another ran for a doctor. The rest gathered around to observe and offer their concerned stares, but the efforts to revive the elderly gentleman didn't look promising.

The Carters, watching serenely from a short distance away, held hands.

● ● ●

That night, after a romantic dinner in their condominium, the Carters sat down on the couch to enjoy some wine and a slide show. The wine was red, and so were most of the slides. The light reflecting off the screen bathed the darkened room with a rosy glow.

Mr. Carter operated the projector with his wife cuddled next to him. Between slides he would use his free hand to stroke their black-and-white cat, Mittens, who never purred no matter how much affection was lavished on him. Mittens had been stuffed and mounted for three years now, ever since the Carters found him lying by the curb, fresh from a fatal encounter with a Buick. The physical damage to Mittens had been minor, so the Carters adopted him and kept him in their freezer for a week until they could get down to the taxidermist. Their expressed desire to immortalize their beloved kitty wasn't questioned, even though the Carters had never met Mittens before he used up the last of his nine lives. Since then, Mittens had assumed his new permanent position, curled into a ball as though he were just sleeping. When not sitting in the Carters' laps like a plush toy, Mittens was mostly used as a novelty throw cushion.

Despite the entertainment value of the Bordeaux and projected pictures, Mrs. Carter was distracted.

"We can't just let it go at that," she said.

Mr. Carter didn't care for what his wife was suggesting.

"If we get another letter, fine. But I'm not comfortable dipping into the man's family history. Especially when it was probably someone in that family who bumped him off."

"He called us his dear friends in the will. No one's going to be suspicious if we politely ask a few innocent questions."

"Details like what sort of exit wounds he and his wife got off on?"

"Wouldn't you like to compare notes?"

"If anyone knows about their fetish, I'm sure it's a dirty little family secret."

"Perhaps we can find someone who's open about it. Maybe they'll talk if we let on we already know. Think of the possibilities. They may have been into all sorts of things we haven't even thought of yet. Things that could spice it up for us."

"Bored?" asked Mr. Carter.

"Maybe a little jaded. I'd like to go further towards the edge."

Mr. Carter advanced to the next slide and the room lit up with a dark red tint much harsher than the others had offered.

"Nasty!" cooed Mrs. Carter.

"I thought you'd like this one," said Mr. Carter. "Aluminium smelter accident. The guy fell into the rolling machine. He was alive up until the moment they cut him out. It seems the roll of metal encasing him was the only thing holding him together."

"Worker's comp must have paid off like the lottery," Mrs. Carter noted pragmatically.

"Actually no. He was a non-union scab."

"Well then," she said, "I guess he had it coming."

● ● ●

The Carters pulled up alongside the curb in front of the late Andrew Farkas's home. It was a large, stately house that flirted with the title of "mansion" without stepping over that line of opulent pretentiousness. Dating back to the roaring twenties, the house might have included a servant's door had it been built just ten years earlier. As it was, it only had the one front entrance, but it was a double door which made the movers' job easier.

The place was bustling with activity as half-a-dozen men in overalls came and went in singles and pairs, carting furniture and possessions big and small down the path to a waiting van. The truck was a twenty-five footer and nearly full. Judging from the volume of boxes still pouring out of the residence, the movers would have to make another trip, perhaps two, before the place was emptied for the new owners.

A "For Sale" sign hammered into the front lawn had a "Sold" sticker plastered boldly across it. The sign served no other function than being a real-estate agent's bragging rights. The property had sold before it ever officially made it to market. Priced low for its size and location, it was recognized for the bargain it was by the second couple to be offered a sneak preview by a well-connected agent. A bid was made for ten thousand dollars above the asking price and was accepted by the family lawyers before any rival bids had an opportunity to cross their desk. The paperwork was already underway and the entire transaction would be settled before the junk mail began to clog the letter slot. The new owners weren't moving in. The sole occupants of the house for the next three months would be a small army of painters and handymen assigned to spruce the place up, add some colour and modernize the fixtures. The property was expected to be back on the market and turned around for a six-figure profit before the year was up.

"I don't think anyone's home," said Mr. Carter, as he stepped out of the car and assessed the line of movers who were making the house increasingly barren and uninhabitable.

"All the better," said Mrs. Carter. "We can go through his private papers."

"If anything's left."

No one questioned the Carters as they made their way up the path, shuffling out of the way of two movers who were excavating the third couch of the day from the property. Stepping inside, they could see four large chambers branching off from a grand hall. Nothing was where it should be, with furniture and boxes collected into islands of disarray in the middle of each room. Slowly but inevitably, the daunting task of taking it all away was accomplished a piece at a time. As the isles of personal possessions eroded, so did the character of the house.

Elaine stood in the centre of the hall, her back to the Carters, watching her father's life being disassembled and sold off. Mrs. Carter recognized her immediately, even without seeing her face. Her expensive designer shoes were a dead giveaway, even if they weren't a precise match with Mrs. Carter's own taste in fashionable footwear.

Mrs. Carter turned on her social smile and strode up to Elaine, beaming, "Elaine! Wonderful to see you again. How are you holding up?"

Elaine turned around. The tears on her cheeks were nearly dry, but had been plentiful enough to erode a pair of matching river beds through her makeup. Her eyes were red and irritated from a long nostalgic cry.

"Oh. It's you," said Elaine simply, not trying to hide her indifference that bordered on displeasure at seeing the Carters again.

Elaine mopped away some residual moisture from the corner of her eye with the back of her hand and made a brave effort to improve her manners.

"Pardon me," she said, "I'm a sentimentalist. It breaks my heart to see all these old memories sold to any dealer who will have them. But it's what Daddy wanted."

"We understand he wasn't big on remembering the past," said Mr. Carter.

Elaine nodded, "Since mother died. Everything he owned reminded him of her, but he couldn't part with any of it. Not until he joined her."

"They were very close, weren't they?" stated Mrs. Carter.

"Oh yes. They shared everything—had all the same interests."

"Interests?" said Mrs. Carter, fishing.

"Oh, you know. Gardening. Travel. They liked to bowl together."

That wasn't what the Carters wanted to hear, but Elaine said it so honestly, it was instantly apparent she didn't know anything about her parents' secret life.

"He scattered her ashes on his last trip to Egypt," explained Elaine. "Of course, I don't expect you to arrange for something so exotic for Daddy."

"We have a nice spot with a view in mind," assured Mr. Carter.

"He must have thought a great deal of you—both of you," said Elaine as she eyed the Carters, perhaps hoping to discover some quality in them—any quality—that might have left a positive impression with her father. She came up empty.

Mrs. Carter probed further, "We were wondering if your father had maybe left a letter or a note with you. For us?"

"A letter?" said Elaine, taking a mental inventory of what was left in the house. "No, nothing like that. There's still a box or two of old tax returns, receipts, a few bills. Nothing very interesting."

"Could we have a look?" asked Mr. Carter.

Elaine stared at the couple for a long moment, her suspicion growing, before she finally, reluctantly, invited them upstairs.

The room Elaine led them to had nearly been emptied, but enough furniture was left to identify it as a study. There were a few boxes stacked high, and paper littered the floor. An antique secretary, sitting in the middle of the room, had its drawers pulled out and piled next to it. Their contents appeared intact.

The Carters split up, picking through the dregs of a man's life like a couple of hounds sniffing out contraband. Mrs. Carter dove head first into the boxes, digging deep in a search that lacked any pattern other than wanton greed. Mr. Carter took to upending the secretary drawers one by one, scattering their contents across the floor. Elaine stood back, watching the intrusion with increasing discomfort.

Mr. Carter was down to rifling through the secretary's numerous cubby holes, pulling the tiny drawers out one by one in quick succession. They were all empty, but the last of them had a small envelope taped to its underside. "A. Carter" was handprinted on the front.

Mrs. Carter abandoned the boxes of paper refuse as soon as she saw that her husband had found something. He passed the envelope to her and watched closely as she opened the flap and poured the contents out into her palm. It was a single key.

"What's this for?" Mrs. Carter asked Elaine.

"I don't know," said Elaine, looking at the simple unmarked key. "I've never seen it before."

"Is there something left in the house it would fit?" Mrs. Carter asked hopefully.

"My parents didn't keep things under lock and key. I can't imagine what it might be for, unless..."

"Yes?" asked Mrs. Carter when Elaine trailed off.

"My parents kept a safe-deposit box for years. I don't know where, or what was in it. But it must have been important to them because they had the number inscribed on..."

Elaine trailed off again as her eyes fell on Mrs. Carter's left hand, focusing on her ring finger. She glanced at Mr. Carter's hand and found its twin.

Fresh tears started to trickle down Elaine's face.

"He gave you the rings?" she said, her voice shaking with emotion. "And now he wants you to have what's in the box, too?"

Elaine was wavering between grief and anger. Anger was starting to win out.

"Who are you people?" she demanded. "I never saw you before in my life and now you're inheriting everything in the world that was important to my father. The lawyers won't even let me keep the family photo albums!"

"I'm sure your father knew what was best," Mrs. Carter tried to assure her.

"What's in the safe-deposit box? What else won't he let me have?"

"We honestly don't know," said Mr. Carter.

"Give me the rings!" Elaine demanded furiously.

"What? No!" cried Mrs. Carter, but Elaine was already upon her, clawing at her hand, gripping her wrist, trying to pull the ring free. The struggle quickly grew violent, and when Mr. Carter tried to separate the women, Elaine lashed out at him as well.

Elaine, sobbing uncontrollably, finally managed to wrench the ring away from Mrs. Carter. Mrs. Carter responded by tackling Elaine, throwing her arms over her shoulders and attempting an improvised choke hold. Elaine bucked hard, nearly shrugging Mrs. Carter off. Looking to her husband for help, Mrs. Carter worked her arms around Elaine's neck and pulled her head back sharply. Mr. Carter took advantage of the tempting target and grabbed the largest of the secretary drawers. He brought the drawer down on the back of Elaine's head with enough force to splinter it. All the joints in her body went limp in a split second and she collapsed like a rag doll stuffed with lead.

The ring leapt free of Elaine's hand as she hit the floor, rolling across the ceramic tiles and stopping abruptly as Mrs. Carter stomped her foot down in its path. Only after she bent to retrieve the ring and slip it safely back on her finger did she turn to check on Elaine and her husband.

Mr. Carter sat down heavily on the floor, staring at Elaine where she lay. Mrs. Carter flipped Elaine over on her back, and observed her closely. She put a couple of fingers on the side of her neck, feeling for a pulse. Blood trickled freely from a gash in the back of her head, pooling on the floor. The rate of blood loss might have been a concern if the crushing blow hadn't already propelled bone fragments into soft brain tissue. Elaine's eyes were fixed on two slightly different points in the room, and she wasn't breathing. Her leg spasmed, twitching once in an unnatural way that suggested more than simple unconsciousness, and then settled at an angle that would have been uncomfortable had Elaine still been alive.

Mr. Carter looked at his handiwork, astonished.

"I've never killed anything before," he said, and then added after much reflection, "I think I liked it."

The Carters sat together in the barren room for a long while, watching the body cool while they caught their breath.

• • •

It took the Carters another few minutes to compose themselves. At last they emerged from the study with clothes straightened and heart rates back to a reasonable pace. As they shut the door behind them, one of the movers approached.

"There's nothing left in there," Mr. Carter said, warding off the man. "Try that room down the hall."

The mover did as he was told and the Carters hit the stairs, walking briskly, but keeping their pace slow enough so as not to attract attention. They passed other busy crewmen on the way, but none of them gave the couple a second look. Apparently the sounds of murder had not penetrated the thick oak of the study door.

"You think we're going to get into trouble over this?" wondered Mr. Carter aloud.

"No one here knows who we are."

"That's true. But just in case, I think we should swing by the bank right now while we have the chance. Before anyone asks us any questions."

"Sounds good. But which bank?"

"That's a five-digit number on our rings. I only know one bank with that many safe deposit boxes."

Arriving at the bottom of the stairs, the Carters froze. Through the yawning front door they could see another car parked behind their own. Two burly men dressed in plain suits and ties were coming up the path. Their profession was obvious to the Carters long before they arrived in front of them and flashed their badges and accompanying identification.

"We're here to see Elaine Farkas," said one of the police detectives.

"Oh?" said Mr. Carter, in a somewhat failed attempt to sound casual.

Over the banister, up the stairs, the Carters could see one of the movers making a room-by-room sweep of the building, opening and shutting doors, checking for remaining pieces of furniture bound for the truck outside. He was only a couple of doors away from discovering Elaine's body.

"We'd like to talk to her about her father's death," the detective elaborated.

"Tragic, untimely," said Mrs. Carter, momentarily locking eyes with her husband. They exchanged a look of panic so subtle, it took a connection on a deeply intimate level to recognize it.

"I think she stepped out for a moment," Mr. Carter offered.

The mover was just opening the door to the study, seconds away from exposing the scene of the crime to the whole household. Mrs. Carter interrupted him by shouting, "Excuse me!"

The mover paused in the doorway, "Yes?"

"Have you seen Miss Farkas recently?"

"She was downstairs five, ten minutes ago. Maybe she went out back."

"Which way is that?" asked Mr. Carter.

The mover leaned over the upstairs banister and pointed, "Through that door, down the hall, and out by the kitchen."

"Could you show us, sir?" said the detective.

The mover shut the study door again and came downstairs to show the policemen the way out back. The detectives thanked the Carters for their assistance and let the mover lead the way. As the trio disappeared into the heart of the house, the Carters seized the opportunity to leave. Once the cops were out of sight, they broke into a frantic trot that became a flat-out run as soon as they were safely outside. The Carters leapt into their car and peeled away the instant the engine roared to life.

• • •

The bank was a cathedral built to the glory of old money. Everything in sight was either marble or mahogany, with a ceiling mosaic highlighted in gold leaf arching so far above the floor, it was impossible to appreciate the finer details without a good pair of binoculars or some very tall scaffolding. This was not a corner branch for people to withdraw a convenient twenty dollars to see them through the weekend. Clients who came here had serious business in mind for serious sums of cash.

The Carters only had to wait in the queue a few moments before a teller was free to assist them. Mr. Carter placed the key on the counter in front of the wicket and stated, "I'd like to check on the contents of my safe-deposit box. Number one four eight seven three."

"Yes sir," said the teller. "Your name?"

"Andrew Farkas."

It took only a few more lies and one loosely forged signature for the Carters to get themselves escorted into the vault. They sat down at a long table that was set out for customer convenience while their teller scanned the thousands of armoured boxes, searching for the correct number. Scaling a footstool, he retrieved the Farkas deposit box from high on one wall and then carried it to the table, where he placed it in front of the Carters.

"Ring for me when you're done," instructed the teller, who then gave the Carters their privacy, leaving the vault and shutting the thick air-tight door behind him. The Carters were alone, with only the hum of the air vents breaking the deathly silence. Together they stared at the box on the table. No words passed between them.

Mr. Carter pushed the key into the lock—a perfect fit. He gave it a quarter turn to the right and the latch released, allowing the top to pop open. Swinging the lid back on its hinges, he took a look inside. Sitting on top of several personal journals was a letter addressed to Mr. and Mrs. Ashley Carter.

Mrs. Carter was into the journals like a shot, poring through them like a speed reader, trying to absorb as much as possible in a rush of images. She couldn't contain her enthusiasm enough to focus on specific content or context—there would be time enough for that later—but her first impressions were promising, thrilling, titillating. From what she could gather as the pages flipped by, here were a series of recollections and experiences, a scrapbook of necrophilic delight, detailing the factual, the anecdotal, and the intimate from a lifetime of personal research.

Mr. Carter concerned himself with the letter first, wanting to be more methodical and restrained in his approach to this great bounty that had arrived on their doorstep. For him, stretching out the anticipation just a few minutes longer would make the final reward all the sweeter. He opened the note and read it aloud.

"The obsession we share has led you here as I expected it would. As you look through the years of notes and reminiscences Emma and I accumulated in our time together, you'll understand why I couldn't entrust them to anyone but a like-minded couple. Allow me to share this legacy with you: you must let the past die. I believe that absolutely, but I couldn't bring myself to destroy these mementos of our happy marriage in my lifetime—a lifetime I plan to end myself, tonight."

Past the journals, near the back of the deep deposit box, Mrs. Carter spotted a small collection of trinkets and souvenirs, all of it dead flesh. None stood out so much as the one large oval centre piece that dominated the collection. It was a human head—distinctly feminine—mummified by time and the dry climate of the vault. Mrs. Carter looked into the concave sockets of the skull, deep into the dusty eyes that hadn't lost their character even as they dried out and collapsed in on themselves.

Mr. Carter stopped reading.

"This would be Mrs. Farkas," he ventured.

"I guess the good bits never made it to Egypt."

As Mrs. Carter stared at the dead woman's remains, fascinated, Mr. Carter read the rest of the letter.

"For obvious reasons, I can't face the prospect of them falling into anyone else's hands, especially my daughter's. She knows nothing of our interests, and that's the way I want it to remain. To assure that, I had to arrange for the contents of this box to be burned. That task falls to you, with my thanks. As you have done me a service, so shall I do one for you. I leave you this gift which I know you will appreciate. It is the fondest thing all couples of our particular bent might wish for—what my wife and I were denied—to die together."

Mrs. Carter was just lifting the dried head out of the box for a closer look when her husband came to the end of the letter. The ominous conclusion inspired quick nervous glances between the couple, and then a closer inspection of the box's contents. Mrs. Farkas's head had been sitting upon a small incendiary device: two sticks of dynamite wired to a digital timer that was hooked, in turn, to the armoured box's hinges. The clock had been activated and was running down the last five seconds to double zeroes.

The Carters spent three of those final five seconds staring blankly at the bomb that was about to go off in their faces, then at the vault door, shut and locked tight. Husband and wife fumbled for each other's hand, holding on tight when they found a firm grip.

Mrs. Carter beamed at her husband, radiant, "How romantic!"

Mr. Carter returned a wavering smile. It always took him a little longer to come to grips with a new stage in their relationship—a deeper intimacy, or a greater commitment. Two seconds hardly seemed enough.

A bright flash and a loud bang moments later resolved any lingering concerns he may have had.

Saltwater Shark

MAX DERNSTON WAS THE SALT OF THE EARTH. Ask anyone.

If you were in a tight fix, short on cash, short on luck, he'd be there for you, and everyone knew it. Now, some might say as a loan shark, that was kind of his business model. But let me tell you, not all sharks are so approachable. They're not like those fuckers at the bank, who want to go probing up your sphincter for your credit history from the moment of conception to ten seconds ago. But they still want to make sure you're a good investment. Only the sick ones are in it for the hurt they'll put on you if you're short. Most of them expect to get paid back in full, and teeth aren't worth shit unless there's gold fillings in them. An ass-whupping here and there is good for business. It sets an example. But a successful entrepreneur does not build his empire on a hill of whupped asses.

If Max had to put the hurt on, he did it dispassionately, professionally. Hell, some might say compassionately. Depending how beat down you were once he was done sending you a message, he might even drive you to the hospital himself, provided it was on the way to his next call.

Take Karl Neelon for instance. Karl was in to Max for six figures, going on a quarter of a million. Max carried him for as long as he could—almost three years—but Karl could never scrape together more than fifty bucks at a time. And fifty bucks didn't come anywhere near putting a dent in the interest that was compounding every week. People started to talk, and Max was in danger of looking like a pushover if he didn't set an example. Sure, Max had been breaking plenty of bones and working him over with everything from an aluminium bat to a cinder block. After one round with a lead pipe, Karl even had to have his spleen removed. Max sent flowers and let up until he was out of intensive care, but Karl's problem had become Max's shame. It was time to put his foot down.

The desert is full of bad debts—deadbeats who got planted when they weren't worth squeezing anymore. Max had never had to put one of his clients in the ground before this, but when the time came he did it good and proper. Karl knew his moment had arrived, but when Max drove him out to his final resting place, he didn't have to ride in the trunk like so many who went before him. He sat right up front with Max like a regular human being. Sure, Max had cuffed his hands behind the passenger seat so there wouldn't be any embarrassing and futile attempts to run, but the gesture was a thoughtful one and I'm sure Karl appreciated it. Now, whether Karl expressed this appreciation or spent the whole trip begging for his life is a matter of some debate. Max, of course, said nothing about how Karl conducted himself in these delicate moments out of respect for the dead. That's the kind of class act he was.

This was how Karl Neelon was safely delivered to his hole, with a measure of care and consideration. But that wasn't the thing that impressed everyone the most. What really knocked our socks off as word of Max's settling of affairs spread was this: when they got there, the grave was already dug. This may not seem like a big thing to a lot of people, but believe me, it's a rarity. Anyone who has to commit an act of murder by abducting someone and driving them way out into the middle of nowhere usually feels that's work enough. The end of the job typically features a gun pointed at the victim's head while they're forced to dig their own grave. So for Max to have already gone out into the desert in advance to select a good spot and dig it himself was an act of unparalleled decency.

I'm sure Karl knew that much as he took a dive to the bottom of the ditch with a .38 slug flattened out inside his brain.

If you had to be indebted to a shark, you wanted it to be Max Dernston. That's why I went to him when times were tough and I needed a stack of cash to keep the repo men from taking my car, and my landlord from changing the locks and dumping all my shit at the curb. It had been a long stretch of bad luck, but I knew I could get back on my feet, if only Max would help me buy the time I needed to turn things around.

"Not the face, Max!"

He was winding up for his next punch, but stopped to see what I wanted. He knew I wouldn't interrupt him while he was working unless it was important.

"I got a job interview tomorrow," I explained. "I need to look my best."

Turning things around had taken me a little longer than I'd expected. The interest had compounded, payments had been missed, and Max had to take action. I knew it was coming and I accepted it. Max even called ahead to book an appointment for my beating. I invited him over to the apartment, the same one I would have been evicted from if not for his loan. It was better to take care of this sort of thing at home. I made sure to have ice packs and aspirin on hand for when he was done.

Max considered my request and nodded. He understood. Salt of the earth.

"Where do you want it, then?"

I had to think. He'd been hammering on my gut and kidneys pretty good already, and Max didn't like to repeat material. Barring anything from the neck up, the options were pretty limited.

"Balls good for you?" I asked him.

Max nodded. "Balls it is. Spread 'em."

I took half a step to the side, standing so my legs were wide open, offering him the most convenient target possible. I wasn't about to do anything to cushion the blow. Max was paying me a professional courtesy, so it was only fair I pay him one in return.

He took a few steps back. Max was only going to take one shot at the boys, but he was going to make it a good one. I closed my eyes so I wouldn't see it coming. Max didn't leave me in suspense. A moment later he kicked me with enough force to leave a criss-crossed imprint of his shoelaces on my nutsack. Even if my knees hadn't turned to jelly, I would have let myself drop to the floor just the same. There was a thick rug waiting to catch me, and in moments like this you take your comforts where you can get them. My stomach wanted to turn itself inside out, but I forced myself not to vomit, swallowing the acid at the back of my throat. Patching myself up after our session was going to be rough enough. I didn't need to compound my troubles by leaving a puddle of puke that would need to get scrubbed out of my shag carpet.

"That's ten thousand you owe," said Max, keeping me current with where the accumulating interest had left us. "I know you don't have it, but I can't let that much slide. You get together whatever you can by next Monday. However many G's you're short, that's how many fingers I'm going to have to break."

He didn't need to tell me the breaks would be bad—fractures all. Probably done with a hammer, several shots per, until what was left was a mangled mess. You could splint that sort of thing, but the fingers would never work right again, and they would ache every day for the rest of my life.

"Thanks, Max," I grunted at his shoes as I watched them walk to the door. He let himself out and left me alone with my pain.

I only saw Max one other time after that. Like Karl Neelon before him, Max didn't come to a good end either. He had debts of his own and, as so many of his clients did, he'd fallen badly into arrears.

Just like little banks borrow from bigger banks, the same goes for sharks. Max Dernston had money, but not enough to bankroll as many people as he loaned out to. To cover business expenses, he had to go higher up the food chain. In order to feed crumbs to the minnows, sharks have to borrow from the whales. Such is the natural order of things.

Max's ultimate downfall was his big heart. Always a soft touch, he'd carried too many deadbeats—loaned out too much cash to bad players who skipped town, or used the borrowed money to buy enough junk to overdose themselves beyond the reach of any IOU. Eventually, it had to catch up to him. All the whales knew he was a stand-up guy, but once Max was maxed-out, someone upstairs decided it was time to make the call. Muscle was dispatched, Max was intercepted on his way home from collecting nowhere near enough to settle his own affairs, and he was relocated to someplace remote and private where the deed would get done—where all outstanding debts were neither paid nor forgiven.

Max didn't get a hole in the ground. He got chucked in the ocean. Fish food.

I heard they chained a spare motorboat anchor to one ankle and tipped him off the back end once they were a few miles out. He managed to grab hold of the side of the boat before he was all the way in the water. Nobody tried to peel him off. The goons who were sent to take him out just sat there and laughed while Max struggled to pull himself back up on deck. Between them, they polished off most of a six-pack before the weight of the anchor and his soaking clothes finally wore Max out and dragged him straight to the bottom. This was years ago now. No remains ever washed up anywhere, but the story is probably true enough.

The last time I ever saw Max Dernston, he was carrying a ballpeen hammer. It fit in one hand, but I could see the weight of it just by the way he held it. You wouldn't want to drop that thing on your toe. And you certainly wouldn't want it landing blows on your digits with intent.

"How'd the job interview go?" he asked, after I let him into my apartment.

"I got it."

"Good for you," he said. "Doing what?"

"Data entry."

"You got a lot of typing to do?"

"Nothing but. It's boring as hell, but it's paying the bills."

"Not all the bills," he reminded me.

"I got some money for you. Not all, but most."

I'd pulled out all the stops, borrowed from any family or friends who were still talking to me, asked for as much of an advance at work as they would give me. I even went to the bank, hat in hand, to see if they'd make me a deal in light of my new gainful employment. They gave me a modest credit line, and I immediately transferred the full amount to my chequing account and pulled it out of an ATM that same day. For the rest, I'd pawned off anything I owned worth a damn. By the time I'd raked in every available dime, I had eight grand. It was all stuffed into a single fat envelope. You'd think eight thousand dollars would look like more money once you stacked it all together.

Max counted it twice to make sure and gave me his final tally.

"That's two fingers I have to take."

I nodded.

"You going to be okay to type at that new job of yours?"

I wasn't exactly a touch typist. Mostly I relied on my thumbs and the first couple of fingers on each hand to see me through. The rest were pretty optional.

"Depends," I said. "Can I pick which ones?"

Max gave it some thought.

"Sure," he said. "I don't see why not."

Salt of the earth.

Dealers

"WHAT DO YOU THINK OF MURDER?"

The question, he had to admit, was not the opener he had anticipated at the job interview.

"What do you mean?" was the only thing he could think to say in return.

"Are you for or against?"

"What kind of a question is that?"

"A perfectly straightforward one."

This was the twenty-seventh job interview the man had had since being laid off from his previous position as the floor manager of a big-box department store. Most of them had offered to keep his name on file if anything came up. None of them had called back. Eventually he had to look at want ads farther afield from his former work experience. At this point, he was so far afield, he was booking interviews for jobs that didn't even specify what the position was. All that had been required to get through the door for this interview was an online questionnaire. It was the typical collection of aptitude tests, along with a lengthy string of queries that seemed to emphasize the psychological makeup of the applicant more than usual.

"I heard you were some sort of dealership," he told the other man who was conducting the interview from across a desk in a private office. It was something he had overheard in the waiting room.

"We are," the interviewer confirmed.

"I thought you dealt in goods."

"No," he said. "Services."

"So not cars or kitchen appliances."

"No. We deal in death."

"Like a funeral home?"

"No. Although, I suppose, from that industry's point of view, we manufacture product. That would fall under 'goods.' But to our own clients, we supply a service."

"What sort of service?"

The interviewer smiled and didn't answer. Instead, he asked another question, which might have been an answer in its own right.

"Have you ever killed anyone before?"

"No."

"Would you like to?"

"Wouldn't everybody? At one time or another?"

"Not someone you knew," the interviewer clarified. "Or someone you were angry at. A stranger. Just a name and photo in a file."

"I wouldn't like to do that at all."

"No?"

The interviewer sounded ever so slightly surprised.

"Of course not. I mean, what's in it for me?"

"Ten thousand dollars."

The man considered the sum, and how much he was behind in lost wages during this protracted period of un-employment.

"Is that what a human life goes for these days?"

The suit behind the desk very nearly chuckled. At least, the unevenness of his next breath seemed to belie amusement.

"Don't be silly. Most human lives aren't worth a thing. Maybe a ten-cent bullet, but few are even worth that much. It's why we drop bombs on so many of them. Nobody calculates the cost of shrapnel."

"So why pay ten thousand dollars to make somebody dead?"

"Because this is the first world, and some people need to be gotten rid of. The reasons are unimportant. I don't pay attention to them myself. All I know is that there's a client out there, somewhere, with twenty grand and a problem."

"I thought you said ten thousand."

"Ten thousand goes to the trigger man. The other ten thousand is for the facilitator."

"Who's the facilitator?"

"An agency, of sorts. My employer. And yours if you're interested."

If he wasn't very mistaken, he'd just been offered a job. If he wasn't further mistaken, he'd been offered a job murdering people.

"Why would I be interested in a job like that?"

"You're saying you're not?"

"I didn't say that. I asked what makes you think I would be."

"I have your application," said the interviewer. "And your profile."

There was a single sheet of paper on the desk, but the print was small and it was upside-down from the man's perspective. Too difficult to read from that angle and distance. The page included the results of his psychological assessment following the extensive online test. That, plus all his personal details like name, address, social security number, background, education, work experience. Even at a small font size, the man felt vaguely disappointed that it was all summed up on a single sheet of paper—one-sided.

"Your profile says you have psychopathic leanings," the interviewer informed him.

"How do you mean, leanings?"

"There's a forty-point scale for grading psychopaths. True psychopaths are up in the thirty-plus range. Normal people are down near the bottom, generally less than eight. You're somewhere in the middle. That's a leaning."

"I'm not a psychopath."

"I never said you were. I said you were leaning."

The man felt he should explain himself further, in case that single sheet of paper didn't summarize his life well enough—didn't explain it.

"I spent a few years in my teens under psychiatric observation. There was an incident. Several incidents. They determined I might be a sociopath. A leaning one at any rate."

Such additional specifics didn't impress the interviewer.

"Psychopath/sociopath, nature/nurture, tomato/to-*mah*-to. It's all the same to us. The specific differences are tediously academic. The important thing is that you have leanings, and fairly strong ones at that. We can use men like you."

Despite his need for an income, a desperation to return to the work force and provide for his family, the man felt he should at least attempt to talk his way out of the job offer. He expected there should be, at the very least, certain moral considerations.

"I'm sure there are plenty of genuine psychopaths and sociopaths and other sorts of paths you can recruit on short notice. A bunch of thirties, thirty-fives, maybe even a full-blown forty."

"Those tend to be quite rare. And when you find one, chances are they're either in prison or gainfully employed in banking or politics. Even if we found one unencumbered, they're not desirable applicants."

"Too stabby?"

"Too uncontrollable. Relatively few psychopaths are the stabby kind, but we can't have them too engaged in their own antisocial agendas. We need them focused on *our* antisocial agendas."

The man had been sitting forward in his seat for the entire interview—an anticipatory stance. Now he sat back. Not relaxed, but contemplative.

"Ten thousand for a murder—for a human life—it still sounds like so little."

"Would you do it for a million dollars?"

"I guess I might. For a million."

"So you admit you're a killer. Now we're negotiating price."

"If this is a negotiation, I guess I might kill someone for nine hundred thousand."

"The price is ten."

"I thought we were negotiating."

"We are. I'm just better at it than you. Ten thousand is my one, my only, my final offer."

The man considered this offer. Not for long.

"It's not much."

"It adds up."

"Does it?"

"You kill one, all goes well, we assign you another. Business is brisk, contracts are plentiful."

"You're trying to turn me into a mass murderer."

"A wealthy mass murderer. Six figures a year is a simple matter. Seven figures is possible if you're prolific."

It all seemed unreal. Surely, he thought, this was a test.

"Do I seriously look like a killer to you?"

"No," the interviewer assured him. "Not at all. And that's exactly what we want. You're blandly ordinary. A ghost of a man. Invisible."

"I wouldn't know the first thing about assassination."

"It will come to you naturally enough. It's an instinct ingrained in all of us. A human trait. Plus you have the right mindset to deal with it. You lack empathy, which means you won't be troubled by guilt."

"Still, the actual act... I have no training."

"Guns are simple tools. Idiots use them proficiently all the time. If that doesn't appeal, we're perfectly willing to accept stabbings, bludgeonings, poisonings. The method is entirely up to you. It doesn't have to be clean, it needn't look like an accident. It only has to get done. The important thing is you remain a ghost. Nobody sees you. Nobody remembers you."

"What if I screw up, get caught, get arrested?"

"We never met and this conversation never happened."

"I might talk, tell them everything. I could convince them to look into it. Without a motive, they might come to the conclusion I wasn't acting alone even if I don't say a word."

"These things happen from time to time. It gets taken care of. Cops are bought cheaper than murder. We rarely need to dig deeper than petty cash."

There was a long silence in the office.

"Do you need time to think about it?"

"No," said the man.

"I didn't think so. You can pick up your first assignment at the reception desk on the way out. Name, address, photograph, deadline. An advance will be transferred to your bank account. The balance will follow upon completion. Good luck."

The man got up, as if in a dream, and walked to the door. His hand was barely on the knob when he was stopped by second thoughts. Ten thousand dollars was a lot of money for so simple a task, and yet...

"I was wondering..." he said.

The interviewer had already tucked away his profile in a file stuffed with a great many other pages filled with small type.

"Do you have any jobs that pay more?" the man asked.

The interviewer smiled and retrieved another brimming file folder from a desk drawer. It wasn't unusual for their contract killers to moonlight.

"We have a sister company."

"Do tell," said the man, taking the seat in front of the desk again.

"What do you think of arson?"

Special

GODDAMN, MY LEOTARD ITCHES.

It must be the detergent they use at the hotel. This is one of the reasons I hate trusting my suit to the laundry service, but what choice do I have? By day three, the costume is getting ripe. The cape is creased from sitting on it for eight hours at a stretch, the inside of the hood is greasy from my hair, and the sweat stains have left salty white lines after drying overnight.

The costume is one of a kind. It's hardly an original, but I only have the one, and if the laundry service fucks up, I'm screwed. I can't very well sit at the table and sign T-shirts and glossies and magazine covers as myself. The fans all want to meet Captain Sandwich Board, not his alter-ego John Doe Whatshisface. I may be the man behind the headlines, but the costume is what makes me marketable. At ten bucks a signature, twenty for a photo, there's real money to be made during the convention. And the lawyer fees keep on stacking. I can't afford to stop cashing in.

I do all the comic cons, flying here and there on the cheap, signing and posing everywhere from Buttfuck Nebraska to Who-Gives-a-Shit Saskatchewan. Money is money, but the real cash can be found on the coasts. This is my third time in San

Diego, which means I've been at it for three years now. Time flies when you're wasting your life.

Not that my time was well spent when I was gainfully employed at what could charitably be called a real job. Shilling on a street corner for some short-order feedbag paid the bills, but came at the high price of personal humiliation. The sandwich board I had hanging off my shoulders advertised the daily special which never seemed to change. Neither did my routine. I'd walk up and down the same block until my feet were raw and my back was threatening to snap in two under the weight of a wooden advertisement that grew exponentially heavier as the day dragged on. I'd answer questions from the public, take a lot of insults, and hurl a few of my own back. It could have been worse. I had the mask to protect my anonymity, I had the cape to keep me warm when the wind was blowing, and at least I didn't have to dress up in a chicken outfit like that poor bastard two streets over who was doing the same gig for a wings joint.

I'd been at it for six weeks when I got caught up in The Incident. In all that time, the daily special changed maybe four times. Mostly they'd swap it out for something new when they had to rewrite the sandwich board that was made of two wood-framed chalk boards held together by a couple of leather straps. The special and other menu highlights were scribbled on, front and back, in a variety of colourful chalky hues. Denise, one of the younger waitresses at the restaurant, would write it up in large flowing script with just enough flair to suggest her community-college arts degree wasn't a total waste. She'd touch it up every few days to deal with any fading or erosion. If I got caught in the rain, she'd have to redo it entirely, and that's when the special would change. We'd hang out and chat while she worked her magic. Those breaks, with Denise doing her street-art thing with a box of broken chalk nubs while I kicked off my flashy rubber boots and sat in a booth, were the highlight of my public-relations career. Other than The Incident, of course.

Hang on, I've got someone at the table who wants a signed photo. This'll only take a minute.

My fan is wearing some sort of costume I can't quite place. I think she's dressed up like the angst-ridden sullen chick from one of those fantasy love-triangle book series that's popular with the kids who can still read. Or maybe she's a genuine angst-ridden sullen chick. I can't tell the difference anymore. The geeks and the nerds let it all hang out at these conventions. Half of them are dressed up as superheroes and all of them look more like the real deal than I do. They put all their love and obsession into their crazy costumes. Me, I can't even be bothered to spring for a strip of fabric softener.

"Could you personalize it?" she says, like it's a request more than a demand.

Oh God, here it comes. When the hell did parents start misspelling their kids' names on birth certificates? Nobody's happy with traditional names anymore. Now they all have to fuck with them, swap letters around, replace or drop others. If I meet one more Cristian or Nicolas, I'm going to take this ball-point pen and etch the letter "H" into their foreheads until it forms a permanent scar. Who has it in for the letter "H"? When did that get dropped from the alphabet? And don't get me started on all the newfangled ways you can spell "Catherine."

"Sure," I reluctantly agree. "Who should I make it out to?"

"Catherine."

My posture instantly goes to hell and I slump in my chair. I feel like an idiot for asking, so I do it avoiding eye contact.

"How do you spell that?"

"K…" she begins. I barely hear the jumble of letters that follow so I just write it however I want to. Fuck her, and fuck her new-age parents and their gleeful butchery of common-sense spelling. I take her money and send her on her way with an insincere smile. Hopefully she'll be back at her hotel before she notices how I mangled her name.

Where was I? Oh yeah, The Incident. I don't know how much you heard about it, but all the parts that aren't bullshit are way overblown. I was just about to start my lunch-to-dinner shift. Denise was touching up the specials after a late-morning drizzle ran streaks through her previous masterpiece.

"There you go," she told me, making sure she'd dotted all the "I"s with a happy face. "Try not to go swimming with this one."

"Looks like a scorcher," I said, looking up at what was visible of the cloudless sky between buildings.

"Then try not to sweat all over it either," she said, with what I'm pretty sure was a flirtatious wink. What can I say? Some women really go for the low-rent, painfully primary-coloured superhero look.

The wink and the smile were gone a moment later, replaced by a look of irritated concern.

"What's that fuss?" she wanted to know.

An alarm had just gone off outside, somewhere nearby. It wasn't the usual noise-pollution car alarm howling because somebody looked at it the wrong way. This sounded a little more serious, like a real alarm system for a home or business. I was just as determined to ignore it anyway.

"It's our new ad campaign. The boss wants everyone to know we changed our daily special for the month."

Satisfied I got Denise to put her smile back on, I picked up the board and went to patrol the block. Outside, in the light of day, I didn't put it on right away. Instead, I stood there like some sort of half-assed art critic, admiring how Denise had filled out all the dead black spaces with vibrantly coloured promises of cheap food that actually looked edible. She had a flair for making some seriously greasy shit sound promising, and I guess that put a smile on my face too. I was still standing there, grinning like an idiot at her rendition of a bacon burger that could clog an artery at thirty paces, when the droning alarm down the street was interrupted by screams and shouts.

Three guys came dashing out of a nearby bank branch wearing hoodies and ski masks despite the summer heat. I knew the bank well. The ATM outside was my first stop after each paycheck. It didn't take much deductive reasoning to figure out these guys had just knocked the place over. Or least tried to. It was equally obvious that it was amateur hour over at the scene of the crime. With the exception of the one holding a gun, they were leaving empty-handed. The alarm must have really spooked them. The two lead runners piled into a waiting double-parked car that peeled away before they could even get all their arms and legs inside. The driver never waited to do a head count, and that left the third man—the one who was packing—alone on the street with nothing but fear and bullets to keep him going. Bad combo.

With his ride gone and getting more gone by the second, he started running in the opposite direction, probably figuring he should put even more distance between himself and the car the cops would likely be chasing. With lunch hour coming up, there were a lot of civilians milling about—too many to give the gunman a clear path. He decided to convince everyone to get the hell out of his way.

Aiming at nothing in particular, the bank robber pulled the trigger and the gun went off several times—a curt pop-pop-pop. Unfortunately, real guns sound much less impressive than movie guns, so no one noticed the wild gunfire until one of the bullets shattered the windshield of a parked car and set off a second alarm. That's when it got noisy enough for everyone to turn and look. Once they saw there was a masked man sprinting down the street, waving a gun, shooting off random rounds in all directions, there was chaos. Pedestrians scattered. Some went diving for cover, others fled down the nearest side street or into any available storefront.

And then there was me. I just stood there like the world's biggest dumbfuck. I could have been watching it all unfold on TV. Maybe it was all that time I'd clocked on the street, people-watching and taking abuse, safe behind a cape and a cowl. Nothing that happened between one corner of the street and the next seemed real anymore. All it meant to me was an hourly wage.

But I'll tell you, once that armed and dangerous and panicking would-be desperado was twenty feet away and still running right at me, it suddenly seemed very real. All I could see behind the ski mask was the wide eyes and the grimacing teeth. I'm sure it was fear I saw, but it could just as easily have been interpreted as rage. Subconsciously that might have been how I read it. I don't really know, because consciously all I was concerned about was which way the gun was swinging and how many bullets were left.

If I had just held still, he might have passed me by, like a no-parking sign, or a fire hydrant, or a piece of advertising—which is exactly what I was—part of the scenery, an inanimate object. But instead I reacted and swung out with the only weapon I had—a sizeable hunk of wood and chalk board. It nailed him square in the face, although he did most of the damage himself by running straight into my swing.

He landed heavily, flat on his back, and was clearly dazed and disoriented by the impact. It should have been over, but in his delirium, he raised his gun hand and pointed the wavering barrel of his weapon at me like an accusing finger. I didn't want a fight, but I knew I was committed at that point. For my own safety, I had to be the one to end it, so I hit him with the board again. And again.

Without the gunman helping me out by ramming his own head into my sandwich board at high speed, I was doing considerably less damage. In fact, as he recovered his senses, I think I was mostly just irritating him. Only when he flopped over on his side and tried to raise himself up did I try a new, desperate approach. His profile presented a tempting target, so I turned the sandwich board ninety degrees and brought the lower corner down on him with as much weight as I could put behind it. The blow landed on his jaw, shattering it. Teeth flew everywhere and blood pooled in the gutter immediately. He passed out on contact, turning into a floppy slab of meat so instantly I thought I'd killed him.

I stood over my defeated adversary for several long minutes, staring, disconnected by my handiwork. It only felt like a few moments to me, but it was long enough for a crowd to gather, and for some of them to snap pictures with their phones.

One particularly well-framed picture was sold and ran in the local daily. Due to declining sales and budget cutbacks, the newspaper had reverted to printing all their photos in black and white. Too bad. If it had run in colour you could have seen the blood stains on the costume. Long crimson steaks punctuated by drops of spatter, soaking into the cheap blue fabric. Maybe the imagery wouldn't have seemed so heroic then and the whole ugly incident would have been forgotten in a week like every other tawdry little crime story. But no, the photo and the story circulated far and wide on the Internet, and that's when those fuckwits at CNN picked it up. They cover about one Canadian story a year and I won the newsfeed lottery. I might have escaped the notice of the American news media if only there had been a hockey riot. That would have covered their quota and they could have skipped me entirely. But no such luck. Once I was famous in America, I was famous everywhere.

For the record, the character I was playing was supposed to be called "Captain Coleslaw," but thanks to a few smartass news reports, I was re-christened "Captain Sandwich Board." Now there are lawyers bickering about who owns the trademark to "Captain Sandwich Board"—me or my ex-employers. Technically, the costume design is still theirs, but apparently the suits agreed that it was so derivative, all we had to do on my end was change the shades of yellow and green to sidestep any copyright violation.

Between lawyers endlessly bickering about trademarks and intellectual property in order to run up their fees, and the pain-and-suffering suit filed by the vanquished bank robber who turned out to be seventeen with no priors, it's been very hard to make any dough cashing in on my instant fame. The talk show interviews have long since died down, the paid personal appearances have dried up, so now I'm stuck signing random crap with my face on it at the San Diego Comic Con. It's the only gig I can still count on for quick cash.

The convention is a circus sideshow by way of an unmedicated madhouse. If you look hard enough, you can still find some comic books for sale, but most of that shit has been eclipsed by marketing. Each year, Hollywood pulls up its stakes and drives a couple of hours down the coast so it can promote every big stupid movie and every little stupid TV show to its target audience. If it has a costumed crime fighter, a vampire, or an alien in it, it's there pitching hard, trying to rev up the hype machine so it has a shot at a record opening weekend, or a season renewal from a broadcaster.

It's hard not to get lost in the middle of all that pop-culture clutter, but fans of fantasy-come-to-life still seek me out.

"I think it's great what you did, man. You totally kicked major ass," is a typical refrain I'll hear from my male followers.

"What are you doing later?" is what I prefer to hear from the female fans. Particularly the ones dressed in something enticing, be it leather, lace, or spandex.

If you have a fetish for that sort of thing, the comic shows are an open buffet. If you don't, you'll develop one over time. I used to keep track of how many Supergirls or Catwomen or Wonder Women I banged, but they all got jumbled together in my memory by the end of year two. I know I fucked a Xena once. Or maybe she was a Red Sonja. I don't remember her hair colour. I just remember she had a Brazilian, so I couldn't tell if she was a natural blonde, brunette, or redhead. Whoever she was supposed to be, she wanted to stay in character and left most of her armour on during our hotel-room tryst. I still have a lump on my head from where she whacked me with her cast-iron bra.

Some of my friends are envious, but I keep telling them that screwing groupies doesn't pay my legal bills. It doesn't exactly fulfill me emotionally either. All they want to do is live out some twisted sex fantasy that involves them—or whoever they're dressed as—going to bed with a real-live caped crusader who put some stupid kid in the hospital with a jaw wired shut. The sick ones fetishize the board. It was kept in police lockup for a few weeks until public opinion swayed them against charging me with assault. Once their potential evidence was cleared for release and the restaurant expressed no interest in getting it back, I went down to the cop station and picked it up myself. By that time I had realized there was a buck to be made from all this mess, and where would Captain Sandwich Board be without his board?

"My hero!" says the next girl to approach my table. The words are meant as a joke, but the husky tone is dead serious.

"Would you sign this for me?" she pouts overtly. It's like she learned her seduction technique from a bad parody of a dirty joke. It shouldn't work, but it does.

She hands me an issue of some mid-level superhero rag I've seen a thousand times before. Captain Sandwich Board makes a cameo appearance on page ten, for which I was all too happy to cash a cheque. It was decent money, but they didn't pay me enough to actually read this shit.

While I sign the page in question, I check out what she's wearing. The costume is typically hypersexualized, with lots of exposed flesh and curves that are exaggerated by extra padding, but I can't figure it out. She looks like a slutty robot, but there are a lot of prominently featured car parts worked into the mix.

"And what are you supposed to be, young missy?" I ask in exactly that same way you would talk to a five-year-old who showed up at your door on Halloween in a homemade hobo costume.

"I'm a Transformer," she says, like it's the most obvious answer in the world.

A sexy Transformer. That's a new one. I can honestly say I've never had one of those.

It's not something I can say three hours later.

Getting ready to join her in my freshly made hotel-room bed, I take a moment to unstrap my sandwich board so I can be as physically flexible as I'll need to be. She doesn't take her eyes off it.

"Can I have a closer look at your board?" she asks.

Of course. She's one of the sick ones. It's not what I was hoping she'd want to have a closer look at, but if it's what gets her in the mood, it's all hers.

Taking the front half of the advertisement in hand, she runs her finger slowly along the edge, drinking it all in with her eyes. Denise's last daily special is still there, although it's largely illegible now. The chalk has faded, and indelicate hands have accidentally wiped away bits and pieces of the design over the last few years, but I've been careful to try to preserve it as it was on the day of The Incident. Some fans are particular about authentic details like that. Most importantly, I've managed to keep it dry. All my appearances are indoors and I haven't been caught in the rain yet.

The girl—whatever her name is—reverently touches the surface of the black board, tracing the outline of a large dent in its surface.

"Is that where you hit him?" The pseudo-seductive voice is gone, replaced with one that suggests genuine sexual excitement.

"That was the first point of impact, yeah," I confirm. "There were others, but that's the only one that left a mark."

Catch it in the right light and you can tell the sandwich board is permanently branded with the distinct imprint of a human face. All the sick ones need to see it first. It's their idea of foreplay.

There's a long silence I let happen before she can finally tear her eyes away from the trace evidence of a violent assault that's three years healed now. Setting the board down at last, she reclines on the bed and moves on to the second half of her agenda.

"Want me to leave the costume on?" she asks quite plainly.

"Sure," I said. It did nothing for me, but what's the point of banging a Transformer out of character?

Twenty minutes later, our transaction is complete. It's getting dark out, so she asks if she can grab a shower and crash in my room until morning. I say it's fine since I don't much care. It's a rented room and a big bed.

"Something wrong?" she says, after she gets her autoerotic-bot rig over her head and sees the look on my face.

"Nah," I tell her. "I just expected you to transform into a hotter chick."

We don't really talk after that. She's already asleep by the time I finish my own shower. And when I wake up she's gone. So is my sandwich board. I nearly have a fit, and I'm just about to call the front desk when I spot it. She hasn't taken it, merely moved it.

The board is propped up on an end table. Denise's old artwork is gone, wiped clean. A large clump of soggy toilet paper by the bed tells me it was wet-washed away. There's new writing on the board. I guess my Transformer seductress was short on chalk, so the message is written in lipstick.

"Fuck you needle dick! Your not special!"

The only new information her message conveys is that she can't spell. I already know the rest.

I check my wallet and find she's left me my cards. The cash is gone, including my take for the whole week. I never call the front desk, never speak to security. What would I say? I got ripped off by a sexy robot chick. No, I didn't catch her name, but she may have folded herself into a Lexus and driven off.

The trip home is long and depressing. The whole week is a bust and I can't even pay for the charged plane tickets when my credit-card statement comes in. I swear I'll never go back to San Diego and know I'm lying even as I tell myself that. There are still lawyers to be paid and there's still cash to be made as Captain Sandwich Board, although the returns are diminishing fast. I come up with a different promise to myself to compensate. I swear I'll leave the groupies alone from now on. No more Barbarellas or Aeon Fluxes or Lara Crofts for me. It's a promise I think I can keep. Unless maybe an Elvira, Mistress of the Dark comes by my table. A man's will is only so strong.

Safely back north of the 49th, I take the weekend off. Then I take another two weeks to top off my long-weekend vacation. I figure I've earned some recovery time. During this break from being a superhero and just trying to live my secret identity minus any secrets, I try to restore the vandalized sandwich board to its former glory. The lipstick smears and fights me when I try to scrub it off. I probably let it ferment on the blackboard for too long. There's no trace at all of what Denise had sketched there so long ago, and it proves difficult to remember despite having looked at it nearly every day for three years. I try to copy her work from various pictures I have lying around, but the photos are too small to make out the details and I lack the drafting skill to make it resemble much of anything.

By the time I declare an end to my perpetual weekend, I've given up. I decide the only way to resurrect Captain Sandwich Board is to commission a whole new daily special from the source.

I drop by our old restaurant for the first time since I collected my final cheque. Most of the staff has changed and I'm told Denise hasn't worked there in years. After much pestering, one of the long-time short-order cooks digs out some employee records. He won't give me her number, but dials it himself and passes me the phone.

What used to be fun and easy conversation between us is now halting and awkward. It takes a while for us to fall back into our old banter, but once I tell Denise what it is I want, things go a lot smoother. She invites me over to her apartment and says she'll see what she can do.

It's rush hour at this point, and it's a long haul trying to bus it across town with a big heavy sandwich board in hand and a lot of commuters sardined together. When I finally arrive, I'm hot and disheveled and worse for wear. Denise doesn't seem to care. She invites me in and I see her loft apartment is full of her own work. She's turned her living space into a studio, and her paintings and sketches show a lot more development since her days of happy-face I's.

Denise takes the sandwich board off my hands and sits down with it and a cup of tea. She has a good long look at it, getting reacquainted, while I scan the apartment and try to catch up with her last three years.

"Fuck you, needle dick," Denise announces.

"Say what?" is the best response I can come up with.

"It's written on your board," explains Denise.

"Oh. You can still read that?"

"Lipstick doesn't wash off so easy. Someone close?"

"A fan."

"She doesn't sound like much of a fan."

"An angry, disappointed fan."

Denise makes a slight "hmm" noise I can't interpret and sips her tea silently. She considers my last feeble attempt to mimic her style and the old hint of spite that remains just under the surface. After a few excruciating minutes, I can't take it any longer and break the silence by repeating my humble re-quest—a request that seems foolish now in light of all the more ambitious work she's accomplished since the last time she undertook this menial commercial-art task.

"So Denise," I say sheepishly, "Do you think can you redo my sandwich board for me? I tried, but I can't make it look right."

"Yes, you really made a mess of things."

She tells me how my handwriting is atrocious and I can't draw for shit. She says it with a smile so I don't take offence. Having sufficiently admonished me, she gets up and scrounges some disused art supplies.

Upon returning, Denise sets down a box of chalk—the same nubs of various sizes and shades she used to work with—and attends to her canvas. She wipes away my sad chicken-scratch remnants with a damp rag, taking extra care with the edges and corners. When she's done, the board is black and spotless.

"There," she says, "clean slate."

And then we start over.

Wetwork Warrior

THE FIRST THING MURDOCK NOTICED, the moment he stepped onto the property, emerging from the treeline that had been cut back a precise fifty yards from the house, was that the motion detectors were off. No floodlights snapped on, no guard dogs started barking. If an alarm had been tripped, it was a silent one, because the hushed night remained undisturbed by his intrusion.

Either Garrison was getting sloppy, or he knew Murdock—or someone just like him—was on the way, and a trap was already set.

If Garrison even suspected somebody from the agency was coming for him, was on the grounds right now, the odds of success had just dropped precipitously. Sure, Garrison was retired, but he wasn't an old man. He'd gotten out early and took his pension at a relatively young fifty years of age. Anyone else who had made it as far as that, and had been as successful as Garrison had been, would have stuck it out for a few more years at least. No need to step away unless there were health issues, like weakening vision or tremors in a trigger finger. But Garrison's final medical exam had been clean. Men half his age wish they were as spry, as solid.

Patrick Garrison was a legend, with a confirmed-kill count of eighty-seven. All the other hatchet men in the business were stunned when he announced his retirement. The smart money was on him continuing until he at least had his centennial and became one of the elite few in the agency to have taken it to three figures. True insiders knew, however, either officially or through word of mouth, that eighty-seven was only the number on the books. Off the books, Garrison's count was much higher. Maybe even double that. Some kills were not for the accountants, the record-keepers, or even the eyes-only crowd. There were bodies nobody ever had to know about, and would never be unearthed in some future audit when the next round of elected jackasses went snooping into operations that were none of their damn business.

Garrison had not been retired long, but so far he'd kept his mouth shut. Regardless, someone high up had dispatched Murdock to retire him the rest of the way. All the way to a flag-draped box and a hole in Arlington. Why it had come to this was none of Murdock's business. He had his orders. But if he had to guess—and he preferred not to—it was something to do with one of the unaccounted bodies north of the confirmed eighty-seven.

Expected or not, trap or not, Murdock was committed now and working on a deadline. He only had three confirmed kills to his name, but those were on top of an uncertain number of insurgents he'd waxed in his Marine days. Who knew how many he was personally responsible for with that much ordnance in the air? Probably one or two dozen. But they didn't count. Garrison was pegged to be number four of the counted kills, and so in he went.

There was no need to kick in the door or pick the lock. It was already open.

Trap, Murdock thought, *definitely a trap*.

"Put your weapon on the floor," said a voice, behind him in the dark, before he was more than six steps inside.

Fail. That Garrison hadn't already blown his head off was professional courtesy. It looked to Murdock like he was never going to make his centennial. Not even close.

Setting his SIG Sauer on the rug underfoot, Murdock slowly stood up straight again.

"Hands in the air and turn around."

Murdock did as he was told and the lights snapped on, revealing Patrick Garrison standing right in front of him, looking just about the same age he was in the last file photo taken of him. And he wasn't armed.

"You here to deliver me my gold watch?" Garrison asked him.

"You could put it what way," Murdock confirmed.

"At least at my last retirement party, they had a cake. Did you bring cake?"

"I have an energy bar in my flak jacket."

"Pass."

Garrison was dressed for bed. He was wearing a bathrobe with deep, loose pockets. There was room enough for any number of concealed weapons, but so far Garrison wasn't reaching for one.

"You haven't been at this long, have you?"

With no gun trained on him, Murdock dared to lower his hands and let his arms hang at his sides. He was confident he could retrieve his pistol from the floor in a second or two if he had to—less confident he could beat Garrison to the draw.

"It's early days," Murdock confirmed. "This time last year I was working roadblocks and checkpoints in Iraq."

"So you were a grunt."

"I was."

"But somebody saw more in you."

"I suppose they did."

"The new career isn't going so well, is it?"

"Not today it isn't."

"It gets better," Garrison said. "I remember my first few assignments. They were rough. It took me at least half a dozen to get my footing, and none of those set me against a seasoned assassin."

"I guess I got the short straw."

"Maybe," said Garrison, like he was putting some real thought into it. "Or maybe this is trial by fire. Sink or swim."

Murdock had considered that possibility himself. Surely someone with more experience and a better track record was available to take on someone of Garrison's reputation.

"Tell me," said Garrison, "how did your other jobs go for you?"

There was no point in obfuscating. Garrison had already guessed. He knew from experience.

"Like you said," Murdock answered, "rough."

"I don't envy you recruits coming up today," sighed Garrison. "In my day the home office was demanding, but a little more forgiving. They always expected competence, but not perfection. Nobody gets it one-hundred-percent right the first time out of the gate. Not even the first few times. However rough it went before, this job they gave you is a vote of no-confidence. If I kill you, then I'm only taking some dead weight off their hands. If you kill me, then maybe you've proven your value, and you have a career worth cultivating. This is your make-or-break moment."

Garrison walked across the room, his hands in his robe pockets. Murdock tracked his every movement closely.

"You can pick up your pistol if you like."

It was an invitation, casually issued, that Murdock was reluctant to accept. Bending over to retrieve his weapon might give Garrison an excuse to start blasting away. Of course, if he had been inclined to do so, he could have done it already, without all the conversation.

When Murdock straightened up again, the SIG Sauer firmly in his grip, he slowly and deliberately holstered it, clearly stating his intentions to Garrison. He was more interested in listening than shooting.

"We're warriors, you and I," Garrison said. "Like the samurai of old, we follow a code. Or at least the goods ones do."

Murdock had read Garrison's file. Mostly to memorize the face in the profile picture, but also to get a few details that might tip him off about what to expect. He'd noticed Garrison had served in the east for years, running ops all through the South Pacific. It was probably where he picked up this bushido bullshit. They used to call it "going native" when an agent started taking on the attitudes and philosophies of the locals where he was stationed. They didn't say that so much anymore. Probably because somebody wrote it down in a report once and one of the elected jackasses read it and decided it was racist.

"From time to time, through political machinations and drama within the corridors of power, it would become necessary for a *daimyo* of feudal Japan to order one or more of his samurai retainers to commit ritual suicide. Even those most loyal to him. Sometimes due to a point of honour, sometimes to smooth over an intrigue that happened at a higher level the samurai would never know anything about. And do you know what that samurai would do?"

Murdock knew.

"He'd cut his own guts out."

"*Seppuku*," said Garrison, keeping to the correct terminology and spirit of the act. "A final act of loyalty, done without hesitation or question. Because that was their way. Live to serve, live to die. When their service was over, so too was their life."

"They were also big on duelling," noted Murdock.

"Oh yes," agreed Garrison. "Plenty of that in those days. Two samurai, standing in opposition, their *katanas* drawn or sheathed depending on their preference. They would size each other up, alter their stances, anticipate the first move of their opponent and their own countermove. This could go on and on until the tension became unbearable. And then they would move in unison. With a single sword stroke it would be decided. One man would live and one would die."

"Sounds like gunfighters in the old west."

"The mythical version of gunfighters, perhaps. The samurai were the real deal. And they were at if for centuries before there was any such thing as a gunfighter or the old west."

"That was back then, and this is the here and now. It's all gunplay these days."

"Is that how you want to handle this?" Garrison asked.

"Is that how you want to go out?" Murdock replied.

"If you kill me, that will be the end of it."

"And if you kill me?"

"They'll send somebody else," said Garrison. "Somebody better. Carlson maybe, or Dupont. You met Dupont yet?"

Murdock shook his head no.

"He's very good. There's no hiding from him. I could disappear tomorrow, down the deepest darkest hole on the other side of the planet, and Dupont would find me. He would find me and he would get me and I would never see it coming. Carlson is also very good, but a complete sociopath. Him you see coming. He likes to work up close. Better Dupont from half a mile away with a sniper rifle than hand-to-hand with Carlson and a knife. Or a hammer. Or a pair of pliers."

"Sounds like we have some real upstanding patriots in the community."

Garrison sounded resigned to the way things were. The way things had to be.

"You have to expect that with people who murder for a living. Some do it for love of country. Some do it for the money. Some do it because it's what they're good at. They enjoy it, they need it. I try not to judge."

"But those types aren't warriors," said Murdock.

"No they aren't. They're not like us."

"Okay, I get it. We're kindred spirits."

Murdock wasn't sure if he believed it, even as he said it, but Garrison seemed to think so.

"I'm not carrying," Garrison said, turning his pockets inside out for Murdock to see. "I could drop the robe as well, but you get the picture."

"So what then? Do you expect me to just let you go?"

"No," said Garrison. "You can't do that, and I don't want it. Better this comes from you than the likes of Dupont or Carlson."

"I don't much like the idea of shooting an unarmed man who knows it's coming and is okay with that."

"Of course you don't. You're a warrior. It wouldn't sit well with me, either."

"What do you have in mind, then?" asked Murdock.

"It would be easier for everybody if I suicided."

"I was going to stage a bungled robbery, but yeah, a suicide would be best."

"There's a loaded pistol in my desk drawer, upper left, if you would allow me."

Trap, Murdock thought, *definitely a trap*.

"I can't let you have a gun."

"Understood," Garrison said. "Rope it is, then. Unless, of course, you would prefer me to bleed out in a bathtub."

"Hanging works for me."

"I think I'd prefer that myself. I never really understood why anyone would slash their wrists as an exit strategy. Sounds like a lot of needless pain right at the end."

"So's cutting your own guts out."

"I can admire the samurai of past centuries," said Garrison. "It doesn't mean I want to emulate their every custom."

Murdock took his pistol out and kept it trained on Garrison while he rummaged around for some rope that would support his weight. There was a coiled length on a shelf just a few steps down the basement stairs. Once he found it, Murdock watched Garrison carefully tie a proper hangman's noose. He was well-practised, like he'd done this before, many times.

The spiralling staircase in the front hall was crowned by a wrought-iron railing that could serve as an appropriate gallows. Garrison mounted an ornate wooden chair in order to fasten his rope eight feet off the floor, around the base of several different rails to better distribute the burden. When asked if he'd like to write a letter or some final declaration, Garrison politely declined. A suicide note was, he advised, an unnecessary prop in a well-staged suicide. Besides, he added, he saw little benefit in spending his last moments on earth writing a piece of fiction.

Every step of the way, Murdock remained on high alert. This was Patrick Garrison after all. Such a man would not go out so easily.

Trap, Murdock thought, *definitely a trap*.

Somehow, someway, he was being played. Maybe he was too new at this game to understand all the angles, and knowing this was making him paranoid. Or maybe, three official kills in, he'd already been at it too long to trust anything on its surface. That could make a man just as paranoid.

Garrison remained perched atop the chair as he put his head in the noose and adjusted it to fit snugly around his neck.

"This is a very nice chair," Garrison said of the furniture underfoot. "An antique. I wouldn't want to damage it. Do me a favour and set it on its side on the floor gently so it will look like I kicked it over."

"Yeah," agreed Murdock, his finger on the trigger, waiting for the trick he knew was coming.

"You'll be the only person in the world who knows how I went out," noted Garrison.

"This one will be on the books," Murdock informed him. "I have to write up a report."

Disposing of used-up assets or defunct agents was not considered so shameful it needed to be hidden away. This regrettable necessity would merely be accounted and filed away in a box nobody would ever bother to look at.

"If you're clever about it," Garrison said, "you'll lie. Say you did it and then staged this yourself. Such a convincing suicide of so challenging a target, they're sure to promote you."

"To what?" wondered Murdock. "One of the paper pushers who send guys like you and me to do their dirty work?"

"Exactly," said Garrison. "But only if you're clever."

"I don't think I'd like that line of work very much."

"You have time to think about it. Years if your luck holds up. Watch those paper pushers at the home office carefully. When they finally retire, you'll notice they all have one thing in common."

"What's that?"

"They get to die of old age."

Garrison took a deep breath, shoring himself up for whatever stunt he was about to pull. Murdock was ready for it, on edge, as if he were perched on that chair right next to Garrison.

"Congratulations. Your first staged suicide. It will never go this easily again," Garrison said, lifting a foot off the chair, leaning forward, still hesitant to take that step towards oblivion, stalling. "The problem with staged suicides is that they never really want to...

Murdock kicked the chair away, sending it clattering across the hall.

Garrison dropped several inches before the rope snapped taut. It wasn't far enough to break his neck, but his windpipe was crushed. Murdock stared intently as Patrick Garrison, the legend, the unofficial centennial by a wide unknown margin, strangled to death. The noose wasn't some sort of elaborate slipknot. It held firm as the body caught in it went through its involuntary struggles and convulsions. They stopped after the first minute. By the end of the third, even the micro muscular twitches had ceased.

Any notions that Garrison might be faking it were dispelled when his bladder and bowels released, evacuating out the bottom of his dangling robe. Murdock had heard of agents faking their own deaths before, and had seen his fair share of soldiers in the heat of combat play dead quite convincingly. But nobody went this far.

There was no doubt about it. Patrick Garrison was dead. And now he was Murdock's number four. Confirmed.

Garrison was right. Nobody else needed to know he had done it himself. Murdock would accept credit for the kill, and maybe even the promotion that came with it—one step up the ladder towards a desk job.

He hadn't had to put a bullet in Garrison's head after all. But Garrison had fired a shot into Murdock's. Not a bullet, but a thought.

Maybe that was the trap. The idea of another path. A chance to walk away from the life of a warrior, and the day that would inevitably come, when he'd have to fall on his own sword. Or cut his guts out.

Murdock willingly walked into it.

Three Point Seven

"WELL THAT'S SUBTLE."

Lemmy Brix's crew had just taken their first look at the getaway car they were expected to use for that afternoon's heist. A second look didn't improve their opinion any.

"We're not going in with this car," Lemmy told the driver. "Ditch it, get something new."

"Is there a problem?"

Duggart had done twenty jobs with the same set of wheels since he'd bought it brand new off the lot six years ago. He figured he could squeeze another twenty out of her before it was time to swap for a newer model.

"It's fucking *orange*."

"You have something against orange?"

Was this guy stupid in the head? Lemmy didn't know. He'd never used this driver before, but Duggart had come highly recommended. Supposedly he was some sort of legend. Dozens of jobs—maybe a hundred or more—and no one he'd ever driven had been pinched. At least, not while they were in his hands. Robberies, hits, fire bombings—everyone knew, if Duggart drove you away from your crime, you got away clean.

He was magic. But the four-door compact that was waiting for them in the parking garage right around the corner from the bank they were about to roll didn't look like magic. It looked like a clown car.

"We're going to get made by every cop and civilian in the city in this thing," said Vin, who was an artist with a scattergun, but had a real talent for stating the obvious. Or was it more an annoying habit?

Bollo nodded his jowls in agreement and said nothing. Lemmy rarely heard him say two words unless it was to order a teller to empty the fucking till, command a security guard to get on the fucking floor, or demand a manager open the fucking vault.

"What do you have under the hood?" Lemmy asked, sure he had to be missing something.

"Factory standard."

"Are you shitting me? How's that supposed to outrun a cruiser?"

"I get by," Duggart shrugged.

When Lemmy had asked his fixer to pair him and his two wingmen with a driver, he'd had to stifle a sharp intake of breath when he'd heard Duggart was available. He didn't want to sound impressed, even if he was. Now, face to face with the little man and his stupid orange traffic-cone of a car, he wasn't so impressed.

"Tell me this heap has some tricks up its sleeve."

"It has a sunroof."

"A fucking sunroof isn't a fucking trick," Bollo interjected.

"No. It was an option. It cost me extra, but what can I say? I like to feel the wind in my hair."

Go-time was an hour away. Everything had been planned down to the second weeks ago. Scrubbing the job wasn't an option. There were debts to be paid, and legs that would be broken if Lemmy and his boys didn't come away with at least six figures to split four ways.

Duggart knew the options were few to none. They'd do this on his terms or not at all.

"Your call," he said.

Lemmy shook his head like he was bailing, but it was a concession just the same.

"Orange it is," he agreed reluctantly.

• • •

The bank went exactly as Lemmy liked banks job to go. Smooth, easy, clockwork. One security guard didn't get on the fucking floor when Bollo fucking told him to, but a sharp tap with the butt of a Glock put him there. The guy wasn't trying to be funny, they'd just caught him by surprise. The blow would leave a mark, but not a concussion. After that, the rest of the staff was professional, courteous, and cooperative. The three men were back outside with two duffel bags of cash a full minute ahead of schedule.

Outside, the sirens were distant. Lemmy took the passenger seat next to the driver. His men piled in the back, each holding a small fortune of cash in their lap. No one buckled up. There was still plenty of time to pull away, nice and quiet, low-key.

Duggart hit the gas. Hard. The rear wheels spun on the pavement, kicking up a squeal ten times as loud as all the approaching sirens combined. The street filled with smoke and the stink of burning rubber before the treads found their grip and launched the car towards the intersection like an orange bullet. Lemmy and the boys were thrown back into the upholstery as an abrupt dose of G-force sat down on their chests.

The stop sign on the corner flew past them and Duggart tugged hard on the wheel, whipping them onto the cross street. The needle tipping the upper limits of the top acceleration speed barely backed off as the car performed a ninety degree drift and straightened out again.

The getaway car only made it half a block.

With another hard pull, Duggart pointed the nose of their ride down a narrow alley next to the parking garage where they'd first connected. He squeezed it between the buildings on either side as snugly as a cork being pushed down the neck of an unfinished bottle of wine. A medium-sized cargo truck was blocking the far end of the alley, its loading ramp down, its bay empty—presumably following a delivery at the back of one of the avenue's stores. At least, that's how it was meant to look.

At a swift but more moderate speed, Duggart took the ramp and loaded the car and its occupants straight into the back of the truck, stopping with no more than a few inches to spare between the bumper and the back wall of the cargo container. There was exactly enough room to fit one vehicle into the other, Russian-doll style. Opening the doors was impossible.

"Stay put," Duggart told the others, cutting the engine and worming up through the sunroof of the car.

He climbed off the back, retracted the ramp, and pulled the loading door down from the inside, plunging them into darkness. The car bucked gently as Duggart walked back across the top. Lemmy and his crew were blinded by a ray of light that shone briefly through the windshield as their driver pulled aside a narrow partition between cargo and cab. Once he slithered through, he pulled it closed, and it was pitch black again.

The truck's diesel engine roared to life and they were on the move once more, edging out onto another street and carefully merging with traffic. Even through the car and truck walls, Lemmy could hear the converging sirens. More than one seemed to pass right by in the opposite lane of traffic, heading for the bank that was growing more and more distant by the moment.

The ride was long, dark, and dull. Duggart had taken the keys with him, so they couldn't even play the radio. By the time the truck stopped again, the three men in the back were dozing lightly. Bollo snored.

The loading door rose once more, though the light it let in was dim at best. Night had fallen and they were indoors. Either a warehouse or garage, Lemmy couldn't say. Duggart pulled the truck's ramp down into position, climbed over the car, and slipped back into the driver's seat through the sunroof. Without a word, he started the engine and backed them out so the others could at last free themselves and unload their take for counting.

Lemmy looked around. He had no idea where they were, but they were alone, without so much as a hint of outside traffic noise.

"That's it?" he asked.

"That's it," Duggart confirmed.

"What the fuck kind of wheelman are you?" said Vin.

"A successful one," Duggart told him.

"I was expecting more action."

"You want an adrenalin rush, take a skydiving class. Car chases with cops are dangerous. People get arrested. People get killed. Me, I'd rather stay alive and out of the can so I can spend my money."

"The cops are still going to be looking for that car," Lemmy reminded Duggart, like he needed to be told his business.

"They've already found it," he said.

Bollo and Vin looked around like they were expecting a SWAT team to come kicking in the doors. They didn't. Everything remained still, quiet.

"By now they're thinking they got a bum description of the vehicle seen leaving the crime."

"How do you figure?" Lemmy asked.

"Because I arranged for another car—similar model, exact colour—to be passing through the area at the same time as us.

A nice old lady who thinks she won it fair and square in a mail-in sweepstakes contest two months ago. The police will have pulled her over within five minutes of us leaving. They may even have arrested her. They'll find no warrants, no priors, and maybe two outstanding parking tickets tops. She plays her cards right, she might win the wrongful-arrest sweepstakes next."

There had been a table waiting for them to dump and divvy up the cash. When Lemmy, Vin, and Bollo left separately with their quarter shares, no one questioned Duggart's twenty-five percent, even though he hadn't broken a sweat and hadn't even driven them one full city block during their high-speed getaway. The whole gig, he'd been more of a trucker than a wheelman.

Twenty-one jobs. Duggart's baby was now officially in the back half of her life. He'd miss the old girl when the time came, but they still had plenty of adventures to look forward to.

He checked the odometer. Three point seven miles.

They'd come a long way together in the last six years. To-morrow he'd get busy painting her for the next job when it came. That was the hardest part of any gig—choosing colours. Right now it was a hot competition between canary yellow and lime green. It would depend on his mood in the morning.

Lines on a Map

"O-RING WAS A DEGENERATE JUNKIE SCUMBAG, but he was *our* degenerate junkie scumbag."

The man in the chair just nodded. It was the end of my pitch. He'd either take the job or he wouldn't. I didn't know what was going to happen if he didn't take it. We'd probably get wiped out by the competition. Derek Dunlan might do it himself, then and there, if he'd taken offence to anything I'd said. You never knew. That's how his rep rolled.

"I'll handle it," he said at last.

Everyone else in the room exhaled at the same time. We were still in business.

All our liquid cash was invested in this move—in what one lone contractor could do for us. It was a hard sell to the rest of the crew, but one by one they'd signed on and ponied up. The old-schoolers who already knew about Derek Dunlan were easy to convince. Once the others asked around, started hearing the anecdotes, the testimonials, the ghost stories, they were onboard too. It hurt every last one of us to dig so deep into our personal reserves, but what choice did we have? It was this or lose everything. We weren't big enough to go to war. What we needed was a one-man wrecking ball.

In retrospect, it was our own fault. You could say we were victims of blind ambition. You could also say we'd fucked ourselves by way of greed and arrogance. Any way you put it, we'd screwed up. Our piece of the pie, selling smack and prescription painkillers, had always been small but lucrative. But the crew had grown. Someone's cousin just got out of jail and needed to earn, somebody else's brother got old enough to get in the game and needed an entry point. There's strength in numbers, but more mouths to feed meant smaller shares. And lighter paydays led to questions about how we might pull a few more sales, move a bit more product.

We'd tried to push the limits of our territory, move the line on the map just a smidge. Half a block, no more. The Knuckleduster crew was still working the top of E-Street. We thought we could pick up the slack down the bottom half. They had a dealer named Bigtop selling there, but he was a lazy, fat slob, and he didn't hustle like he should. Buyers were drifting elsewhere, unable to score when they needed to because Bigtop had waddled away to refill his Big Gulp and pack another pound onto his fat ass. We saw an opening and we took it. Once we hustled Bigtop off his corner, we braced for a pushback. There'd be threats and posturing. Maybe someone would get their ass kicked. Maybe someone would need a new grill after getting their teeth kicked in. When the dust settled, we'd either have a quarter mile of new territory or we wouldn't. We thought it was worth the risk to find out.

The Knuckledusters didn't fuck around. On the second day we had O-Ring working the corner, he got clipped. No warning, no threat. Not even an ass-kicking. A car pulled up—what he thought was his third sale of the day—and the banger riding shotgun literally shotgunned him. A sawed-off blew out his intestines, and O-Ring got to watch himself bleed out into the sewage drain two feet away from where he fell. It took an hour for an ambulance to respond. They'd only come into the hood with a cop escort, two cars at least, and that takes time for 911 dispatch to organize. O-Ring was long gone before then.

There was no use asking for help from on high. Our suppliers weren't going to be impressed with us rocking the boat this way, and then losing our petty turf dispute over the course of a single weekend. If it had worked out, we were hoping to be rewarded for our initiative. Now that it had blown up in our faces, we were worried about getting whacked and replaced by our own capos.

"You ever hear about a man named Derek Dunlan?"

This is the topic I dared to broach less than a day after O-Ring got his ticket punched. He wasn't even in the ground yet. There was still a lot of anger and tears in the room, and it would have been best to let things settle down and even out. But time was short and we had to make a move, a statement.

"He's a fixer, ain't he?" said one of the boys who didn't know for sure. The ones who did already know stayed silent.

"Like a mechanic?" asked another one of the ignorant masses.

"He fixes things for people like us. Businessmen, entrepreneurs. He figures out what's broken and he—you know—fixes it."

I didn't need to elaborate. We all knew how things got fixed in our line of work. There was nothing wrong with the distribution model. It was tried and true and had worked just fine going back generations. It was the people working within the model that gummed up the works. They were the moving parts that made mistakes, got out of line, ground the machine to a halt. The best way to fix those parts was to remove them entirely, take them out of the equation, make sure they stopped moving permanently.

"You sure you want to do this?" came a question from the back. It was Binker, and he looked solemn when he asked it.

Binker and I went back. All the way back to the playpen in
his family home, where I used to get dropped off for the day
while my parents worked long hours to put food on the table
and junk in their arms. We were like brothers, and he was the
only one in the crew who was permitted to openly question me
because it was understood he would only do so when I was
way out of line. Binker hadn't said shit about my move on the
Knuckledusters. This, however, he questioned.

"Dunlan's the nuclear option," he said. "That motherfucker's a stone-cold psychopath."

Hardly anyone had laid eyes on him in years, and the kids
coming up didn't even know his name. But the word was he
was still out there, still active, still doing jobs if you had the
right connections, knew the right numbers to phone, had
enough favours to call in. Most people who'd seen his face
lately had ended up with theirs blown off. There were stories
going back to Derek Dulan's early days, his mad-dog days,
when he could walk into a bar full of armed men and walk
back out again the sole survivor without a scratch on him.
Yeah, they were just stories, legends. But I'd seen newspaper
clippings from the last gang war that happened before most of
today's bangers were even born. Stacks of bodies. Entire crack
houses and biker clubs and mob fortresses wiped out. The
local police actually ran out of crime-scene tape before the
massacres ended. Somebody had to have done all that shit.
And one name kept coming up, repeated over and over, always
whispered like if it got said too loud, it might summon the
devil.

"You think you can hit the Knuckledusters hard enough to
keep them from coming after us?" I asked.

Binker hung his head in shame. We all did our fair share of
posturing, but none of us had ever been in a real gunfight.
Shooting rats down at the dump was as badass as it ever got.
The only reason we'd never been moved on before was because we kept a low profile, did our jobs well, and had the

backing and support of bigger fish. Now all that was in jeopardy.

"We need to hit them so hard, they'll never dare come back at us. That might mean wiping them all out to a man. We're talking at least a dozen guys, maybe more these days. You know anyone else who can get that done, quick and decisive, so it don't make waves?"

If the man we were talking about was as good as they said he was, we could still come out on top. And if he made a crater where the Knuckledusters once stood, we could take over the entire territory, not just that postage-stamp on E-Street. If that happened, it would be worth the price we paid many times over.

"We need to get in touch with this Derek Dunlan," I decided. "See if he'd be willing to settle this thing for us. Hire him if he'll have us."

It would take every stack we had on hand. The entire payroll for the week, including the fifty Gs we were expected to kick upstairs. Everyone would have to eat a lean month or two while we played catch-up. And we would have to negotiate the interest we'd owe the capos, which wouldn't come cheap. Someone would have to volunteer to get kneecapped for late payment, and they'd have to be compensated for taking one for the team, of course. Price of doing business.

I had a number from a friend of a friend. I'd never called it because I wasn't stupid. It was understood: this was for extreme emergencies only. All there was on the other end of the line was an answering service. No message, just a beep. I explained the situation in general terms, keeping the specifics vague, making sure to never say anything that could come back to haunt me in a court of law. Details could wait for a face-to-face meeting. I left a number I could be reached at and then spent the next hour trying not to stare at my phone, willing it to ring. It never did. It was the doorbell to our hangout that rang.

We were set up in a house. Nobody owned it. Like dozens of others in the neighbourhood, it had been abandoned, neglected, vandalized. Nobody was interested in the place, not even the banks. Estimated market value was about a hundred bucks, that's how undesirable the lot and location was. The place was likely to fall down around our ears one day, but the plumbing still worked and the price was right. We kicked out the meth-head squatters and called it our own. The power company had cut the place off years earlier, but we ran an extension cord to the next house over and powered a few essentials off that. Apparently we were getting enough juice to make the doorbell work. I'd never heard it before. Nobody ever rang it, nobody who wasn't on the crew dared come up the path.

There was a man on the front porch—somebody I'd never seen before, who was too well dressed to be from anywhere around our hood. I didn't ask who he was or what he wanted. I already knew those things. This wasn't a random visit from someone who'd got lost and gone knocking on the wrong door. Derek Dunlan hadn't bothered to call me back, he'd tracked me down in person.

● ● ●

Introductions were not made, but an invite was extended. It was polite, professional, courteous. Nobody offered Dunlan drinks or a snack. This wasn't a social call. The only thing I offered was a seat, and he took it, saying nothing.

"I got your message," were the only words to come out of his mouth at all. It was just enough to confirm who he was— that we weren't being played. I didn't dig for more. Once he was settled, I sat across from him. Everyone else stood, in doorways, up against walls, giving our guest as much space as they could. They didn't want to get close, and they sure didn't want him to feel crowded.

I went into as much detail as I could, hitting every point I thought might be pertinent, skipping the parts that might not be relevant. Boring Dunlan with needless colour commentary wouldn't have been helpful, and I didn't want to waste any of his time. He listened to everything I had to say whether he thought it was worthwhile or not, and never said a word, never asked a question, never asked me to elaborate on any facet. When I was done, I waited for a response, or even a hint he'd heard me and understood. After a long stretch of nothing, I threw a direct question into the empty air between us.

"Can you fix it?"

We all waited expectantly for our guest to answer. He took his time, letting us hang while he gathered his thoughts. At last he spoke, in a slow, measured tone, like he was explaining simple math to idiots.

"Seems to me, it's you lot that's gone wrong. You forgot your place. You tried to take something that wasn't yours. You put your entire operation on the line, and for what? Access to a few more smackheads who are too lazy to walk another block for their hit? The way I see it, it's you and your crew that needs fixing."

I half expected him to start executing us, one after the other. Dunlan worked as a fixer from the top of the food chain, all the way down. He'd done jobs for our own capos before this. Maybe word of what happened had already reached their ears, and they'd hired Derek Dunlan to resolve the problem by taking us all out and cleaning house.

"That said," he added, after letting us worry about our fate for a punishing amount of time, "the Knuckledusters overreacted. Normal protocol is you break an arm, break a leg, kick in a few ribs. Message sent and received. You don't go filling graves because some fat fuck can't hold his corner for more than twenty minutes without taking a piss. Yeah, I figure you overstepped and they overreacted and now we've got a mess that's bound to get a lot messier before it's sorted out."

"How messy?" someone in the room dared to ask, voicing the infectious worry.

"Here's what's going to happen," Dunlan said. "Now that you've been pushed off the block, the Knuckledusters are going to keep pushing. They'll take your territory a street at a time, and they'll clip any of your guys who take one step off the boulevard. By this time next week, you'll be down to one pusher slinging dime bags out of the alley behind the laundromat on Draper."

Everyone in the crew knew it, but hearing someone from outside spell it out for us made it real. Nobody was working the disputed E-Street corner, but the Knuckledusters were bound to have a dealer and some muscle staking their claim again by the end of the day, once they were sure we weren't going to escalate. Then it would be a waiting game. They wouldn't let it rest there. Things weren't going back to the status quo. When we didn't respond, they'd smell weakness. And then they'd come for a piece of our territory. And another, and another. As much as they could grab. So long as they paid off the bosses and there was no interruption in the flow of commerce, no one would care it wasn't our crew running those few measly blocks anymore.

"We can't have that," I said.

Dunlan nodded knowingly. So did some of the crew. Their necks were in the noose, their future hung in the balance. Some of them didn't have any future to look forward to, uncertain or not, if we got pushed out. At least a few of them would catch a bullet on their way off the block.

"What do you want to happen?" Dunlan asked me.

I swung for the fences.

"I want those motherfuckers dead. All of them."

His face was sympathetic, patient. It was a tall order. I was waiting for him to explain how that was an unrealistic option. Overblown, out of line, out of the question.

"I can do that," is what he said instead.

Dunlan rose to his feet and looked down at me.

"Let's go."

"Now?" I said, remaining seated.

"Right now."

"We didn't settle on a figure."

"One hundred large," said Dunlan, like he had his rates posted on a shingle for all to see. "For that, consider everything handled. Once and for all. Permanent."

I looked around at the rest of the crew. We'd all pitched in and I knew we could cover it. But it wasn't like the money was all stacked and counted in one spot. Dunlan knew it and told me as much.

"You'll pay me when the job is done."

"You want an advance?" I asked, sure I could lay my hand on five figures then and there. "A down payment?"

"Not worth the time and effort to split it off and count it out. I'll be collecting in full before the hour is out."

"You packing?" I asked, wondering just how heavily armed he'd been when he walked through our door. No one had patted down Dunlan when he came in. No one would have dared, even on my say-so.

"I have everything I need," he said.

• • •

At Dunlan's insistence, I came along, alone, belted into the bitch seat of a car that would have been boosted in five minutes flat if anyone else owned it. I didn't need to give him directions. Dunlan knew exactly where he was going. The Knuckledusters operated out of a former storefront on the main drag. The windows were boarded up and reinforced with steel sheeting. There were two lookouts on the door who weren't shy about letting everyone know they were armed, plus a security camera to give those inside a heads-up if shit went down that the guard dogs couldn't handle.

"Coming in?" Dunlan asked me, as he pulled up across the street and killed the engine.

"In there? You shitting me?"

"You've invested a lot of capital. Don't you want to keep an eye on your investment? See how it plays out? Make sure you got your money's worth?"

"I don't want to get caught in any crossfire."

"You won't. I guarantee your safety."

He was out the door and crossing the street before I could answer—not running, not storming the place. Just walking, bold as can be. And I followed him like I'd been issued an order rather than an assurance.

The boys on the door took their positions between the street and the entry when they saw Dunlan coming. Both of them had their hands on their gun grips before he'd crossed the solid white line in the middle of the road. It didn't slow him down any. He only stopped when he was within arm's reach of the pair.

"I'm here to see your boss," he said.

"And he knows you're coming?" said one of the guards, because it sure sounded like he did.

"Nope."

"But you have an appointment," said the other.

"I don't need one."

The two lookouts were only looking at each other by then, trying to figure out what their partner thought about that particular statement. The problem with dealing for the capos uptown is you never knew who they were going to send down to check on things. If someone showed up on your doorstep with an attitude that suggested they were not to be fucked with, chances are they were someone you didn't want to fuck with. A pinch of respect in such cases went a long way towards keeping you healthy. A good doorman knew it.

"I have to pat you down," said one.

"No you don't," said Dunlan, like it was never going to happen in a million years.

"Rules is rules."

"And I'm telling you, whatever you find, I'm going to stick it up your ass. Not metaphorically. Literally."

Dunlan spread his arms; a welcoming gesture. It was an invite, a challenge, a dare. And the doorman hesitated, which was smart, but also an admission that he wasn't going to lay a hand on him. Just in case he'd have to answer to a higher power than the boss inside. Just in case that higher power was standing right in front of him now.

Not more than five seconds later, the buzzer on the door sounded, indicating it was unlocked. And that buzzer kept going, loud and irritating, as Dunlan stared down two men with one eye per.

"You going to get the door for me?" he asked, lowering his arms.

And they did. Holding it open for the both of us like we were some high rollers checking into a fancy Vegas hotel-casino. Whoever hit the buzzer for the door was watching on the camera overhead. It switched off as soon as we were in.

The interior of the old storefront was dingy, badly lit, and filled with tatted up bangers who looked like their face ink was designed to help them blend into the shadows. There wasn't much in the way of furniture. The counters and display stands had been ripped out long ago. Now there were only a few chairs that looked like they'd been lifted from the Goodwill, and a metal desk that had once been fashionable office fare before any of us were born.

I recognized the man behind the desk as Reaver, head of the Knuckledusters for the past year after inheriting the position from his old boss who had turned up dead in a shooting gallery. The gang's previous leader may have been sticking needles in his arm, but it was the knife stuck in his belly that had finished him off. Rumour was Reaver was the one who put it there, and he'd done nothing to discourage that impression over his twelve-month-and-counting reign.

I could see Reaver recognized me, too, though we'd never had cause to socialize or occupy the same place at the same time before. He didn't give me more than a glance. It was the man I was with he was interested in—the man he'd recognized through the grainy image on the security monitor in the corner.

Dunlan took a seat in the armchair in front of the desk without it being offered. I followed his lead and sat next to him on a scavenged wooden stool that creaked underneath me.

"What can I do for you this fine day, Mr. Dunlan?" Reaver asked, trying to sound casual. He didn't. I could see he was bouncing his knee under his desk. And he kept one hand out of sight, like he was already fingering a piece strapped under the middle drawer. Dunlan couldn't have failed to notice, but he didn't seem the slightest bit concerned.

"So you know me," he said. "That's good. You must also know my close personal friend here."

He tilted his head ever so slightly in my direction.

"What did you say your name was?" Dunlan asked me, never taking his eyes off of Reaver.

"Trip," I said. Not my given name, but the street name everyone knew me by. Almost everyone.

"My close personal friend, Trip," said Dunlan.

"Yeah," Reaver said cautiously. "You two sure are close, I see."

"Oh we go way back, don't we?" Dunlan elaborated. "All the way back—what's it been now—twenty minutes? Long time. Lotta history between me and my close personal friend, so I know you'll extend him every courtesy you do me."

"Okay," Reaver agreed, like he was being given a choice.

"Goddamn," declared Dunlan, looking around Reaver's crib. "I haven't been here in such a long, long time. And I can see why. It's a real shithole."

Reaver bristled. You could see it if you looked close, but he tried to keep it under wraps.

"This neighbourhood's gone to hell," Dunlan lamented. "I watched it go there, one step at a time. And then I got out. And I stayed out. And I stopped watching. But seeing it all again, it brings back memories, you know?"

Reaver nodded like he did, indeed, know.

"This place," said Dunlan, "this exact place, this used to be a fruit and vegetable shop. I used to come here when I was a kid. You know how much an apple cost back then? Ten cents. Pack of beans? Ten cents. A nice fat cauliflower? Ten cents. That was the seasonal price, of course. Other times of the year, it would run you a little more. But whatever was in season was usually just ten cents. I buy an apple or a few carrots now, it doesn't seem right paying more than ten cents. But then, hardly anything is worth only ten cents anymore."

Dunlan reached into his coat and everyone in the room went stiff. Nobody pulled a gun. Nobody so much as moved a finger towards their piece. Depending on what Dunlan pulled out of his inside pocket, it was going to be life or death for a lot of people in that room. Maybe they'd take out a legend in the middle of all the shooting, but sure as shit he was going to take a lot of them with him if it came to that.

A moment later, his hand came back out of his coat without a gun, and everyone tried to uncoil their muscles without letting on how tense they'd been for the last few seconds.

Dunlan leaned over and set something on Reaver's desk. It was a bullet, standing up on end. Small, plain, unremarkable. Potentially deadly if loaded into a magazine—harmless otherwise. I'd seen a million of them just like it in my life.

"See that?" he said, pointing at the head of the bullet, almost touching it. "That's a nine millimetre, 115 grain, FMJ Wolf cartridge. Steel case, with lacquer and sealant. They mass produce them in Russia, and they sell them here in bulk. You buy them by the box. You can buy them by the crate if you want. Depends how much shooting needs to get done. You buy enough, the cost goes way way down. Know how much that one bullet cost me? Ten cents."

Dunlan sat back in his chair like he was relaxing.

"That's how much your life is worth to me. Normally, for a hit, I'll do a double tap in the brain, minimum. But not you, because you're not worth it. One ten-cent slug through the head is all you get. And if you pull through by some miracle, I'll let you be a retard eating your meals through a tube up your nose for the rest of your miserable life. That's how little I give a shit."

Nobody moved. Not their hands, not their legs, certainly not their mouths. But if you listened closely, the room was so silent you could hear the eyeballs. They were moving plenty as Reaver's crew looked at each other, one by one, wondering what happens next. Eventually they all locked on Reaver himself, waiting for the word that would make all hell break loose.

But Reaver didn't say shit. Once Dunlan gave him all the chance in the world to fuck everything up until it could never get unfucked, he continued speaking.

"I look around, I see a bunch of ten-cent vegetables in the making. Just like the ones I used to shop for with my mama in the good old days."

"There's ten of us," said Reaver, reminding his guest of the headcount in the room. The odds.

"Hear that?" Dunlan asked me. "Ten. I like round numbers. Makes the math nice and simple. We didn't talk expenses. Expenses are extra, on top of the fee you're already paying me. Think you can swing one more dollar?"

"Yeah, I can do that," I said, through a mouth that had gone bone dry.

"I know who you are," said Reaver. "I've heard the stories. Even so, you can't take ten of us."

"We're going to find out. Or, at least, some of us are," Dunlan told him. "Not you. You get to go first."

Reaver tried to keep his poker face on, but I could see him chewing the inside of his lip. It was nerves, a bad habit, a sign of weakness, and Dunlan spotted it too.

"Or we could sort this thing out," he said. "Sort it out, not shoot it out, yeah?"

Reaver took his hand—the one he'd kept hidden for the entire conversation—out from under his desk so slowly, I'm sure I've seen statues move faster. He placed it flat on top, fingers wide, and I could see the cold metal surface fog from his sweating palm. He said nothing, but bowed his chin slightly to Dunlan. It wasn't a nod so much as a twitch.

"Here's what's going to happen," Dunlan began.

• • •

Dunlan didn't negotiate the peace. He stated the terms of the ceasefire like it was a done deal—a binding contract signed in blood and sworn on our mothers' graves, valid and unbreakable until the end of time, amen. O-Ring never happened. The push up E-Street never happened. All was forgiven and forgotten about and everything went back to normal. The gears kept turning, the poison kept flowing. Everybody earned, and everybody stayed alive.

All the way back to the car, I waited to catch a bullet that never came. But I didn't dare look back, terrified of showing fear. And Dunlan certainly didn't look over his shoulder. He walked across that street like there was an impenetrable aura around him that no one would or could violate.

Only when we were back in the car and a block away, well past the mark where even a lucky shot from a handgun was likely to hit us, did I say anything.

"I couldn't help but notice," I said, "that the Knuckledusters—every single one of them—is still alive."

"You told me what you wanted to happen," Dunlan replied. "Doesn't mean it was ever going to. I said I could do it. I didn't say I would."

There was no refuting that, and I wouldn't have argued the point if I could.

"You sure they won't cross you?"

"Would you?" was answer enough.

We were back in front of my own crew's digs in less than five minutes. The entire hiring process, summit, and two-way trip had come in at well under an hour. I got out, but Dunlan didn't follow me in.

"Payment. In full, in my trunk, now," he said.

You never saw a hundred G's counted, recounted, and triple checked so fast in your life. I would have bet my soul that it was all there, down to the dollar. At the very least, I knew I was betting my life on an accurate count. I brought the money to the curb myself, alone, stuffed into three plastic shopping bags. The weight stretched their handles to the breaking point, and I barely made it before they snapped and let the stacks spill out all over the sidewalk. The car trunk was open and waiting.

In the time it had taken to bundle it all together, a few of the guys had asked how the job went down, and I gave them the broad strokes. No one questioned me, or the payout, but I knew there were concerns. It was a huge pile of cash, and we were all wondering if we'd really got our money's worth. The coming days and weeks would tell us if Derek Dunlan still commanded enough fear to keep the peace he had dictated that afternoon. No one could predict the future except, apparently, Dunlan—who took his money and drove away with it.

Every penny of it.

And we didn't say shit.

Chick Magnet

THE HOOK WAS IN. I'd caught her eye and now, despite herself, she was staring. Not at me. At the bait.

It takes her another two minutes to come on over. Resistance is futile.

She opens with what is, for me at least, the most cliché pickup line of them all. She doesn't know it's a pickup line. Not yet.

"Boy or girl?"

I have no fucking clue.

"Girl," I tell her, figuring my coin-flip guess won't suffer a spot check. Goddamn gender-neutral baby clothes.

"She. Is. Adorable!" is the verdict once my mark has had a long close look at the infant strapped into the stroller. I'm not one to judge. All babies look the same to me. Unless they're deformed or something. Most aren't. And if they are, they probably don't get taken out in public in strollers for all to see.

"Hi," I say, by way of introduction. "I'm Mike."

I say my name is Mike a lot. It's generic, forgettable. She tells me her name like I give a shit. We talk baby stuff. The heavy burden of being a single dad. The tragic circumstances that turned me into a widower with such a little angel to protect from the big bad world. It tugs on her heart strings. I play them like a harp.

The clock is ticking on the amber alert and I have to get off the street soon. I'm blocks away from the scene of the crime, but the cops cast a wide net once word is out. This I know from experience. It's not my first kidnapping.

I'm no master criminal. I've never made a dime off of any of the kids I've stolen—borrowed, really. The thing is, I'm no master pick-up artist either. Every guy has his shtick, his moves, his play for a hot girl he wants to bed. I'd always had problems putting an effective song and dance together until I discovered having a baby on hand was my ticket. It was a lucky accident, really. I'd been asked to mind my cousin's kid in a park for ten minutes while he ran an errand. When one of the local soccer moms sat down on a bench next to me and started asking questions about this child she assumed was mine, I was happy to tell her a bunch of lies. By the time my cousin got back from the store, he found his toddler unattended in a sandbox. I was busy getting my dick sucked in a public toilet. There was a lot of harsh language waiting for me once I was done, and no one ever asked me to babysit again, but I knew I'd struck gold.

People can be awfully cagy about letting you borrow their kids—even the very young ones that don't do much more than sleep, cry, eat, and shit. It's not like I want to do anything nefarious with them. I just need them to serve as my wingman long enough to seal the deal. So now, whenever I spot some young lovely creature I fancy, I go looking for the nearest baby I can liberate from a parent or guardian for a few minutes—a few hours, tops. Stealing is a crude term for it, but I don't exactly ask permission either. Mostly I linger in the area until mom or dad's guard is down for a few moments, their hand is off the baby carriage, or the little tyke is taking a few first steps out of their line of sight. That's when I make my move. If I'm lucky, the girl I'm after is still where I last spotted her, and I can make my flyby as a newly minted father.

The baby usually catches their eye, if only fleetingly. But when I set up shop right in their line of sight, and loiter with purpose, nine times out of ten I can reel them in for a friendly hello. The script does the rest.

Twenty minutes of cooing and consoling is average to put us in a hotel room. I try to let my mark pay because I don't like to blow the cover on one of my stolen credit cards unless I have to. It never seems to ruin the mood.

This girl from the coffee shop is textbook. She was still nursing her cappuccino when I returned with the first available baby I could pilfer. The first time I saw her, I was invisible. Once I was fake-waiting for a bus only a dozen paces away, I was superdad with an irresistible bundle of joy she just had to see up close.

Babies. They're even better than puppies. Nobody is allergic to babies.

What might have been a quick exchange drags on. Every time she looks like she's willing to politely let me get on with my day, I draw her further in with another leading hint of my lonely burden, or a cute baby-related anecdote. It shouldn't work, but it does. Something way deep down in the most primitive part of her brain is busy pushing buttons, telling her to go after the provider, the nurturer, the promising mate who might care for her and her own eventual offspring. That little ancient nugget of instinct is telling her to bag that provider every bit as hard as mine is telling me to fuck the hot chick.

She likes the grief-stricken-widower-with-infant-child routine. She's so in love with the idea, she doesn't question the little things. Like why I have some brand-new condoms waiting in my wallet when we check into a room a block away.

Baby or not, there are things we're going to do to each other that no child should see. I leave the kid bundled in a blanket on the bathroom floor. Bawling while we're balling.

The woman grunts out her words, two at a time, between thrusts. I answer in the same rhythm.

"She's crying."

"She'll stop."

"Does she need to be fed or changed?"

"No, she's good."

Eventually the baby stops crying and I can focus on me. The relative quiet of two adults moaning at each other clears my head and lets me finish in a timely fashion.

"Call me," the woman says, slipping me the phone number she just wrote on a hotel notepad with a hotel pen.

"Absolutely," I assure her before she's out the door. I flush the number along with the used condom. Then I shower and dress.

I leave the "Please Make Up Room" sign dangling from the door knob. Housekeeping will find the baby on the floor in the bathroom, next to the damp towels—probably hungry, fussy, irritable, but otherwise fine. They'll call the police. Child Protection Services will quickly match the baby with their amber alert, and the family will be tearfully reunited before the day is done.

A bored desk clerk will give the cops an unhelpful description of the average couple who checked in, paid in cash, and vanished without fanfare, never officially checking out. In less than a day, there will be any number of awful crimes with blood and real victims to monopolize the attention of the police department. No one's going to care about the mysterious one-hour kidnapping case that had a happy ending.

By the time I return home that night, the whole thing is an anecdote to the police, and another pleasing memory to me. My wife greets me at the door with the big news.

"I'm pregnant," she tells me.

It's the happiest news of my life and I tell her that.

She smiles, glowing.

Nine months, give or take, I'm going to get so much pussy. Hassle free.

I don't tell her that part.

Crocodile Tears

THE FUNERAL WAS ORDERLY, respectful and, most notably, quiet.

The eulogy, delivered by the presiding minster, had been safely generic, taken from a playbook of basic eulogies that only needed a few blanks filled in with specifics like names, accomplishments, hobbies, and surviving loved ones. As the decedent was utterly unloved, the names of his successors sufficed. They amounted to a third wife and four children, two of them step. The seating at the funeral home was filled out by friends who were never too friendly, associates who were never close, and co-workers who only ever interacted with the dead man on a strictly professional level.

The whole event went like clockwork. Many there looked forward to going home immediately following the ceremony. Some would return to work. The family would accompany the hearse-led convoy to the nearby cemetery for burial. A few hangers-on would last through to the reception, where there would be kind but empty words, graciously accepted in exchange for a refreshing buffet of coffee, tea, and cake.

Liv Vaughn checked her watch. She was the last of the wives and the only one to make it all the way to widowhood and the inheritance at the end of the rainbow. Her chair in the front row was pinching and uncomfortable, but she figured this leg of the wake would be done in ten more minutes and then she would be on her feet again, bound for the plush back seat of a limousine that was included in the cost of the funeral.

The minister finished his latest round of prayer and flipped through his notes for a verse he knew would sound personal and intimate, even though he'd repeated the exact same poem at hundreds of prior funerals. In that brief pause, while the assembled mourners waited patiently for him to find the correct page, there came a noise from half a dozen rows back, somewhere in the middle of the crowd of disinterested spectators. It was a sharp sniffle.

Liv's first thought was that someone must have a cold or an allergy. But then the sniffle was followed by a sob, and she was taken aback by something that sounded like a genuine outburst of emotion. Liv resolved to ignore it. Funerals were always a time and place for repressed feelings and memories to surface. If someone was, indeed, crying at her late husband's funeral, she was certain it had nothing to do with him and everything to do with how the trappings of the event dredged up painful memories of past loss.

Liv's capacity to ignore the occasional sob from behind her was tried by the open weeping that followed, and completely shattered when this anonymous person broke out into inconsolable crying. There was a murmur in the room as others reacted to the demonstration of grief. Finally, Liv was compelled to turn around to see the source of the commotion. She couldn't spot the person—a woman by the sound of the blubbering—because the perpetrator was stooped over in her seat, loudly honking her nose into a hankie. Her neighbours on all sides looked away uncomfortably, but none of them knew where best to put their eyes. Some seemed to be diligently counting ceiling tiles.

Liv turned back to the minster, who had stopped in mid-stanza at the jarring sound of the mourner. She glared at him until she caught his eye and he took his cue to get on with it. When he resumed reading, his pace was brisk and he sounded hurried. The final minutes of the ceremony seemed interminable—at least twice as long as the rest. At last, it was time for the funeral-home attendants to wheel the casket to the waiting hearse. Everyone stood for the departure, and the sight of the dead man's vessel on the way out inspired the lone woman to cry at twice the volume, with tears more copious still.

Again, Liv craned her neck to identify the source, but the woman was short enough to be lost in the shoulder-to-shoulder sea of men in dark suits. A glimpse of black mourning attire, pitch as though she were the grieving widow herself, was spotted between the shifting bodies, but Liv saw nothing of the woman's face.

Who the hell was it, Liv asked herself over and over again. A mistress? A secret daughter? A hidden wife? Each possibility seemed more improbable than the last. Merle Vaughn had been an extremely bland man, a boring lover, a dull conversationalist. Absent as both a husband and a father, emotionally and physically distant, he redeemed himself by working long hours and filling the void with a mid-six-figure salary. His money was comforting in all the ways he, as a man, was not.

In the wake of the vacating casket, the crowd began to thin. The mourners evacuated the funeral home, making their way to their cars in the lot. Some would reconvene at the graveside service, but Liv knew they would lose more than half the attendees, who would sagely judge that they had paid all due respect by attending the funeral proper, and had absolved themselves of further commitment. Amidst the migration of people, Liv lost track of the incongruous woman in black. For propriety's sake, she relocated herself to the lobby, where she could better accept the string of condolences from her husband's associates who would not be joining her at the cemetery, but were polite enough to say a few words before skipping out. The mystery woman was not to be seen there either, and although curiosity picked at Liv Vaughn's mind, she was content to never see or hear from her again.

There was no conversation in the limousine. Liv sat between Merle's two stepsons from his second marriage, and across from his two boys from his first. They were practically strangers, and there was nothing to talk about, unless the terms of the last will and testament proved unsatisfactory for any of the parties. Then they would talk to each other through lawyers.

Liv was still a couple of years shy of sixty. Time had been relatively merciful to her, and she retained enough of her looks to suggest the beauty she once possessed without taxing the imagination too much. She was trim to the point of being a tad bony. Liv preferred to think of herself as angular. Attracting a young lover to her bed was not out of the question, especially once the lion's share of the assets had been transferred to her name. Yet Liv felt indifferent to her prospects. She had been wealthy as Merle's wife, and would be wealthier still as his widow. There was little to gain from any further romantic entanglements. Money had always held more appeal than sex, and at this point in her life, she had plenty of one, and her fill of the other. Still, she couldn't help but feel ever so slighted by the absence of flirtations from Merle's business associates. Liv had been under the impression that most widows could look forward to one or more men at the husband's funeral offering their assistance with "anything...anything at all" in ways tasteful, respectful, yet tellingly more suggestive than mere practical offerings of handiwork, lawn mowing, or car lifts.

Two of Merle's sons escorted Liv down the cemetery path, one on each arm. The other two marched along their flanks, blocking the rest of the path, and setting the pace for the trailing mourners. The stone at Merle's grave was already engraved and in place, the hole dug and waiting. The hearse had come in through another gate and was parked nearby. Liv was pleased with the efficiency of it all. With the casket already poised over the hole, balanced on wooden slats, this next step of the ceremony, the most solemn and final of the bunch, would be short. The sky was overcast, but if the weather held for only a quarter of an hour more, everyone would be back in their cars before they felt a single drop of rain.

A small but dense group clustered around the grave, and the minister ran through one more short sermon before four of the funeral directors raised the casket a few inches with two ropes slung underneath. Two more men from the funeral home quickly removed the planks that had been supporting it, and the box was lowered to the bottom of the pit.

There were a number of other women dressed all in black at the graveside ceremony, but so far there had been no notable tears or distress. The loud one—whoever she may have been—appeared to have abandoned the procession before the cemetery. That suited Liv fine, as she was able to concentrate on the next duty of her newly minted widowhood—being the first to cast some earth onto her husband's coffin.

A carpet of green Astroturf had been laid out around the hole, covering the unsightly mud beneath the tear in the cemetery greenery until it could be replanted with fresh sod. Only the mound of dug-up earth had been left exposed. The minister took a sample of soil from the pile, digging it out with a silver scoop, and handed it to Liv. She looked down into the hole and dumped the contents of the scoop onto the casket lid, which responded with a hollow thud and the trickle of loose earth rolling off the sides. Merle's sons were next to take part in the symbolic burial, followed by anyone else who was interested in tossing in their own handful of dirt before the gravediggers took over in earnest.

One of the attendees—a rather short woman in a black dress, a black hat, and a black veil—took her turn and then began to break down before her contribution to the hole had had time to settle. She tossed the silver scoop aside and, to the gasping dismay of everyone in attendance, threw herself into the open grave, landing on top of the sullied casket with a heavy thump the thick wood handily withstood.

The crowd pushed forward to stare into the hole. Down at the bottom, the woman gripped the edges of the casket and planted her veiled face on the polished oak surface, staining it with her tears.

"Why? Why? Why?" she bellowed between sobs.

Merle's two sons had to step down into the grave to peel the woman off the casket. They hauled her out of the hole by the arms, delicately but firmly. Everyone wanted the ugly scene of unbridled grief to end, but no one wanted to look like a bouncer ejecting a drunk from a club. Compassion—or at least the appearance of compassion—took precedence. Once she was returned to the surface, the woman assumed her place among the other mourners, weeping and sniffling all the way. For a brief moment, she turned back, like she meant to cast herself down the hole again, but Merle's oldest boy blocked her and held her close, as though comforting her. Assuming the role of human straightjacket, he made sure there would be no repeat of the scene by wrapping his arms around her. Once she settled, he continued to hold her by the arm for the rest of the ceremony, ready to tighten his grip if she started to edge towards the abyss once more. The two of them stood there, watching shovelfuls of dirt being dumped onto the casket lid by two groundskeepers, until the grave was filled, and there no longer existed a hole to leap into. Only then was the women released. She had cried her eyes out through the entire burial, but her tears, much like the supply of earth, seemed to have finally run out.

Once his grip on the woman's arm was loosened, Merle's son hardly noticed her fade into the crowd. Liv saw him hunting through the retiring heads, trying to track her in case she was about to cause more trouble—like throwing herself under the wheels of the departing hearse as a new wave of grief seized her—but she was nowhere to be found. There was another burial happening that day, mixed with assorted other random visitors. With so many people wearing formal dark attire on so grey a day, she had melted away into the herd, camouflaged.

The scene at the burial had held up everyone's departure an extra five minutes, and although Merle's mourners made their way back to the parking lot at a brisk pace, none of them arrived before the skies opened up. The limousine driver from the funeral home was quick to intercept the widow with an umbrella, but he was too late. Liv was thoroughly soaked by the time she made it to the car. She and her stepsons would have to share a soggy backseat ride together, followed by an unpleasant reception in damp clothes.

Liv resolved to give the anonymous woman a piece of her mind should she choose to show herself yet again at the reception, but she already knew the opportunity wouldn't present itself. The damage was done, and the woman, attention hog that she was, would not seek to dominate the less formal event, where she might be confronted for her overwrought behaviour.

Just when she was certain she would never lay eyes on her again, Liv spotted the woman as the limousine pulled onto the boulevard that bordered the cemetery. She was waiting in a shelter at a bus stop, out of the rain, sitting patiently on the bench in her full mourning attire, as though commuting to or from work with the rest of the nine-to-five wage slaves. It was a strange sight, but that's not what caught Liv's eye. It was the woman's black skirt, hitched up so it wouldn't drag on the dirty concrete floor of the bus shelter, leaving her legs exposed.

She was wearing kneepads.

● ● ●

"Before we begin, I have a small point of business."

The notary opened a folder and retrieved a slip of paper from the top of the stack inside.

The will reading for Merle's estate took place five days after the funeral, in the spacious conference room of an otherwise small notary office. Liv was in attendance, as were the boys. Merle's two ex-wives had materialized for the occasion, having long since burned through their divorce settlements and years of alimony. They were both sniffing around for a post-mortem handout and Merle, Liv expected, had probably included them somewhere in the will out of a misplaced sense of obligation. She hoped their inheritance wouldn't amount to more than one or two personal items that dated back to their failed marriages. A piece of furniture perhaps, or a painting. Hopefully one of the ugly ones. Beyond the two ghosts of ill-conceived nuptials past, there were assorted family members, extended family members, and some who were extended to the breaking point. Few had come to the funeral, but a number of out-of-towners had made the trip for the will reading.

"Is there a Tracy Poole here?" asked the notary, reading from the slip of paper that had become the preamble to the main event.

"That's me," came a faint voice from the back.

"I have a cheque for you, signed by the late Mr. Vaughn. The memo space states, 'final payment.'"

A young woman, small and unfamiliar, with jet-black hair and tattooed arms, stepped forward and joined the notary at the head of the table. He handed her the cheque for her to confirm the sum.

"That's correct," she stated.

Without another word, she pocketed the cheque and left the office before the reading of the actual will could commence.

Liv was so preoccupied turning the name "Tracy Poole" over in her mind, she hardly heard any of the terms of the estate detailed by the notary, and had to later pay her own lawyer to reiterate the contents of Merle's will one-on-one.

Tracy Poole. It had to have been her at the funeral.

Liv knew the name, but she'd never heard it spoken aloud before that day. It took her all afternoon to remember where she had seen it before. It had appeared somewhere among Merle's papers when she was picking through his various legal documents during the final weeks of his terminal illness. The one page she remembered had nothing to do with medical care or finances. It had just been a random name on a random piece of paperwork, set aside to be shredded along with any other outdated or irrelevant pages once the estate had been settled and gone uncontested and unaudited for the appropriate number of years to make it final. When Liv finally found the slip of paper, lost at the very bottom of the very last box she picked through, she discovered what looked like a basic invoice. There was a sum to be paid up front, and another to be paid on delivery. Delivery of what was not specified.

Liv realized, to her surprise, that she was jealous. Fiercely jealous. The entirety of her marriage to Merle had failed to spark even the tiniest hint of passion, but this—this had inflamed her. Who the hell did this woman think she was, mourning her late husband more than her? Mourning him harder than all his wives combined? And then for this woman to collect a special dispensation right off the top of the estate, above and beyond what would be calculated, counted, and divided in the coming months. Why should she be paid and provided for first? It was all too much.

Liv kept the invoice nearby for the rest of the evening as she drank alone from a bottle of brandy that had been in the liquor cabinet for the past three years. It had taken that long to use up half of it. The remainder of the bottle would not survive to see morning. Between rounds, sometimes between sips, Liv would return to the page once more. She had read it dozens of times. Now, when she looked it at, she didn't read it so much as try to stare a hole through it.

There were only two fingers of brandy left sloshing around at the bottom of the bottle when Liv picked up the phone and dialled the number in the top corner box of the invoice. It was long past regular business hours, and well past the time when it was considered polite to phone anyone at all. Nevertheless, the call was picked up after only a single ring.

The woman's voice on the other end said, "Hello?" as though this call, or any other call at so rude an hour, was not unexpected or unwelcomed.

"Who are you?" Liv asked straight away.

"Would you like to make an appointment?"

"What were you to my husband?"

The accusatory question was taken in stride. Liv might as well have been asking a take-out restaurant if they delivered as far as her zip-code.

"This is my professional number," the woman explained. "I can answer questions, but only in person and with a consulting fee in hand. Would you like to make an appointment?"

Liv thought about it. Not for long.

"Yes."

"Cash only. If you create a new account with me, I can accept cheques, money orders, and all major credit cards."

• • •

They met in a small café the next afternoon. Liv brought the stated consulting fee with her in an envelope and pushed it across the table at the young woman, who was working her way through a latte that Liv had also paid for. Other than the briefest of introductions, the two had barely spoken to each other. They had, in fact, said more to the waiter who took their orders. Only once she was at the bottom of her drink and had leafed through the contents of the envelope to ensure the correct number of twenty-dollar bills was inside, did Tracy Poole cross her hands on the table top and get down to business.

"You have questions," she reiterated, correctly. With that statement, the dam broke, and the first few came spilling out of Liv's mouth.

"How did you know Merle? Why were you at his funeral? What was he paying you for?"

The woman who had collected her consulting fee answered with a query of her own.

"Did you love your husband?"

Liv paused at the direct question before deciding stark honesty would lose her nothing.

"No. Did you?"

"No," answered the woman. "I only ever met him once, when he retained my services."

"Are you a prostitute?"

It was a pointed question, bitingly stated. The woman seemed to take no offence whatsoever.

"No," she said. "I fake tears, not orgasms."

"I don't understand."

"I'm a moirologist. A professional mourner. I'm paid to attend funerals, memorials, burials, unveilings—and cry."

Liv thought she had never heard of anything so preposterous. Before she could say as much, the woman explained herself in a way that seemed well-practised.

"Would you have shed any tears at the funeral? Would anyone? I filled a void."

"I don't understand," said Liv.

"There are certain people in this world who pass unloved, unmourned. Sometimes the family hires me. Sometimes the people themselves retain me in anticipation of their own demise. With me in attendance, they can be certain that at least one person will be showing a respectful amount of grief."

"You call that ridiculous display respectful?" asked Liv, remembering the embarrassing spectacle all too well.

"I often need to compensate for the lack of emotion from everyone else present. If I make a big enough scene, that's what's remembered. And no one notices the indifference from the rest of the attendees."

"You threw yourself into my husband's grave!"

"At his specific request," the woman explained. "It's an extra service I offer for an additional fee. There's a certain risk involved, and protective gear is required, but it does make an impression."

Indeed it had. Liv would never forget it. Nor would anyone who had been there, she was sure. In the coming years and decades, if Merle was remembered by his associates at all, he would be remembered for the grief-stricken woman at his funeral who had mourned him so passionately.

"This world is filled with people who have emotionally distanced themselves from everyone," Tracy Poole added. "Or have outlived anyone who once cared. Don't they deserve to have some tears shed for them, too? The contracts I offer are simple. The pre-need retainer is, I think, reasonably priced. Many of my clients aren't even around to feel the pain of paying the balance."

"I couldn't find Merle's contract with you, only the invoice."

Tracy dug into the bag next to her chair and produced a clipboard with a small stack of documents fixed to it. She placed it on the table between them so Liv could have a look.

"I always keep the standard form handy. As you can see, it's all straightforward without any legalese. Discretion is assured, and most clients prefer not to involve lawyers. I suppose they're a bit ashamed to need my services and don't want to be judged by outsiders. Ironic, really. If anyone can understand being unloved and unmourned, it would be a lawyer."

Liv's hand edged towards her purse. Her fingers slipped past the open teeth of the zipper, probing for the nickel-plated .22 she kept in there. She'd brought it in case this Tracy Poole person proved to be a dangerous lunatic, but she had turned out to be so much worse. She was a parasite, a predator, preying on the lonely, the forgotten. Liv felt disgust, revulsion, and the need to act.

She ran her fingers across the barrel of the gun, then dug deeper until she touched the barrel of another weapon. Liv took hold of it and drew it from her purse. It was a rather ornate fountain pen she'd owned for many years. In her life, she had done much more damage with it than she ever could with a pistol—to herself, and to those around her. A marriage licence, a pre-nup, a power of attorney, a DNR...

"Where do I sign?" she asked.

The View from Inside the Pocket

SHE WANTED TO LEAVE THE LIGHTS ON and open a window. Bright lights, fresh air, and a good view. It sounded nice enough.

Her name was Tina, and she was a candidate groupie. Her and so many other girls who had picked a party, blue or red it didn't matter, and showed up at the rallies and speeches with buttons and hats and signs to show support. At that age they should have been following rock stars on tour. But for whatever reason they were drawn to the glitz and glamour of political conventions. It's not as crazy as it sounds. The rallies have their own mystique, their own razzle dazzle. And the music's better if you're into oldies.

They were young, still in school, still learning. Some of them had read the right book, listened to a good speech, watched a compelling podcast, and come away with a cause that resonated. They were idealistic and naive enough to think they could change the world. If they followed the campaign long enough to see their candidate elected, they'd have that notion crushed out of them by the end of the first term. But while it lasted it was cute, endearing. You couldn't help but fall in love with their enthusiasm and remember a time when you were young and stupid enough to believe the system might work.

"I could use a drink," she said.

"I'll see what's in the minibar."

"Fix me something tasty."

I was just another campaign minion, running the call centre. Nobody really, but she came back to my motel room just the same to sport-fuck our would-be congressman by proxy. She reminded me of a missed opportunity in college. How could I say no? Why would I say no?

I brought her a Scotch. Her hand slid down between my legs. Her mouth soon followed. The lights stayed on and we screwed across from the open window that let in a night breeze and the peering eye of a cameraman with a big empty memory chip and plenty of batteries.

I had a visitor come to my table over breakfast. I didn't know him, but I recognized choice moments from my night with Tina. There were photographs by the dozen that captured every contortion and made sure our faces were featured prominently. He also showed me a scan of the girl's driver's licence, with a birth date that indicated she'd only qualified for one a few months ago.

He said very little, reminding me of certain laws and statutes that sounded antiquated, even quaint, but remained on the books and were enforced vigorously. Contributing to the delinquency of a minor. Transporting a minor across state lines for immoral purposes. Supplying drugs or alcohol to a minor. Statutory rape.

"Who are you?" I asked him.

"An admirer of your work."

"What do you want?"

"Your attention."

There was no more for months. Years.

It's like they knew I would run for office long before I did. Or maybe they just hedged their bets and sought leverage with every up-and-comer. How much did the girl and photographer cost that night? Very little, I expect. I was a cheap investment that paid off big. It was only once I put the incident behind me, almost dared to forget it ever happened, and was millions of dollars into the hole on my own promising campaign that I got another visit.

"Remember me?" said the man.

"Yes."

"Remember our last conversation?"

I nodded and he told me I would receive calls from time to time. Calls I should take. Calls I should listen to carefully.

They had me tucked in their pocket, good and deep. And the phone rang often.

"Thank you for taking my call, Senator. Our mutual friend, Tina, says hello."

"What can I do for you today?" I asked in my official capacity.

"You have a vote coming up and we wish to express an opinion."

Somehow I knew the anonymous stranger's argument would sway me.

The pocket was deep and dark and I couldn't see who else was in there with me. But I knew we were packed in tight.

Shell Game Eight

SHELLY FLAGHER WAS THE HARDEST HARD-ASS in the checkout lanes of Murray's Miraclemart. Nothing north of eight items made it past her pricer. Only bar codes under the high-water mark tasted the laser. Anything more than that could get the hell in line over at lanes two through six. Shelly ran the express lane, and you slowed the flow at your peril.

She could count the contents of a cart, basket, or bag at thirty paces, and she could spot a violator in her lane before they ever even committed to choosing the wrong line. Shelly would let them make their blunder, wouldn't stop them as they piled item after item onto her conveyor belt, wouldn't say shit until she was finished her transaction with the customer ahead of them. Only then would she tell them, firmly and without pity, "Eight items or less."

"Aw, c'mon," was a common retort.

"Oops, I forgot," was another.

"Right, I'll remember next time," was pretty common.

None of them held any sway with Shelly.

She would stand there, eyes of steel, and stare down the violators, the rule breakers, degenerate scum that they were, until they collected their items, one through eight and beyond, and relocated. Some would do it sheepishly, some spitefully, but relocate they would.

Occasionally there was a bargainer. Some fool who thought their presence in the express lane was a negotiation. They'd pick out a few products above the eight-item limit, set them aside, and tell Shelly to ring up the rest. They'd take their staples now and come back for the impulse buys later.

No deal. In Shelly Flagher's world, nobody got to unbreak the rules.

"I'd like to speak to the manager," was a stubborn measure from the few who questioned Shelly's absolute authority over the express lane.

"There's his office," Shelly would say, pointing out the plain white door between the can-crusher machine, and the pyramid of empty five-gallon water-cooler bottles.

She could have summoned the manager and owner of Murray's Miraclemart with the store's PA system, but she never did. Shelly already knew she was in the right. Sometimes the complaining customer would walk off in a huff and go knock on his door. Mr. Murray never answered it. It's like he had a sixth sense for knowing when it was a customer coming to complain about Shelly kicking them out of the express lane. If he was in there—and he usually was—he'd remain hidden, silent, and would refuse to come to the door. Two or three knocks later, the customer would give up and walk out. More often than not, they'd be back shopping for groceries in an-other day or two. Lesson learned, they'd choose a lane other than Shelly's, even if they had just a few items.

Mr. Murray had responded to a customer complaint about Shelly. Once. And once only.

"We need to talk about your attitude," Mr. Murray had said on that fateful day.

She was invited, firmly, to come speak in private inside the little managerial office. Shelly followed without a word and let

Mr. Murray station himself behind the pressboard desk that held nothing more than a phone, a pad of paper, and a pen. A lot of talk ensued, but it was mostly one-sided. Mr. Murray made his case about good business practices, respecting their clients, serving the community. Shelly listened to it all, her face blank and monumental, her eyes ever steel—piercing, never distracted, rarely blinking.

Mr. Murray had not built this business himself. He had inherited it. The Murray on the supermarket sign referred to his late father, not him. When the elder Murray owned the place, having worked his way up from the position of store clerk in its five-and-dime days, there had been a game plan. A blueprint for a supermarket empire that would create generational wealth for his family. Murray's Miraclemart was destined to be a nation-wide chain in those days, supplying fresh produce and breakfast cereal and canned soup to a hungry populace. This location was only the starting point of something vastly bigger and infinitely more ambitious.

While scouting locations for a second outlet across town, the elder Murray suffered a stroke that left him paralyzed all down his right side. He made a brave face of it, saying—when he could speak—that this was only a minor setback. He would throw himself into physical therapy, work hard on recovery, and get back to building his empire before the year was out.

Before the week was out, he had a second stroke in the hospital, and died a few hours later.

Among his unfinished business was the job of making a bigger family to enjoy the fruits of his labour. One son was all he had managed at the time of his death. The second Mr. Murray dropped out of university to come home and head the business after his father's death. Less ambitious and rather unassertive compared to his old man, the dream of empire went to the grave with the elder Murray, and the supermarket remained a lone outlet, serving a tight local community for roughly six or seven blocks in all directions.

"Do you understand what I'm saying?" Mr. Murray asked Shelly, once he was done with the speech he had written down and practised for an hour before summoning his surly clerk. He'd been careful to tear the page with his speech off his pad and crumple it into a tight ball before depositing it at the bottom of his trash pail. Even so, he was concerned Shelly might spot the impression of his pen tip into the next sheet of paper in the stack, recognize a word or two from his statement, and know he had not been speaking off the cuff. He had prepared for this confrontation with his minimum-wage employee because, on some fundamental level, Shelly Flagher scared the bejeezus out of him.

"The customers are always right," he said, grasping at that one final adage desperately.

"No," said Shelly, speaking for the first time since the office door closed behind her, "they're not."

"That's not how the saying goes," replied Mr. Murray, trying to smile, trying to make light of the moment. The attempt bounced right off of Shelly's stern face and ricocheted around the room. Mr. Murry had to resist the urge to duck.

"The express lane," Shelly explained, "isn't."

"Isn't what?"

"Express."

"It's one to eight items," said Mr. Murray. "So it should move pretty quick."

"It doesn't," said Shelly. "It's the slowest lane in the store. Anyone with half a brain knows that. But the idiots haven't figured it out, and idiots can't count, so they slow it down even more by bringing more than eight items. They need to be set straight."

"Um," began Mr. Murray, and decided that wasn't a strong opener for his counterargument. He tried again. "I don't think you should be calling our valued customers 'idiots.' But that's beside the point. How can the express lane be the slowest lane in the store?"

"All the other lanes do is total up groceries. Even if everyone in line has fifty items, they all move faster because they don't have to do the other dumb crap the express lane does."

Mr. Murray didn't see how a few extra duties could account for very much time lost, but Shelly didn't wait for him to ask before enlightening him.

"Every two minutes, I have to stop, turn around, and deal with someone at the back counter who wants to return bottles or buy lottery tickets or a pack of smokes."

"We have the express lane deal with those transactions because the eight-item transactions are so short."

"Only they're not because of all the interruptions—like the granny who just won a free Bingo Bucks three times in a row, or the dumpster-diver who's wheeled in one of our stolen shopping carts with thirty bucks worth of beer bottles that need to be counted."

"They're valued customers as well."

"Sure," said Shelly. "Which is why eight items or less needs to be enforced. Otherwise it's chaos and we're no better than wild animals."

Mr. Murray was slow in responding, and in that pause, whatever power he wielded in his tiny office leaked away under the door, or up through the ventilation system.

"Rules," stated Shelly in that void, "are rules."

The sudden vacuum in the room made the air feel cold. Like a tiresome transaction at one of the cash registers, with a customer who insisted on paying in exact change, pulling random coins out of their change purse until they got lucky, Mr. Murray just wanted this to be over.

"Try to be nicer to the customers," he said vaguely. And Shelly left with no hint of acknowledgement or agreement.

Mr. Murray never invited her to another private meeting in his office, never praised or admonished her work ever again. Instead, he looked forward to the day when he could replace all the lanes in his store with automated checkouts. Customers could scan their own barcodes, bag their own groceries, pay by credit or debit card, and get the hell out. No fuss, no bother. Some people thought replacing low-skill, low-wage jobs with machines was dystopian. Mr. Murray thought it sounded like heaven, and he longed for that bright, shiny future. The technology was already here. He only needed to secure a big enough bank loan to make it happen. It might be another year or two, but it would be soon.

It could never be soon enough to see the ass-end of Shelly Flagher, on her way out of his supermarket with her pink slip and her attitude.

Ten months later, Murray's Miraclemart became the scene of the most furious gun battle the town had seen since warring factions of two rival mobs lit up a nightclub parking lot in the upper east end at three in the morning. It had taken police two whole days to locate and collect every bullet and shell casing from that gangland exchange. By comparison, no one ever accounted for every projectile from the supermarket showdown. Even a year out, customers were still finding lead fragments at the bottom of the candy-bar bins, and no amount of mopping had managed to wipe away every last dried drop of blood spatter. There were doubtless still some fluids left under the shelving units, or speckling the acoustic tiles in the ceiling, blending in with the rest of the brown stains up there.

Nobody saw the shootout coming, or the impending robbery that incited it. Three men, similarly dressed in dark jackets and woolen caps, took their place in three different checkout lanes, with no regard as to how swiftly any of the lines were moving. None of them pushed a shopping cart, carried a basket, or held a single item for purchase. A fourth man, only identifiable as part of their group through his choice of garb, took a position at the sliding doors, loitering for no obvious reason—or at least no reason obvious to the untrained eye. A security guard would have spotted the setup immediately, stepped outside, and put in a 911 call before the first gun was ever drawn. But Murray's Miraclemart had no such person on staff.

The men positioned in the lines advanced, one customer at a time, until they were all close enough to their respective tills to make their move. In a synchronized maneuver that must have been rehearsed, they pulled the rolled-up brims of their caps down, making sure the eyeholes were well placed and their noses covered. Then they took out their weapons. A second earlier they were anonymous customers, easily ignored, instantly forgotten. Now they were masked gunmen, and the only thing witnesses would remember about them when they made their statements to the police would be the masks and the pistols.

"Everyone on the floor!" the men yelled in unison, and customers started dropping in waves when they saw the guns.

Most of the cashiers started to drop as well, but the three in the targeted lanes were given different instructions.

"Not you," a couple of them had to be told.

Only the third one hadn't been headed to the floor, hadn't raised her hands in surrender or defence, hadn't so much as changed her expression from the same blank work-a-day look she always wore on the job.

"Empty your register into the bag!" said one of the robbers, producing a sack that would be able to securely hold all the pending loot.

Shelly's response was immediate, calm, and non-negotiable.

"No," she said.

"What do you mean, 'no'? Bitch, just do it!"

Mr. Murray had chosen the wrong time to be out of his safe-haven office cocoon. Standing off to one side, his hands up, he decided the three gunmen at his cashes and the fourth watching the exit scared him even worse than Shelly Flagher ever did.

"Shelly! Don't screw around!" he hissed. "Give these guys what they want and get them out of here."

The other two cashiers had already popped their drawers and were pounding fistfuls of bills into the sacks that had been shoved in their faces.

Shelly Flagher didn't have a death wish. She didn't want to die or catch a bullet that day. She would have preferred to go home without so much as a blister or a bruise. But there was something deep inside of her that refused to be bossed around. Not by her actual boss, and certainly not by some lowlife hood who had shown up in her lane—her dominion—waving a gun and issuing orders. On her best day, in her most conciliatory mood, she was an immovable object. Pushed, threatened, abused, her fierce unflinching will become an unstoppable force.

When she spoke again, slowly and distinctly, each word was measured and clear.

"Get the hell out of my express lane."

There was no argument to be made against her final statement of intent, her clearly communicated stance that there would be no cooperation forthcoming. Not now, not ever.

No one will ever know if the masked man in Shelly's lane meant to shoot. Maybe he just tensed up. Anyone who ever spoke to Shelly Flagher knew that feeling of tension—the kind that made muscles contract, tighten, even ache. The kind of tension that could make a finger squeeze a trigger, even if there was no conscious intention to do so.

A sharp crack made everyone in the store jump—from the folks up front who saw it all, to the staff in back who were cowering behind a cooling unit stacked high with frozen pizzas on special.

There was no miracle to be had at Murray's Miraclemart that day. Shelly's embossed name tag didn't stop any bullets. The single round punched her square in the chest, about three inches off from the worthless piece of plastic that wouldn't have even stopped a peashooter slug if given the chance. It dropped her to the floor with a hole through one of her lungs, and an exit wound out her back that took a piece of vertebra with it.

The man who fired that deadly shot, purposely or inadvertently, didn't let the ugly incident slow him down long. He stayed professional, remembered why he was there, and stabbed at the buttons on Shelly's cash register until the drawer popped with a ding that sounded almost as loud as the gunshot that had silenced the supermarket.

While Shelly Flagher bled out, flat on her back, the robber-turned-shooter helped himself to the bounty in her register—change rolls included. Much later, when the contents of his bag were collected by police, counted, and itemized as evidence, it turned out Shelly Flagher's life was worth exactly two hundred and forty-three dollars and ten cents.

But Shelly wasn't quite so cashed out. Not just yet. The hole in her might have killed someone who wasn't such a hard-ass. Certainly it would have convinced most people to stay down. But not Shelly. She had a reason to get back up. And that reason was within arm's reach of where she hit the floor, tucked behind the counter, mounted on a couple of pegs where it had been stationed since the last time she'd had call to use it.

There was no heat to be had in any of the other lanes. No Mr. Smith, no Mr. Wesson. No Colt or Remington to be found stashed under the cash drawers. Nothing more deadly than a ballpoint pen or the serrated edge of a register key.

But the express lane, that's different.

There's always some dumbass who waits for the display case to get unlocked before hopping the counter and trying to make off with a handful of Scratch-and-Wins or an armful of cigarette cartons. They never go for the cash. They'd rather try their luck with a bunch of empty promises and coffin nails.

Dumbasses all. That's why Mr. Murray hadn't loaded the 12-gauge he bought for the checkout lane. It was only on hand to scare off the dumbasses. Shelly had never been shy about letting them know it was there. Twice before she'd had it out to wave off counter jumpers in mid-jump. A flash of shotgun barrel pointed in their general direction was enough to make them freeze, a tip of Shelly's head towards the sliding doors was enough to make them run.

When Shelly appeared again, slowly rising from the floor, she was using the barrel of the 12-gauge as a crutch. The relatively short riot shotgun was still long enough to see Shelly, at a squat five-foot-two, to her feet. Only once she was perpendicular again did she lift the weapon. It took all the strength that hadn't already been punched out of her by that bullet. That and a whole bucketful of surging adrenaline. The man who had just shot her—who must have figured he'd killed her dead—didn't even see her until she had the barrel levelled at his head, no more than six inches away.

Mr. Murray had been horrified to see one of his employees shot—even if it was Shelly Flagher. He certainly didn't want to see the thief's gun emptied into her to finish the job. His first instinct was to warn her off, tell her to stay down, wait for help.

"Shelly, that's not even..." he began to point out, but stopped himself so as not to expose her bluff with the empty weapon.

But Shelly wasn't bluffing.

It had never occurred to Mr. Murray to buy ammo for the shotgun, let alone load it. It was for show and nothing else. Shelly knew better than to ask him for a box of shells, understanding that the very possibility of any shooting happening in his Miraclemart was unthinkable to him.

To Shelly, however, there was no point in having any sort of firearm unless it was capable of doing what it was designed to do.

"You want some birdshot, too?" the clerk at the sports-and-game outlet had asked.

Shelly paid out of pocket for the shotgun shells, with no expectation of compensation, even though she considered it a work expense. As such, she was only willing to buy one box.

"You know," the clerk added, when Shelly only stared at him silently, "for warning shots."

Racking the shotgun slide was warning enough as far as Shelly was concerned. After that, the stopping power of buck-shot—and nothing but—would do all the talking.

Waving off counter-jumpers had never involved racking the slide to get their attention. The sight of the weapon was enough to scare them away. But the gunman's eyes were else-where, so Shelly pumped the action, chambering the first of eight shells stuffed down the magazine tube, and that made him turn his head. It was the last thing he ever did.

At point-blank range, there was hardly enough space for the buckshot to expand into any sort of spread. As such, the gunman's head didn't explode all over the store like a bursting melon—it imploded around the more centred point of impact. A split instant after Shelly bore down on the trigger, his frac-tured skull caved in around the crater that used to be his face, and all the brains and gristle contained therein came coughing out the back of his head and over the pickle-jar stand. The spent buckshot pellets still had enough energy to break many of the jars in the display, spilling as much brine as blood.

The lookout at the door, best positioned to witness one of his partners get executed by the cashier, cried out something that sounded half-scream, half-curse. It drew Shelly's attention and she spun around, working the pump-action as she pivoted. She fired without aiming, but was still on target. With more distance to cross, this shell gave a better spread, and the buck-shot caught the man across the chest. He fell back, triggering the motion detector over the sliding doors, which opened for him as if to clear a path for his departing soul.

A single 9mm round, like the one that had dropped Shelly, can do a lot of damage to an organ. A shotgun pellet can't compare. But the thing about shotgun pellets, when they come blasting out of a buckshot shell en masse, is that they tend to hit a little bit of everything. Catastrophic damage to a single organ is exchanged for serious damage to a lot of different organs. Shelly's second volley had torn dozens of holes in both of the lookout's lungs, as well as his stomach, liver, and heart. Chips had been taken out of his sternum and spine, and three different ribs had been blown clear off the cage, leaving bone fragments floating around the man's chest cavity that would have caused him no end of misery if he'd survived his encounter with the express lane. Lucky for him, he was dead before he hit the floor.

In a matter of seconds, two men were down, and a cashier was critically wounded. It would have been enough carnage for one day, and enough paperwork for police to fill their week. But the battle had only just begun.

The two remaining gunmen quit their looting and started to return fire. Both of their automatics spat out the entire contents of their magazines in Shelly's direction, but it was rapid, panicked fire. The rounds chewed up extra-large bags of potato chips, blew apart containers of salads that had been prepared in-house, and absolutely murdered a stand of dishwashing detergent that was blameless of sin.

Shelly, untouched by any of these projectiles, filled the air with her own, racking and firing several times until she caught one of the robbers in the thigh. He went down in the pool of brine and blood and broken glass. There was little time for him to flop around in the mess before Shelly blasted a few dozen holes in his neck. Arteries opened, and a torrent of gore erupted that couldn't have been stopped with all the two-ply paper towels to be had in the household cleaning-products aisle.

The last man standing made it as far as the express lane and tried to wrestle the shotgun away from Shelly. He grabbed at the barrel but only managed to get a hand over the muzzle. Fingers flew when Shelly discharged the weapon again, and her masked assailant fell to the floor, staring at the pulped mess of muscle and bone that was left behind at the end of his wrist.

The adrenaline rush had done its job and seen Shelly through the crisis. Now that the outcome of the battle was decided, it drained out of her as quickly as the blood flow from her chest wound. She pulled another breath to keep going, and half of it went in through the hole in her lung with a nasty slurping noise. When Shelly exhaled again, a gurgle sputtered out, blowing crimson bubbles. This was a sucking chest wound, and Shelly would have agreed: it sure did suck. Every signal her body was sending up to her brain must have been telling her to shut down, take a load off

But Shelly, hard-ass that she was, mustered the will to go on. There was still killing to get done.

Dropping to her hands and knees, Shelly crawled around the back end of her counter, dragging the shotgun with her. By the time she made it to the lane, she was on her side and wriggling forward like an inchworm. Clear of the counter, she pointed the shotgun one final time, taking careful aim at the wounded man who was scrambling backwards, away from her, on his heels and one remaining hand.

The riot shotgun roared.

That last man's skull was tough enough to resist being penetrated by most of the pellets, but the beads flattened out under his skin and muscle, deflecting around the bone. They peeled the flesh off as one big bloody hood that flopped onto the polished floor a dozen feet away in a twist of hair and human features that was still wearing a destroyed woolen cap.

Only then, when the matter was settled, did the express-lane cashier rest, passing out, wrapped around the far edge of the checkout counter, cradling the hot steel instrument that had allowed her to win the day.

I may have already mentioned that Shelly Flagher was the hardest hard-ass in the checkout lanes of Murray's Miraclemart.

Only eight items maximum were ever permitted to cross Shelly Flagher's express lane. She had ultimately sent eight back, shotgun shells all. Technically, it amounted to hundreds of buckshot pellets, but they still only counted as eight in Shelly's world. Even she wasn't hard enough to count a carton of eggs as twelve items. Certain things could be permitted to slide. That was only fair.

As police locked down the crime scene and paramedics plugged the holes in Shelly in order to give her a halfway decent chance of surviving the trip to the hospital, Mr. Murray looked around the ruins of his Miraclemart. There would be expensive repairs to pay for, insurance claims to make, and maybe a few lawsuits to settle from traumatized customers looking for quick cash to calm their jangled nerves. He knew then that the automated checkout lanes he idly fantasized about as he sat alone in his little plain office would have to wait a while longer.

The headline on page three of the weekly free newspaper summarized the carnage as alliteratively as possible.

SHELLY'S SHOTGUN-SHELL SHOOTOUT!

Someone on the editorial staff was trying to be cute. The following paragraphs were less so, detailing the police report, the damage done, and the body count. Other local media outlets covered the story with considerably less flair. The nearest network affiliate tried to interview Shelly in her hospital bed. Respectfully waiting a whole week for her to feel up to talking to them, they found out the hard way that she was feeling well enough to kick them out of her room without comment. Or at least without comment that was fit to air.

Three weeks after the shootout, Shelly Flagher returned to work. Everyone could tell she was still in pain and would be on the mend for months to come. She wasn't so spry, and walked with a slow gait, wincing whenever she had to raise the arm nearest her wound. No one argued with her to stay home and rest, even with Mr. Murray paying her full salary throughout her time off. They all knew better.

Shelly's return was good for business. Once the Miracle-mart had been cleaned up, patched back together, and was no longer designated a crime scene, sales were brisk. Suddenly, people from all over town, well outside the usual range of customers, wanted to come and see where it had all gone down. Most of the lookie-loos bought something after they'd had their eyeful. Even morbid gawkers need milk or a loaf of bread. With Shelly back at the express lane, it lent a certain authenticity to the scene.

Some of the regulars commended Shelly for her heroism. Some told her she shouldn't feel the least bit bad for wasting those dirtbags. None of them dared bring more than eight items for her to ring up.

On her second day back, Mr. Murray invited her into his office for an official welcome home. It wasn't a private meeting—the door was left open. He made sure to avoid the subject of her taking a few more days. She'd have been welcome to if she had asked, but Shelly Flagher would do no such thing.

"I'm glad to see you're feeling..." Mr. Murray began. It was as far as he got.

"There's no shotgun under the express-lane counter anymore," Shelly noted.

"The police have it. Apparently it's still evidence."

"When do we get it back?" was all she wanted to know.

"I'm not sure that we do," said Mr. Murray, who hadn't bothered to ask after the weapon that had turned his supermarket into a slaughterhouse.

"Get a new one, then."

Mr. Murray nodded like that was a good idea, which he didn't think it was. But waiting around for Shelly to tell him a second time seemed like an even worse idea.

"Maybe you should leave this one..." said Mr. Murray. He stopped and let the word "empty" die in his throat.

There had been twenty-five shells in the box Shelly had bought at the sports-and-game outlet. Enough to reload a riot shotgun like the one the cops took twice more. Plus one for good luck. She'd paid good money for those shells, out of her own pocket, and she didn't like to see them go to waste.

"It's good to have you back," Mr. Murray lied.

Shelly Flagher returned to her post without saying anything more, leaving Mr. Murray alone in his office, with his thoughts of automated checkout lanes seeming ever more like the stuff of dreams.

There was, he reluctantly conceded, something to be said about having a real human staff manning his cash registers, dealing with the community, providing customer service.

Besides, automated checkouts don't return fire.

Injured, hobbling around, suffering, Shelly worked through the following weeks without a word of complaint, getting better, stronger, every day. Patiently, she waited for Mr. Murray to replace the weapon under the counter, even though she didn't really need it. On the day before the new shotgun arrived, Shelly stared down some twitchy reprobate she just knew was waiting for her to unlock the display case so he could grab himself a fistful of Scratch-and-Wins. He was a counter-jumper if ever there was one.

"Don't even think about it," Shelly told him.

And whether he was or he wasn't, he didn't. Instead, he took off so fast, he beat the motion detector to the sliding doors and ran face-first into the glass. As soon as they began to part, he forced himself through the breech and was never seen again.

Like we didn't already know it: Shelly Flagher truly was the hardest hard-ass in the checkout lanes of Murray's Miracle-mart. But she wasn't the hardest hard-ass in the whole place.

Don't get me started on Jason Wint behind the meat counter.

The Laundry List

"I DIDN'T DO NOTHIN'."

His eyes were pleading, but not innocent. No one in the business was innocent. Everybody was guilty of something.

"Of course you didn't, Billy. That's why we're here. For all that nothin' you didn't do."

"Is it a hit?"

You had to give Billy Cribbs credit. He was a weasel, but he cut right to the chase. And he wanted it straight. Was he about to get himself murdered or not? The answer put his mind at ease. At least a little bit.

"Nah, Billy. It's just a message," Anthony told him, removing a small folded slip of paper from his pocket.

Marco was finished duct taping Billy to a chair in the workshop. He tore off the final strip with his teeth and smoothed it down in place. That would hold him.

Billy was a notorious runner. Numbers sure, but that extended to his feet as well. He'd been present at ten different police raids. Bookies or brothels, he'd high-tailed it out of there like the wind, and the cops never got a collar on him—never placed him at the scene of whatever crime they were trying to crack down on. Not even that time they landed hard on Jenny Yee's legendary den of sin and pulled fifty staff and patrons out in a whole convoy of paddy wagons. They got every single perp on the premises by blocking every last door and window to the joint. But not Billy. He got out. Ran right across the roof and made the jump to the next property over. It was a long jump, and if he'd missed it, it would have been a broken neck for sure. But he made it. He had the momentum to carry him over, and once he was across, he didn't stop running until he was in a whole other precinct. Rooftops and running shoes the whole way.

"Who's it from?" asked Billy, looking at the paper Anthony was unravelling in front of him.

"You know who it's from if we're the ones delivering the message. And you know what you did for him to send it."

"I didn't do nothin'," Billy reiterated.

"So you've said."

Anthony looked at the handwritten note, not for the first time. He went over it again, silently, until Billy couldn't take the suspense anymore.

"What's the message?" he asked, helpless to do anything but listen. He couldn't do more than wiggle slightly. Marco hadn't fixed his ankles to the legs of the chair, but even if Billy could rock himself forward and plant his feet on the floor, he wouldn't get far, bent over with a heavy hunk of furniture taped to his back.

"You mean this?" Anthony said, waving the slip of paper around in the still air of the dark, muggy shop. "This isn't the message. This is a list. A list of what we're supposed to do to you. What we do to you, *that's* the message."

"Kneecap?" Marco asked, anticipating the most likely item on the list.

Anthony squinted at the handwriting.

"Yeah..." he concluded. "I don't think that's an 's,' so just one'll do."

Marco dragged a stool over and went to fetch the sledge-hammer. Anthony tucked the paper away while he set the heel of one of Billy's feet on the seat of the stool. Billy tried to buck out of his grip, but Anthony held him firm.

"Nononononononono!" Billy stammered, like there was a chance, if he could rattle off enough "no"s in a row, it would stop what was coming.

Marco's hammer blow came without pause or ceremony, folding Bill's leg in half at the joint—the wrong way. Billy's kneecap splintered, digging shards into flesh and muscle. He screamed like a wild animal—a single long bleat, until his lungs were out of air. The pain made him pass out the very next moment. His head nodded forward, his body went limp, and his breathing resumed as a wheezing snore, confirming he was only unconscious, not dead of shock.

"Want me to wake him up?" Marco asked.

Anthony ran his eyes down the next few items on the sheet. Things weren't going to get any nicer.

"Nah, he's best out of it for the rest of the shit we need to do. He wouldn't want to be awake for any of it, and it'll be easier for us to get it done if he's down for the count."

Marco looked over his partner's shoulder and commented, "Jeezus, his handwritin's horrible."

They were both having trouble with one scribble halfway down the page.

"What's a gloogloo simile?"

"Glasgow Smile," Anthony finally deciphered.

"What's that?"

"It's when you cut through the corners of a guy's mouth, all the way back to his wisdom teeth, on both sides," Anthony demonstrated, running his finger along his own cheeks where the incisions would be made. "They'll stitch it back together, but the scars will always make him look like he's wearing a gruesome smile."

"Oh, you mean a Chelsea Grin," said Marco, knowingly.

"What's a Chelsea Grin?"

"Same thing."

"So why's it got a different name?"

"I guess it comes down to where it gets done," Marco speculated. "It's a Glasgow Smile in Glasgow, and a Chelsea Grin in Chelsea."

"We're in fuckin' Hoboken," Anthony reminded him.

"Then I guess we're inventing the Hoboken Grimace today."

Anthony looked at Billy in his chair—his head hanging low, his leg bent backward, a compound fracture pooling blood. His breathing was the sickening groan that always seemed to come with trauma-induced unconsciousness. Anthony had heard that sound often in his career. It was creepy every time.

"You hold his mouth open," said Anthony, "I'll do the cutting."

He had a switchblade in his pocket. It was good for this sort of job and so much worse. He also used it to pick dirt from under his fingernails and, when it had been through a dishwasher between jobs, peel the occasional apple.

By the time they were done, Billy was bleeding profusely out both sides of his face. The cutting had gone smoothly, with their mark sleeping through the surgery, but they had to make sure his head was left tilting forward so he wouldn't choke on the steady flow before it had a chance to clot.

"You're gonna have to help me out with this one," said Anthony, moving down the list.

"Bubble Piccolo," Marco ventured, after trying to sound out the indistinct words for the better part of a full minute.

"Sounds like some sort of instrument. One you blow under water or something."

"That don't make no sense."

"Should we be filling a tub of water or something?"

Marco looked again and finally deduced an order that made more sense.

"Double van Gogh!"

"Ah!" nodded Anthony knowingly, relieved to finally have it straight. Once it sunk it, however, he was troubled.

"Taking both his ears seems excessive."

"The whole list seems excessive," Marco agreed, "but orders are orders."

"You know, van Gogh only cut off one earlobe," said Anthony, as he started to saw through the back of the first ear with his switchblade. "People always think he cut off his whole ear, but he didn't."

"You're a fuckin' well of historical trivia."

"I'm only saying, maybe we can just cut off his earlobes."

"And what if that's not how the boss wants it?" said Marco. "You want him to demonstrate what he had in mind on you, so you get it right next time? That the kind of feedback you're fishing for?"

"No," said Anthony, without further consideration, and proceeded to make his way through the rest of the ear. Then the other.

"What's the next one say?" Marco asked, as Anthony tossed the two slabs of meat into a nearby bucket.

"Poopy," he announced, consulting the list.

"You sure?"

"Looks like 'poopy' to me," said Anthony.

"Geez, you don't suppose the boss wants us to do something fucked up with his asshole, do you?"

"I hope not. I hate doing the ass stuff. It's all well and good telling a guy you're gonna stuff something up his ass—something that don't belong there. But the capos never think it through when they try to make good on the threat. Somebody has to actually go and stuff that thing up an ass, which ain't so pleasant for them, neither. And what if it's something that don't fit so good?"

"Remember Don Palazzo? Dead twenty years now, God rest his soul. In bed, natural causes, ripe old age and surrounded by family, the lucky bastard. Not so for a lot of the unfortunate bastards he ordered hit or roughed up. I was a kid at the time, but I remember hearing about Pete Lucio, who used to set up pins at the bowling alley on fifth avenue."

"I remember that guy, always with a cigarette hanging out of his mouth while he was filling in seven-ten splits. Whatever happened to him?"

"Don't you know?"

"I thought he got retired out when they installed the automatic pinsetter."

"Nah. He was the reason that pinsetter got installed. Better that than hire somebody new. Don Palazzo owned that bowling alley. Not on paper, but he owned it just the same. And he didn't care for Pete Lucio putting cigarette burns in the maple pin-deck. He told him, if he ever heard about him putting a lit butt down on his nice varnished wood again, he'd stuff something where the sun don't shine."

"Bowling pin?"

"Pete Lucio wished he'd said bowling pin. A bowling pin would make sense, given its general shape. Maybe Don Palazzo meant to say bowling pin, but his English weren't so good back then. What he said was 'bowling ball.'"

"That's not good."

"No, it's not. A bowling pin will rip you open. That's stitches and probably the better part of a year on a colostomy bag. You can survive it, though. But a bowling ball? That was a death sentence the moment it came out of the Don's mouth."

"It didn't have to be."

"It didn't. But Pete Lucio was a two-pack-a-day man, minimum. And he was never careful about where he stubbed out his smokes. When they sent a guy over to let his widow know he wasn't ever coming home, he said he saw all sorts of cigarette-burn marks on the kitchen counter, on the table, on the chairs. Meanwhile, there was an ashtray right next to the gas stove. Empty. Clean. Like you could eat out of it."

"Popeye!" Anthony suddenly exclaimed, interrupting Marco's story.

"What that now?"

"On the list. It says 'Popeye,' not 'poopy.' He wants us to take one of his eyes."

"Thank Christ for that!" said Marco with a heavy sigh.

"Just one eye," said Anthony, preparing to go digging behind Billy's eyelids while Marco held his head still.

"Lucky break for Billy," said Marco. "We already made him deaf, at least he still gets to see out one eye."

"We took both his ears. That don't make him deaf. He still has his ear holes."

"Yeah, I guess so," said Marco, as Anthony severed the optic nerve and popped Billy's eye out, straight into the bucket with his ears.

That was the last item on the list. Anthony and Marco stepped back to assess their handiwork, confirming they'd done a tidy, professional job of it.

"Ain't nobody gonna recognize Billy Cribbs after what we done to him," Marco said, with a certain distinct regret.

"Billy Cribbs?" asked Anthony.

He double checked the other side of the paper in his hand.

"That's not the name I got down here.

"Right there," said Marco, pointing to a hastily jotted note on the page they had been assigned only an hour earlier. 'Billy Cribbs.'"

"It says 'Billy Grimes.'"

"That's a 'G'?"

"And that's an 'M' and an 'E,'" Anthony noted, interpreting the chicken scratch.

It was still leaning towards ambiguity, but the more Marco stared at it, the more he suspected Anthony was correct.

"I think you're right," he conceded at last.

Both men gazed on the bleeding heap of a man before them. His broken form would have spilled out of the chair if he hadn't been so firmed taped to it.

Anthony had to hand it to Billy. "He *did* say he didn't do nothing."

"Yeah, but they all say that, don't they?"

A message had been sent all right, but they got the address wrong. Billy Cribs would serve as an example to others, sure. But he'd also be a lesson. Sometimes life—*the* life—wasn't fair, and even people who don't have it coming get it just the same.

"I think I got some remorse about this," Anthony concluded.

"You suppose we should drop Billy Cribbs off at the ER on our way to other Billy's place?" Marco suggested.

"It's the decent thing to do. We won't stop or nothin'. Just push him out on our way past the door."

"Maybe we should pin a note to him."

"Saying what?"

"'Sorry'?"

Anthony thought about it, but not for long. There was the decent thing, and then there was being too decent.

"Nah," he said. "Let Billy Cribbs figure he must have done *something* wrong. That way he'll watch himself, and it'll be less likely he'll ever do *anything* wrong ever again."

"What do we do with the leftovers?" Marco asked, staring down into the bucket of cast-offs.

"Stick 'em in his pocket. Maybe they can stitch some of this shit back on."

"Tough break, Billy," said Macro, tucking the eye and two ears into the breast pocket of their owner's blood-soaked jean vest. He left one ear poking out above the flap so the doctors would be sure to spot it.

"On the bright side, we've already figured out all the shit we need to do to Billy Grimes," said Anthony.

"That'll save us a lot of time," noted Marco.

Anthony took hold of the back of the chair and tipped Billy Cribbs at an angle so he could drag it on two legs, across the floor to the loading bay where their van was parked.

"See? It wasn't all a waste of time."

"Silver linings," agreed Marco. "Silver linings."

A Foot in the Door

THE GIRL ARRIVED BY HIRED CAR. Not an Uber or some filthy taxi, but a nice set of wheels with a driver. Hired cars came at an hourly rate that didn't get discounted if your trip across town only took fifteen minutes. It was an investment. I'd seen it before. The professionals—the real pros—liked to make sure they showed up for their date as pristine as possible. No creases, no ruffles, and smelling of their expensive soaps and perfumes—not whatever piss-stained drunk last rode in the back of the cab. It made for repeat business with the high-rollers, the whales with a fat bankroll. And all the working girls wanted that.

They didn't get it here.

Officially, for legal purposes, their fees bought time and companionship and nothing more. Unofficially, but understood between all parties, they were selling sex. The difference between them and street whores was the difference between a steak dinner and a greasy-spoon burger that may or may not give you botulism. With the sex they were selling came a certain class, a certain poise, and a higher standard of cleanliness. Their lovers were legion and they'd all serviced more cocks than you'd care to count, but there was an effort to keep the numbers down, to be selective, to keep their stable of clients small. Repeat business was the goal. And presentation was key to getting repeat business—to keep those wealthy clients coming back for more.

But I knew better. This place didn't do repeat business. Not one of the girls summoned was ever called back. And not one of them would have come back for any sum of money. If you got your foot in the door of this particular luxury high-rise, that door got slammed in your face right after your first visit. Mind your toes or they might get clipped off if you're not wearing safety boots.

The new girl who walked into my lobby was wearing pumps, not boots, and her polished toenails stuck out the tips of her shoes, exposed and vulnerable. I sighed at the sight of her. Not because she was so pretty, but because I knew she'd be a whole lot less pretty once it was time for her to leave in an hour or two. As usual, I'd be waiting downstairs to call her a cab—a good enough ride for escorts commuting home after a job. And while we waited for it to arrive, I'd perform triage as best I could. An ice pack was waiting in the staff fridge. Disinfectant and bandages were in a first-aid kit. Assuming she was able to speak after her ordeal, I'd ask if she wanted the cab to take her home or to the hospital. If the evening had gone particularly bad, I'd default to instructing the driver to take her straight to the ER.

You'd think word would spread, but there are always new girls trying their hand at escorting, and maybe the network of communication isn't as tight as it might be if there was more longevity in the business.

"Hi," the girl said to me as she approached. "I'm here to see Mister..."

I cut her off with a nod. There was no need to invoke his name. Frankly, I didn't even like to hear it spoken aloud.

"I'll announce you," I said.

I took the desk phone and put in a call to the top floor. The building had a lot of suites, each of them occupied by their own rich asshole. The assholes got bigger and richer the higher up you went. But I knew which one to ring. Only one of them had a regular rotation of hot women, well paid at an hourly wage. He was in the unit that crowned all the rest. The very top. King Asshole.

"Did you request company this evening?" I asked, when the other end picked up.

"I did indeed!" said the penthouse prick, sounding delighted, expectant. "Is she here?"

"She's at my desk now. A car just dropped her off."

"Is she pretty?" he asked. The online pictures of escorts often didn't show their faces.

"Yes, I'd say so," I concluded, after letting my eyes dart up and down the girl's body.

"Is she clean?"

"As far as I can tell."

I didn't know how closely he expected me to inspect her, but she smelled nice.

"Send her up," I was told.

I didn't wear a uniform or a spiffy cap. I wore a suit and tie and sat behind a desk. Officially I was a doorman. What I really was, was a line of defense against the outside world. I protected the tenants of the building against unwanted incursions. I signed for packages, collected parcels, accepted mail, and greeted visitors. I was a doorman who didn't open doors. I buzzed people in, I buzzed them upstairs, and I watched them every step of the way through cameras set in the elevators, halls, and stairwells. That was about the extent of my job, detailed right in my contract with the holding company that owned the property. But there were other aspects to the work that weren't outlined in black and white, weren't part of the job description. These duties were understood, but never spoken of, and were unofficially paid for through tips and Christmas bonuses. Collectively, they could be described as selective blindness. What extra I was paid on top of my official salary came with the understanding that, even as I stood vigil over the property, there were things I was not to see, not to acknowledge. Things I was to wilfully ignore. No one explained what these things would be. Part of being qualified for the job was having an instinct for it, being savvy enough to know without being told.

The comings and goings of illicit affairs was one of the more mundane things I was expected to turn a blind eye to. Certain deliveries was another. It was none of my business what was in a plain brown wrapper, even if it stank of weed or worse. Just like my on-again/off-again eyesight, my sense of smell failed me when it needed to. All these things I had no qualms about. It wasn't any of my business who was cheating on who, or which of the tenants was getting high on what.

It was the violent incidents that troubled me.

Domestic quarrels were common enough. Sometimes they came with black eyes. It wasn't my place to comment on a wife's new shiner, or scratches across a husband's face. And if an ambulance had to be summoned, I left the involved parties to come up with their own excuses for what happened. I didn't see anything, I didn't know anything. Particularly when police or lawyers got involved.

I've got a strong stomach. Strong enough for this sort of work. My first job was working in a butcher shop. If you're not used to the sight of blood by the end of day one, you're never coming back for a day two. The same goes for a doorman, standing as a buffer between the insulated elites, and accountability for their sins. Just when you think you've seen it all, there's some new awful transgression you have to feign ignorance of.

"He'll see you now," I told the girl. "I hope you like heights."

"I love a good view."

"Take the elevator up, all the way."

"Thanks!" she chirped.

Young, reasonably fresh, not so innocent. The best ones could make a thousand bucks in a single night with a single client—more if they went the extra mile for that optional gratuity a generous high-roller might offer after the deed was done. Most of them were college kids, trading a few years of sexual favours for tuition. They'd try to get out before they burned out, with a degree—hopefully a marketable one—no student debt, and maybe not too many ugly memories.

The girl walked over to the twin elevators in a series of short steps, the tight dress clinging around her thighs barely letting her legs swing. She pushed the call button and one of the elevators was already waiting at the lobby level. Stepping in, she pressed the top button on the panel, and spared me a little wave and a sweet smile as the doors closed and the car carried her away.

I swallowed my pity and pretended I didn't already know how her evening was going to pan out. The girls went up, and they came down. None of them stayed more than an hour or two. And an ugly memory that would last them a lifetime was guaranteed. If they ever tried to forget about what happened, it was certain the son of a bitch would leave them with a scar or two that would always remind them.

I didn't know the exact details of what he was into. I just know he liked it rough. Seeing the aftermath sometimes set my imagination into overdrive. As much as I could close my eyes to the pain he inflicted, I couldn't turn off the images it put in my head.

She was a pretty girl. It was probably the last time she'd ever be so pretty. Bruises would heal, makeup might cover the marks, hair pulled out by the roots would grow back, a bridge could make missing teeth look like they'd never been smashed out. But these escorts would all have a certain haunted look about them after their visit. I knew it, even if I never saw them again.

There's always new talent getting into the business. And he'd just keep going down the list. A list that never seems to get any shorter.

Sometimes I wonder, if I were a better man, would I ever go up there and put a stop to it before things got too rough? Before another girl, trying to make a living, trying to get by, got her looks ruined by a sadist who got his kicks by fucking them up instead of fucking them the regular way.

I'd fantasize about waiting outside his door. And at the first hint of trouble, letting myself in with the master key, pulling him off his latest victim, and putting my foot up his ass and my fist in his face.

What a hero. A regular white knight. One that would be on the unemployment line the very next day.

Nobody's hiring knights any more.

I'd entertain these notions from time to time. Play with the idea of doing the right and noble thing. And then I'd do exactly what I did every time there was a girl up there taking a beating. Nothing.

I was in that thought cycle again, running through those same virtuous instincts, those same impotent fantasies that made me grind me teeth at my post, when the lobby windows all wobbled in unison. It was a slight bowing of the floor-to-ceiling sheets of glass, as if they'd caught a strong gust of wind. If only one had done it, it would have been barely noticeable. When a whole row of them on the boulevard-side of the building did it at once, it made me jump in my chair.

I looked up, wondering if some big road-repair vehicle was rumbling by this late at night. But there was no traffic, only blood. Something had smashed itself so hard against the pavement, it had rattled the street-level windows and spattered them with streaks of red that were slowly elongating as the thicker stretches formed drips that ran down the polished glass.

I knew then I'd have to turn off my unreliable senses again that night, to a greater degree than ever before. There would be all sorts of things to claim I never saw, never heard, didn't remember, didn't know about. Our luxury high-rise, for all its past sins and avarice, had finally chalked up its first murder.

I was already blaming myself as I crossed the lobby to confirm what I already knew had happened. It had been only a matter of time before that penthouse prick went all the way. You can only hurt so many people before hurting isn't enough anymore. I just hoped he'd had the decency to snap her neck before throwing her off his balcony. Maybe she didn't have to know the terror of free-falling down the side of one of the tallest buildings in town.

Just past the lobby doors, lying on a stretch of pavement that had been specially crafted by the city to have the high-rise's address etched into the giant slab of granite underfoot, was a purplish-brown lump of meat, glistening under the streetlights. I'd never seen a human sample before, but I knew a liver when one was presented to me. The impact had ejected organs from the body's ruptured gutsack.

My strong stomach asked me for permission to be sick. I refused it.

There was no avoiding it. I'd have to call 911 myself. Beyond that unavoidable task, I'd play dumb, swear ignorance. The prick could make excuses to police detectives through his lawyer mouthpiece. My duty ended with my ignorance. I'd neither help nor hinder the investigation. And while that unfolded, I'd go home each night and drown my guilt with a bottle of bourbon.

I was on my way back to the desk to put in the call on an outside line when a bell rang. It wasn't the phone, it was the elevator, announcing its arrival. Two seconds later, the doors pulled open and the girl I'd sent upstairs less than a quarter of an hour earlier came spilling out.

Her nose was bloody and she was carrying her left arm like an accessory. Her wrist dangled at an irregular angle and I figured it was broken. Rushing to her side, I caught her as she stumbled forward, unbalanced and dazed from the beating she'd taken. Truth be told, she looked better off than most of the girls returning from their visit upstairs. But then, it seemed this one had come out on top in the battle royale that served as foreplay for the penthouse prick. This time, when he got off, he got all the way off. Right off the balcony and through seven hundred feet of open air. The load he shot was a puddle of innards, smashed out by the collision with solid concrete at terminal velocity.

"Jesus, what happened?" I said stupidly, not wanting to know, but failing to stop myself from asking.

"He didn't waste any time," said the girl. "Got the jump on me, even before I could dose his drink."

She was exhausted from the struggle, babbling, in shock.

"What do you mean, 'dose his drink'?"

"Fentanyl overdose is the easiest way," she panted, wincing in pain. "One hit to put him down, then I finish with the spray. A few shots up the nose usually does the trick, and I leave the bottle in his hand for the cops to find."

It wasn't unheard of for some girls to deal drugs on the side and bring along party favours for bonus cash. But I already knew that's not what she'd been up to. I offered to call an ambulance, but she wouldn't hear of it.

"I don't want to deal with the cops," she said. "I'm an escort."

"I know," I replied.

But she shook her head, like I had it all wrong.

"Not that kind."

I helped her to my chair behind the desk. Once she sat down, she kept talking, and promptly began to tell me too much.

"I'm the sort of escort the escorts hire when they have a problem client. 'Escort' means to accompany or guide. And that's what I do."

I grabbed the first-aid kit from the locked cabinet. I wasn't qualified to set broken bones, but I could at least stop most of the bleeding and soak up the spilled blood.

"Regular escorts accompany their clients to bed. But my clients give me a target," she said. "And that target...him I guide to the grave. A glass of wine spiked with poison is a good path. Straight out a high window is another one. Sometimes a better one."

Her gaze drifted to the tall windows at the front of the building, and I was sure she could see the blood streaks across them, even as the flesh around her eyes turned a darker shade of purple and swelled right in front of me.

"More questions that way," she continued, "more ambiguity. And there's your reasonable doubt. Police figure maybe it was something other than murder. Maybe it happened after the visitor left. No need to look for me. No need to figure out which working girl might have been up there before the accident happened."

She'd played out this scenario before, that much was clear. I expected it had gone smoother in the past. A push over the railing if the poison didn't pan out; a forceful shove into oblivion if a simple push wasn't enough. Any self-defence course will teach you to use your opponent's weight against them. That's usually lesson one. But this time the escort had been up against a violent john who was looking to put the hurt on as soon as she was through the door.

"Is the suite trashed?" I asked her. "Can you tell there was a struggle?"

"No," she said. "He came on strong right out the gate, but I played along. I took what he had to dish out like a sport, like I was into it. When he went to get a drink, I let myself onto the balcony. Told him I needed some fresh air before we continued. He came out to take me back inside, and that's when I showed him the exit."

"You didn't leave anything belonging to you upstairs?"

"All my stuff is with me," she said, patting her purse. "I know how to be a ghost."

She was definitely still punch drunk from the fight, but she had enough wits about her to stay professional, to keep a clear enough head to do what had to be done. And so did I.

"You need to go," I said. "And I need to stay and call this in. But I'll wait until you're gone. Put as much distance as you can between yourself and this place as fast as you can."

She rose unsteadily to her feet and took a few trial steps. Her limp was pronounced, but she was determined to keep going.

"I'll flag something a few blocks away," she agreed, and added, "I was never here."

"I wish I could do more."

"Some of the girls told me how you'd help patch them up. How you were kind to them and said nice things."

"Being nice is a small favour."

"It's rare. And sometimes it's enough."

She hobbled off towards the front entrance.

"Maybe you don't want to go out that way," I said, with all too good an idea of the sight that was waiting for her beyond those doors.

"Right," she said, and stopped where she was.

"There's another way out on the south side. Don't use the emergency exit, it sets off an alarm."

She winced as she made a painful one-eighty and limped away in the opposite direction, following my advice.

I let her have a five-minute head start, no more. Any longer and a late-night pedestrian or passing car might have spotted the body outside, and it wouldn't look good if they reported it before me. As I gave the incomplete details to the 911 operator, I erased a few hours' worth of video footage from a variety of security cameras that were hooked up to the hard drive under my desk. Nothing I hadn't done a dozen times before.

Once I was sure I'd handled my end, I went outside to wait for the police I would lie to, and the paramedics who could do nothing but scrape up remains. I figured they'd want me to tell them who had cashed in that night, to identify the body. But if I hadn't already known who it was, I would have been hard pressed to figure it out.

Careful to step around the wet spots, I observed what was left of the penthouse prick. He'd hit with such force he cracked the pavement. The blood that seeped out of him ran freely into the split. The granite slab, engraved with the high-rise's address, would forever be scarred by his eviction.

A fall from that high, it does weird, unsettling things to a body you won't soon forget if you're unlucky enough to see the aftermath. The lower jaw, for one, seemed to be missing. It didn't get knocked off by the impact. It folded in on itself and got rammed through the roof of his mouth. Now he had an underbite—an underbite that was sticking out of his left eye socket. I could count five teeth jutting from a distinct gum line, situated in a place where you would never recognize them unless you were trying to trace where that jaw had ended up. The rest of his face wasn't much better off. Picasso would have been left confused and disoriented.

There was something else on the pavement that didn't belong. This item hadn't been splashed all over the place by the fall. It was light enough to have landed more gently, away from the carnage, and was only mildly scuffed as a result. It was a single high-heeled pump with an open toe.

The escort had been limping from her injuries so badly, I didn't realize half the limp was from a missing shoe. I took it back inside and filed it in the lost-and-found box, next to the umbrellas and scarves and single gloves, before the first-responders had a chance to spot it. By the time I was back outside to greet them, the boulevard was lit up with emergency lights flashing blue and red.

Within the hour, the paramedics had loaded every significant chunk of what was left of King Asshole into a series of bags—small, medium, and large. The pieces would get run through the system. Cause of death was pretty damn obvious, but there was still a process that needed to be adhered to before they could pour what was left of him into a grave. The main thing now was determining if there was any reason to suspect foul play.

The initial line of questioning took place at my desk as a fire engine idled outside, hosing down the pavement, washing all the leftover fluids down the sewer before morning commuters could get a look at the offal by first light.

"Did you see anyone come or go leading up to the incident?" I was asked by the cop taking my statement. "Anyone at all?"

And, on cue, my selective blindness kicked in.

"I didn't see a thing."

●   ●   ●

I thought I'd never see her again. Like the regular variety of escort, I wasn't expecting she'd ever want to revisit the address that should have been blacklisted by every paid hook-up site on the web. But three weeks later, in broad daylight, while traffic through the lobby was at its peak, she came strolling in with purpose, beelining straight to my desk.

She waited patiently for me to get off the phone with tenants on the eleventh floor who were having an issue with a clogged drain they'd been washing too much hair down. I assured them I'd have maintenance come up to take a look and disconnected.

"Has anyone asked about me?" she said, with no need to reintroduce herself.

Her lower arm was in a cast, immobilizing her wrist. She wore sunglasses, but I could see her eyes were still bruised green and blue past the edges of the lens.

"Nobody knows you were here," I said. "Nobody knows you even exist."

"I'm sorry to have involved you."

"Not a problem," I assured her. "I made my statement. They took it right here. I didn't even have to go down to a station."

"Do they have any suspects?"

"They didn't share their line of thinking with me, but no detectives have been back, and all the cops looked pretty bored. Even the paramedics dealing with the remains looked like it was a dull day on the job. Another mundane suicide. Messier than most, but routine."

"Messy," she repeated back to me. "It was a messy job, all right."

"I didn't mean that as a criticism. I'm sure there are unexpected complications in your line of work all the time."

"I'm here about one of those," she said. "It turns out I left something behind after all. I didn't realize it until I was a block away, but the emergency vehicles were too close for me to turn back."

"A shoe," I said.

"I was hoping you'd find it first."

"It was outside. Must have come off in the struggle."

"You hid it?"

"In plain sight. Nobody but me knows where it came from."

I ducked down to retrieve it from lost-and-found, where it remained on the top of the pile. Setting it down on the desk, in the open light, you could see the marks, which looked like regular wear and tear if you didn't know how they got there.

"It survived the trip down well enough," I commented.

"Better than me," she said.

"At least you got to take the elevator."

"You're a prince," she said, stuffing the shoe into her handbag.

"Not really," I said. "But I try."

"That's all any of us can do."

She turned around to go and I realized I never caught her name. Probably for the best. I already had one to remember her by.

"See you around, Cinderella," I said.

And without ever looking back, she raised her good hand to wave goodbye. A few seconds later and she was out the door, walking across the numbered granite slab, stepping over the new crack in the pavement, paying it no heed, like she had no part in putting it there.

I watched her through the boulevard windows. The limp she had the last time she departed was gone. Two firm feet carried her away until the city and the street traffic swallowed her whole and she was gone from my sight, if not my memories.

Ghoul: A Romance

MY HOUSE ISN'T HAUNTED. People ask. Not all the time, but reliably, whenever they find out what happened on the property. The murder took place ten years before the house was even built, but it's still the scene of the crime—a notorious crime if you're into that sort of thing. If you look up my address on Google Maps, there's a little button to indicate that it's where the body of the Lavender Torso was found—in a long since demolished tool shed on an otherwise empty lot. The murder and dismemberment of the girl—a fledgling torch-song singer who could barely book a set in even the crummiest dive bar with a postage-stamp stage and a microphone—was at least a week old by the time it was discovered. Her name was Sally Rhodes. She was twenty-two and dreamed of a life of fame and adulation. Someone stole her life back in the summer of 1948, but she got her fame and adulation just the same.

Yeah, my house isn't haunted, unless you count the gawkers. I didn't really notice them the whole first year I lived here, but eventually I would catch people staring. The slow drive-bys with eyes on my house instead of the road; the sauntering pedestrians on a street with no sidewalks; the people who would stop right in front of my address for a minutes or two and take a picture—or a selfie. There was an unusual interest in my yellow cookie-cutter bungalow, virtually indistinguishable from all the other bungalows it was shuffled between in a late 1950s development that stretched for several blocks in all directions.

It made me paranoid. I thought there was something wrong with the house. Every time a gawker cruised my home, usually, on average, once a week, I'd go out onto my strip of front lawn to see what was amiss. Had there been some act of vandalism that had drawn their attention? Was something untoward spray-painted across my aluminum siding? Had a chunk of landing gear snapped off an approaching overhead flight and imbedded itself in my roof while I was at work? Surely something weird was drawing their eye. But each time, all I saw was my tiny, boring, affordable abode.

Finally it was a simple internet search that told me what the deal was. I typed in my full address. The old real estate listing that had caught my eye when I was in the market came up, but it wasn't the first result. It wasn't even in the top ten. Before it were a dozen articles and entries about the Lavender Torso. There were probably dozens more out on the Web, but these were the ones that mentioned the contemporary street name and number of where the heinous crime had been committed once upon a time. Some had the precise GPS coordinates.

After that, I did my best to ignore the sightseers, the true-crime enthusiasts, the armchair detectives who had their own theories about who among the long list of police suspects—none ever charged or convicted—had done the deed and gotten away with it. I'm sure they would have been happy to talk my ear off about it if I ever confronted or engaged them. I never did.

The Lavender Torso was a cold case that just wouldn't go away. It was a gruesome-enough crime, with an appealing-enough victim, and mysterious-enough circumstances, to have captured the imaginations of subsequent generations of amateur criminologists. And their ranks were always being replenished. I could tell whenever one of the cable networks ran an episode or special about the case—the history channels that rarely touched upon actual history, and only the bloody lurid stuff when they did; the learning channels that emphasized sordid crime and reality shows over teaching or education. They'd fill a time slot with an old rerun about the murder, or a new episode of a new show that offered no new facts or angles, and the visits would spike. That same week, I'd spot four or five tourists going through their routine instead of the usual one or two. Then it would drop off abruptly. The casuals would go away, and the serious kooks would have the street to themselves again.

I've never seen the same person more than once. One pilgrimage to "the murder house," as my friends took to calling my place to get under my skin, is enough for even the most morbid of Lavender Torso groupies. There's really nothing to see. The property looks completely different since that day in 1948, when a passerby caught a whiff of decomposition and spotted three severed human fingers lying on the lot—all pointing towards a tool shed, and each sporting a long manicured fingernail painted a shade of lavender. I don't know what they expect to see now. Probably nothing. Maybe they just want to have stood on the spot where it happened, even if it doesn't really exist anymore.

There were no repeat customers. Except one. Each year, on the anniversary of the day Sally Rhodes's body was discovered, I'd find a single rose. A lavender one, appropriately enough. I understand they're rare, and don't come cheap from flower shops that overcharge for even the most common of colourful weeds. The first year, I didn't know what it meant, and figured someone had dropped it on my lawn at random. By year two, I knew all about the Lavender Torso case, and the sudden reappearance of a lavender rose made a whole lot more

sense. It took me four years and four roses to spot the culprit.
I wasn't purposely staking out my own property, but that year
the anniversary fell on a Saturday, so I didn't have work, and
happened to be up early enough to catch the girl in the act.

She was young, but old enough to know better. Older than
Sally Rhodes ever got to be, at any rate. A Bohemian, artiste-
type, I figured this was some sort of project she was working
on. There was probably a magazine article in the works. Or
worse, a blog.

"Hi," I said, loud enough for her to hear me from the road.

The girl looked up, guiltless, and gave me a smile. I was
standing in my doorway, in a bathrobe, holding my morning
cup of joe.

"Thanks for all the flowers," I added. "They're pretty."

"Do you just throw them away?" she asked, curious but
otherwise indifferent to their fate.

"No, actually. They're too nice. I put them in some water.
They last about a week. Then they're done."

"That's good," she decided.

"Are you the ghost of the victim?"

"Don't be silly," she smiled.

"Family?"

"No, I'm not related in any way, as far as I know. I can't
speak for who might be a third cousin six times removed in
relation to someone who was involved in the case. You never
know when it comes to remote connections like that, but I
have no direct involvement personally."

"So what are you then?"

"Just a fan."

"Of her singing?"

"Of unsolved murders. Solved ones, too, if they're still
mysterious."

"Would you like to come inside?" I suggested. "There's
more coffee."

"Could I? That would be great," she beamed, and walked up my path.

Inside, I showed her to an armchair in the middle of my living room, facing the window.

"Have a seat," I said. "How do you like your coffee?"

"Cream, no sugar."

By the time I returned with another mug, she'd gotten her bearings and was staring at my couch.

"Would you mind if I sat over there instead?" she said, with a nod at the preferred vantage point.

"Suit yourself," I said, remaining standing.

She relocated and sipped at her coffee. Her eyes darted all over the room, ceiling to floor, across my furniture, my every possession. It might have felt intrusive, but she wasn't really seeing any of it. She was looking at how she imagined things once stood, back in the summer of 1948.

"Do you know much about the murder scene?" she asked me.

"Only from a couple of articles I read online. I'm going to bet you know more."

"I've seen the blueprints for your house. They're on file at city hall. I compared them to the surveyor's record of the lot. There's about a seventy percent overlap of where the shed used to stand. This spot right here, where I am now. This is where most of it happened."

"He killed her right there?"

"Nobody knows for sure where the actual murder was committed. It might not have even been anywhere near here. But this is where his workbench was. Just a wooden door laid out across two sawhorses. This is where he mutilated the body. Most of what he did to her was done after she was dead. Killing her was incidental. What he really wanted was all done right in this exact space."

I could see her shiver, even across the room.

"Getting a creepy vibe?" I asked.

"More of a tingle."

She ran her fingers up and down my old couch, feeling the fabric like it was the dead flesh of the Lavender Torso herself.

"Is this where you sleep?" she asked.

"No, there's a little bedroom in the back. But I've napped here plenty of times. Not sure if I'll be doing that again any time soon."

"Have you ever felt anything unusual on this spot?"

"Hungover sometimes."

"You know what I mean. Psychic impressions. Weird dreams."

"Dreams are always weird," I said.

"Ever dream of murder? Blood? Dismemberment?"

"I probably will now, thanks."

There was a long silence that wasn't awkward. We were two people, alone in a room and miles apart. I was having coffee, she was having her moment. She only spoke again when she was good and ready.

"You should probably fuck me now," she said, like it was the next obvious stage of our interaction.

"On the couch? Where it happened?"

"Of course."

"Is that something else he did to her body?"

"No," she said. "Every profile of the killer concurs: he was almost certainly impotent. But the way he penetrated her was infinitely more intimate, wouldn't you say? He wasn't sexually violating her. He opened her up, exposed her completely. There was no part of her, inside or out, that he couldn't see or touch at will."

"And that puts you in the mood?"

Her breathing had quickened and her neck had flushed red.

"Not you?" she asked, like she thought it should.

"No," I said.

"Does this?"

She rose off the couch, unfastened her pants, and peeled them off her thighs until they were bundled at her ankles. I'd already known she was wearing a thong. The straps had been visible above the waistline of her skinny jeans. It came off next.

She stood in front of me, naked from the waist down. Not long enough to catch a chill.

"I'll get a condom," I said, and went to tear one off the roll in my sock drawer.

By the time we were finished, the middle cushion segment under her was soaked through in her juice. The stain would come out; the smell never would. That didn't bother me. It was an old couch, a hand-me-down, and her scent in it was like a trophy, even though her wetness had nothing to do with what I'd brought to the scrum. It was my first and only three-way. Me, this ghoul, and the Lavender Torso. I'd tried not to think about the dead girl while I was getting the deed done, but there was no banishing her presence. I knew the visitor under-neath me had Sally Rhodes on the brain. That's who she was making love to. Me, I was just a convenient warm body and an erection. I might as well have not been there at all. If it weren't my house, I would have been tempted to excuse myself and leave them alone together—the fangirl and the memory of a murder victim who would have been old enough to be her great grandmother had she survived. Maybe I should have stepped out instead of chasing a cheap orgasm. It would have been the decent thing. But then, orgasms and the decent thing are often at odds with each other—mutually exclusive.

"Are you hungry?" I asked, sometime later.

She was still basking in the afterglow. Mine was long gone, and I was more interested in disentangling myself from our tight post-coital position on the narrow cushions than I was in food.

"You don't have to buy me dinner," she assured me.

"I was thinking more about a slice of leftover pizza in the fridge."

"I'm fine," she said. "In fact, I should be going."

Once I was off the couch, and she had room to maneuver, she found her thong and jeans and pulled them back on. I realized I didn't even know her name, even though we'd just fucked. It seemed rude to ask now, so I didn't.

"We should do this again," I said. "Same time next year?"

It was a joke. I figured this personal tour of the crime sce-ne would get her past the Lavender Torso. Sally Rhodes was probably played out. At the very least, the awkward shame of our tawdry fling would put a damper on the next annual visit or two.

"What are you doing Wednesday?" she asked in response.

"Nothing," I said, then clarified, "Work."

"Can you call in sick?"

"I could. Why?"

"Because it's safer to go in the afternoon. Once the sun goes down, not so much. But early afternoon should be fine."

"Go where?"

"Have you ever heard of the Kellerman Court Axe Mur-ders?"

• • •

I hadn't. Few had. Even an internet search offered scant de-tails. This wasn't a notorious murder like poor Sally Rhodes. There was no glamour to this one, no sex appeal. The victims had been children.

No contact information had been exchanged. She knew where I lived and that was enough. With no call or confirma-tion, I took the day of our appointment off, fully expecting to be stood up. But there she was, at my door again, punctually at noon. My ghoul—my murder-scene tour guide.

We took my car, but I had to let her navigate. Despite my best efforts, I'd been unable to locate any point on the map called Kellerman Court, or Kellerman anything. It turned out the suburban cul-de-sac, winding around a small square of grass and four trees, had been renamed decades ago in favour of a more fashionable dead figure from local history. Plus, of course, the name Kellerman Court had suffered a bad reputation following the horrible events in 1961.

"This one, here," she said, prompting me to pull over by the curb in front of one of the half-dozen houses situated around the square. Parking was easy. None of the houses were occupied.

"You been here before?" I asked. The whole neighbourhood had gone to hell. Anybody who could afford to move, sold and left years ago. Many who couldn't afford to move, or couldn't sell, bailed anyway, leaving the bank holding the bag on properties nobody wanted anymore. All the windows were broken and boarded up, but that hadn't kept the squatters out. Come nightfall, the houses were likely to be well travelled by junkies looking to shoot up, or street whores looking to turn a trick—and then shoot up. I could see why a daylight visit was preferable, but it still seemed needlessly perilous.

"Are you crazy?" she said. "I'd never come here alone. I always wanted to visit, but not by myself."

"And now?"

"There's strength in numbers."

"There's two of us," I reminded her. "Two. That's not strength, that's just a potential double homicide."

"Then we'll double the number of victims this place has been home to."

"It was two who got killed here?"

"A boy and a girl. Brother and sister. Bjorn and Mary. Six and seven years old. Today is the anniversary of their death. And it happened in that house right there, in an upstairs bedroom, early in the evening, 1961. Wanna go in and see?"

"Not really."

"Let's go anyway. We're here."

And she let herself out of the car, knowing I would follow.

It didn't take long to find the preferred route trespassers were using to get inside. The front door was still padlocked. So was the back, but the steel plate had been pried out of the wood, leaving the useless bolt dangling.

We stepped inside and found ourselves in what was left of the kitchen. The plumbing was ripped out, and any cabinets that had stood in the way of the plunder were splintered in the process. The floor was covered in debris, and we had to shuffle our feet to plough through the collection of broken glass, broken tiles, and random nails and screws that lay in wait, ready to poke straight through the rubber soles of our shoes if we made an ill-considered step.

"This place is a hazard," I cautioned my companion.

The loose door to the yard swung shut in the slight breeze, and the near-complete darkness that followed made me curse myself for not having the foresight to bring a flashlight. Even in full sunlight, the house was boarded tight enough to keep the interior black as night. No sooner had I admonished myself for failing to guess that urban exploration might be in the offing, than the kitchen brightened under a single beam of illumination.

"That way," said the voice behind the blinding bulb pointed in my face.

I turned and saw the door frame that led out into the hall. Cautiously, I walked through, hoping there would be enough light to spot anything I didn't want to step in before I committed to my next advance. It wasn't only weakened floors and tetanus that worried me. Every room was a mess, used as a pallet for taggers, a source of melt-value metal for looters, and an open toilet for everyone else.

In the silence of the abandoned home, each footstep creaked so loud it was deafening. I thought we might break through the floorboards at any moment. A lot of the slats were warped, and there were signs of mould. The roof had probably leaked for years, with the holes in it getting bigger and bigger with each rainfall. Who knew how much the water damage had destabilized the bones of the place? I wondered what kind of a load the load-bearing walls were still capable of supporting safely.

"Stairs," she said next, swinging the beam to the steps that moaned and complained as soon as I put any weight on them. I wondered what was directly underneath the flight—what would be waiting for me below if the stairs split open and swallowed me whole. I was relieved when we made it to the second floor, even though any tumbles through the failing structure promised to be extra-crippling with the added height.

"If the property value ever comes back, the banks will have this whole block knocked down so they can toss up some condos and turn a profit," my companion speculated. "Failing that, the city will wait until the first one collapses from neglect. Then they'll raze the rest as a public-safety risk, even though the only public at risk are ones who have fallen right out of society."

"And us," I reminded her. "We're stuck inside this death trap if it caves in on us."

"This house has been standing here for nearly a century. It can last twenty more minutes."

There was a bathroom at the end of the corridor. I could smell it before we arrived. Mercifully the toilet lid was closed, but I could tell the drifters and druggies who had passed through the place had filled it before resorting to closets, bare floors, and anywhere else that suited a pressing need to relieve themselves.

"She gave them a bath, right here, in this tub," I was told, as it was lit over my shoulder. I stepped aside so my fellow explorer could have a better look. She was the one who needed to see it. "Other people lived here after the murders, but this is the original, you can tell. The style is old fashioned. See the clawfeet? It never got changed."

There were three other rooms upstairs, but my escort knew which one she was after. Once she led me into the largest of them, her flashlight found the spot beneath the broken, boarded window where the murders happened. There wasn't any furniture to suggest how the room had once been laid out, but I was sure she had memorized any crime-scene photos that were still filed away in public archives or reprinted in obscure case-history books.

"She put them down here, side by side, in her own bed. She waited until they were asleep, and then went to the basement to pick out a tool."

"We're not going in the basement, are we?" I asked.

"We can skip that part. Where the hardware came from isn't important. It's where it got used."

I wondered what sort of selection had been on hand that night, long ago. If there was a choice of tools, why not a hammer or a screwdriver? Surely there had been knives in the kitchen. The woman even had the option of drowning her children in the bathtub right before she went for the much bloodier option.

"She smashed her babies' heads in with an axe," as if there were a logical answer to my unspoken question. "To let the devil out, she told officers later that night."

"So they caught her?"

"She never tried to hide it. A neighbour spotted her sitting on the front porch, wearing nothing but a negligee and blood. Her husband was working a night shift. He came home to police cars and an ambulance. His wife was already in custody, and they wouldn't let him see what she'd done to the children."

"Do you know what happened after that?"

Stupid question. Of course she did.

"There was no trial. Only a hearing. Trista Lucekevic was locked up under psychiatric observation in a county mental hospital for the rest of her life. She died in 1978, believing she'd set her son and daughter free, and that they were happy and healthy, forever stuck at the same age they'd been when they died. She claimed they never visited because they were busy with school."

"And her husband?"

"Fell off the radar. The courts signed single-party divorce papers in 1963. There's one rumour he remarried, another that he drank himself to death. Maybe both are true, maybe neither."

"Awful," I said.

"Awful," she agreed, with a shiver that wasn't revulsion. "A lot of lives were destroyed in this room."

The flashlight remained fixed to the same spot on the floor for at least a full minute more before there was a soft click in the quiet room, and we were plunged back into darkness. I thought the battery might be dead, or maybe this was meant as a sign we were leaving, and that the light would come back on and point the way to the hall in a moment. But we weren't going anywhere. We were only getting started.

Her hand found my leg first. Then my belt buckle. Before I could say anything in protest—as unlikely as that was—my pants were unfastened and dragged down. There was a slight crackle of shifting detritus as the girl set her knees down on the filthy floor and took her task in hand.

There was no foreplay. No tickle or tongue. In an instant, I felt the head of my cock hit the back of her throat. Her lips were buried in my pubes for a moment, then she was all the way back up my shaft. Drawing her mouth off the tip, she took the plunge again, all the way back down, repeating the motion with no flourish or variation. Her pace was swift, merciless, relentless. And I went with it. What choice did I have?

The mechanical momentum of the act, the steady piston sound of saliva and suction, was broken by another noise in the vicinity. Somewhere in the house, a crackhead had just woken up. Perhaps two.

The disturbance was distant, but there may well have been others closer. We might not have been alone in the room for all we knew.

I thought that notion might make me lose my erection. Instead I lost my load.

Reduced to a spasming, twitching mass, I barely kept my footing. The mouth didn't care, and clung on like a barnacle, refusing to disengage. I finally had to take the girl by the hair and shove her off before I tripped backwards over my bunched up clothing and fell.

She leaned back, her palms planted on the grimy floor, and sucked in the first full breath she'd allowed herself in the three minutes it had taken to bring me to climax. I listened to her panting slow and stabilize as I hurried to pull up my underwear and pants, buttoning and zipping everything back into order.

"Are you okay?" I asked, only once I was sure I was collected and reasonably calm again.

What she said wasn't an answer. I don't think it was even directed at me.

"All those potential babies, dying in my stomach acid, getting digested, becoming part of me..."

She sounded like she was in a trance, lost in the maze of troubling thoughts that disturbed and excited her. Dealing with a lover in moments like this, giving them the comfort and support they need while coming down from a dark sexual high— they call it aftercare.

"Um, yeah..." I said.

I'm no good with the aftercare. It didn't seem to matter. She was in her own orbit. I'd helped her get there and now she didn't need me.

I stood quietly in the dark. How long, I don't know. It was too dark to see my watch. Eventually, she stood back up and told me she was ready to leave. The flashlight guided us out. We didn't encounter anyone else along the way, but somebody's coughing fit a room or two over confirmed the sounds I'd heard earlier weren't my own paranoia.

"Thanks for that," she said, out in the sunlight that forced us to shelter our eyes with our hands. "I never would have managed alone."

"You ever go out on normal dates?" I asked. "You must watch movies or have dinner."

"I'm free Saturday night," she said. "Late. Let's shoot for eleven."

"What do you have in mind?"

"The Partridge Street Strangler. Four victims in April to June, 1976."

I didn't want to let my disappointment at the prospect of another murder-themed field trip show. So far our get-togethers were paying reliable sexual dividends, and who was I to complain? Indulging her obsessions was a small price to pay. And the name of this killer already had me intrigued.

"He killed them all on the same street?"

"No. He would have been caught sooner if they were all on Partridge Street. It's not that long of a street. But he earned the name based on the second victim, Elizabeth Dewey. And she wasn't killed on the actual street. She was raped and strangled in the train underpass that runs beneath it. The rest of the victims died the same way at various other points in the neighbourhood, but it was the Dewey case that spilled the most ink on headlines and follow-up articles."

"Why her and not the others?"

"She was the only one who got her picture in the papers. And she was very pretty."

"Of course," I said. Even in an age of new media, things hadn't really changed. Only now it was pixels instead of ink.

"It was also the only murder to be witnessed. That was the testimony that put Boden Todd in the electric chair."

"People saw him in the act?"

"Oh yes," she confirmed. "Dozens, maybe a hundred or more. It only took four, swearing it was him under oath, to get a conviction."

"All those people—and nobody tried to stop him?"

"None of them were in any position to do anything but watch."

• • •

She didn't come around to my place that Saturday. Instead, we agreed to meet on the bridge overlooking the twin tracks that ran under that short section of Partridge Street.

"I've passed this spot many times before," she said, approaching the railing at the side of the road and looking down. "Each time, I've never done more than look over the edge."

We were alone on the street that late at night. The shops in the area were all closed, and most of the apartments above them were either dark, or dimly lit by screens playing to tenants who had dozed off in front of their television sets. She had arrived with no fanfare, no greeting. Instead she came over next to me and peered down at the parallel tracks below, launching into her grim routine.

I didn't say "hello," didn't try to engage her. She'd involve me when she was good and ready.

"It's time to take the plunge," she said at last, and walked to the nearby corner of the bridge, where the safety rail ended and the embankment down began.

There was a gravel base, poised at a sharp angle, uninviting to any foot traffic, outright dangerous for concrete-jungle hikers who dared to try to use it as a path. The stones were old, hammered into the earth by decades of rain and wind, stained nearly black by the diesel exhaust of thousands of passing train engines, virtually glued together by the tar-like residue that had settled across them and fermented. While providing no worthwhile footholds, the layer of grit was firmly set by age and filth, and at least cooperated by not cascading down the side of the slope the moment any weight was put on it.

"Help me."

Words to me at last, as she raised an arm for support, even as she continued to lower herself down. I took her by the hand and grabbed a rung of the rail, serving as her anchor as she stretched and found the corner of a concrete pillar beneath the bridge that offered her a safer route of descent. A full head taller than her, with a much longer reach, I was able to follow, keeping my fingertips hooked over the edge of a steel girder until I, too, was able to set a toe on the support block. From there it was a simpler path, down the underbelly of the bridge, until we arrived at the platform over the train line. There was a dip of several feet to the tracks and ties below.

"Get down there," she told me, but made no move to step off herself.

"There's no train coming, is there?" I asked, looking up and down the tracks.

"Not at this hour," she said. "It's only daytime freight now."

I did as I was told. There was no sound of any traffic coming or going, either on the line or above us on the road.

"Not so in 1976 when Elizabeth Dewey died right where I'm standing," she said. "That's when the 11:15 passed this spot. The final commuter train of the day. Dozens on board—at least the ones sitting on the left side—might have seen it happen. For a moment. Just a couple of people struggling in the dark. Most of them probably didn't even consciously register what they were seeing in those few seconds."

"Yet you said there were witnesses who testified it was this Todd guy they saw attack that girl."

"So they said. But it was dark—like it is now. It was late. These were people coming home from a hard day at work. Thinking about their problems, their next day's commute.

Elizabeth Dewey was on her back. The killer was on top of her."

"Then there's no way any of them could have seen his face. Certainly no way they could have been sure it was him."

"But they fried Boden Todd just the same. Maybe it was him. Maybe it wasn't. His criminal record didn't do him any favours. Neither did his behaviour at his trial. Those were the things that really sent him to the chair. And that's how Elizabeth Dewey and three other victims were avenged. With another death."

"Doesn't sound like justice at all," I said.

"It's not. It's destruction."

She was taking her pants down. I'd already known where this was going.

Judging her position very carefully, like a surveyor with a theodolite, she made doubly sure she was on exactly the correct spot before setting down on the edge of the platform. Pulling her pants off over her shoes, she cast them aside and spread her legs before me. Her raised position on the poured slab of concrete put her at a perfect height for my cock, which was already straining to be released.

"Is that where she was found?" I asked, unzipping.

"I've seen the crime-scene photos," she nodded. "Every one."

She pointed to a large wedge, a couple of feet to her right, that had been knocked out of the slab by some past impact.

"See that notch? It's in all the wide shots. Can't miss it."

"I'm sure you know your stuff," I said, and was deep inside her an instant later. There was no call for foreplay, no need to warm her up. The ghosts in that underpass had done all the preliminary work. I was the tool to finish the job.

You could almost imagine the roar of the engine, the squeal of the wheels, metal on metal, as we fucked in that tunnel. The sounds of a train that had screeched past an act of violence, long forgotten, were mimicked by the grunts and gasps of two humans who weren't recreating that moment so much as summoning its memory, its echo.

"Choke me," she said. It wasn't a request. It was a demand.

I placed my right hand around her neck, cupping her jawline between my fingers, and held her close as I maintained the pace.

"Tighter," she gasped, and I closed my hand around her throat more firmly, just short of discomfort that would be too intense—for her or for me.

"Tighter," said hissed again, digging her fingernails into my wrist, spurring me on until I added a few more pounds of pressure.

Her face turned red, then purple, and it looked like her wide staring eyes would come popping out of her head straight at me. She didn't speak again because she couldn't talk. The panting, the gasping, the whistling in her nose all stopped because she couldn't breathe.

I pounded into her furiously. It was a race between my climax and her brain death, and they were running hard, neck-in-neck. I was in the moment, but that moment took a whole extra minute for me to make it. It was a long time to go without air to her lungs, blood to her head.

The bellow I made as I came was as pure and loud as any noise I'd ever uttered. I let it all out, emptying my mind, my soul, and my balls all at once. There wasn't an ounce of energy or vitality left in me when I was done, and I collapsed across the body that lay beneath me, spent. I barely had enough conscious thought or effort left to release my grip on the throat in my hand and let my arm flop limply across our cold stone bed.

I don't know how long we lay there before I realized my companion, my guide, my lover, had not resumed breathing. I felt her bruised neck for a pulse and thought I found one, but was unsure if I was only feeling my own heart, pounding through my fingertips from sexual exertion and murderous intent. Skipping chest compressions, I went straight to mouth-to-mouth resuscitation, blowing my hot breath into her lungs. As our lips touched, I remembered we'd never even kissed before.

She remained splayed across the platform, pantless and dripping onto the tracks below, while I tried to push some life back into her limp body. At last she sucked air out of my mouth. A small gulp, but it got her started. I leaned back and let her continue on her own, strained though her efforts were.

"Are you okay?" I asked, once inhaling and exhaling seemed to have become a natural, automatic instinct for her again.

"I'm..." she pondered, "great."

"Did you come?" was the only other thing I could think to ask.

"Oh I came, all right. But then I *went*, and that was so much better."

I handed her her pants and hastened to cover up as a wave of shame rolled in.

"You ejaculated inside me," she said, clinically noting the unsheathed penis I tucked back into my fly. I hadn't worn a condom—hadn't thought to bring one, even though I knew damn well how the evening would go. I don't know why.

"Sorry," I muttered.

"It's okay," she said. "It's hotter that way. More authentic."

● ● ●

The climb back up to the road was challenging, with each of us taking turns getting a firm grip and helping the other reach the next handhold. The gravel embankment made for a slippery slope every time a few pebbles dislodged underfoot and threatened to unceremoniously slide us straight back to the bottom. In that last stretch, we just kept our heads down and scrambled on all fours until we found ourselves back on solid pavement.

The Partridge Street bridge offered us two paths away from the scene of our latest tryst. I was parked a block away, on the same side where we'd descended and climbed back out.

"What are you doing Fri...?"

I cut her off before she could fill me in on the details of the next morbid anniversary in her agenda.

"I don't ever want to see you again."

She fell silent for a moment. The abruptness of the breakup hit her like a slap in the face. But she recovered quickly, and slowly nodded as she considered the implications.

"Probably best to leave it where it is," she agreed. "It's been fantastic. The best. I think we both know the only way it's ever going to be better, and maybe that's not a place we're ready to go."

"No," I said. "That would require a certain...commitment."

"Right. We'll call it 'commitment issues' if anyone asks."

"No one will ask. No one has ever seen us together."

"We should keep it that way," she said. "Just in case."

"In case of what?"

"Just in case we ever do hook up again and, you know, *commit.*"

Our eyes remained locked in silence, and an understanding that didn't need to be spoken aloud passed between us. She turned and walked the rest of the way across the bridge, leaving me on my own side to return to the safe retreat of my car.

That was the last I saw of her.

It's coming up on a year since our first meeting. Any day now. Each morning I find myself looking out at my front lawn, wondering if I'll see a lavender rose lying there—wondering if I'll catch her in the act.

And wondering if I want to.

Drill

YOU'VE SEEN THIS MOVIE BEFORE.

The drill sergeant who's singled out one of his recruits—the ne'er-do-well, the big mouth, the smarty pants—and now he's going to give him his free shot. They've been butting heads for weeks, they've come to resent each other, so Sarge will let the malcontent take a poke at him. And that's when he's going to hand the kid his ass.

Oh, he's getting on in years. It's been a long time since old Sarge stuck a bayonet in the guts of some Jap or Kraut or gook in whatever craphole of a war he crawled out of. But he's still got the moves and the training, and he's going to show this young upstart that he don't know shit about shit. Experience, training, discipline wins the day every time.

You've seen this movie before. And so has he. But this ain't the pictures, these aren't actors, and this piss-stinking barracks ain't fuckin' Hollywoodland.

Sarge has his beady little eyes on me as I step out of the line. His fists are already clenched. He's a coiled spring, all muscle and hate, and he's looking forward to what happens next. The prick has probably done this to one poor sap every basic-training cycle. Always early on, to set an example for the rest. It's like his fuckin' Christmas.

He's waiting for me to make the first move—a lunge he can use to push me off my feet, a haymaker he can dodge and reply to with a rabbit punch to the ribs. Some stupid rookie mistake, and then he'll take me to school in front of everybody. But I know what my move is, and I make it. I tell a joke.

"I thought your dance card was full, Mary-Sue," I say, and I can tell Sarge doesn't know what the fuck I'm talking about. Neither does anyone in the line, with one exception. My audience: Hawkins. He's a big dumb farm boy from Nebraska. I wouldn't say shit to him, except he's in the bunk under mine, and he's a talker. Nothing he ever says is worth a damn, but I do remember some of it, including half an anecdote about a girl back home named Mary-Sue, who always managed to fill her dance card at the county fair because she was partial to giving blowjobs under the football stands.

It's not much of a joke, but Hawkins snickers, and that's all I'm after. For a split instant, Sarge turns his head away to see what's so goddamn funny, and that's when I break his jaw. No haymakers or rabbit punches for me. Just a straightforward fully extended jab fired from my right shoulder. I pick my target on the old stripe's profile and aim for a spot in space several inches past that. Then I give him everything I've got.

His jaw dislocates and snaps in an instant. A few teeth go flying before he drops. I drop almost as fast, landing on his chest with both knees. A hand around his throat lets me direct his head where I want it to be as I bring my fist down into his face a dozen times over. A tough bastard like that, you never know. Even with a broken jaw, he could still have enough sense to dole out a dose of hurt something fierce. I take no chances. The next shot breaks his nose. The three after that pulverize it. Then I go to work on his eyes, making sure they'll be swollen shut for the next month.

The whole line of recruits watches me do this, and nobody lifts a finger to stop it. Another few more weeks of basic training, eating rocks and spitting gravel, crawling through dirt and mud at their drill sergeant's say-so, and they'd have come to love him in some twisted fashion. But this is week two. They're still in the hate-and-fear phase, so they let me pound the pure shit out of the man and they enjoy it. They wish they had the balls to join in, now that I have him down and at my mercy.

Once I'm done making him ugly forever, I get back on my feet and busy myself ending Sarge's career. I stand on one of his knees, grab him by the ankle, pull hard and twist. There's a snap and a crunch and I know the first knee is nothing but shrapnel that will cause him pain for the rest of his days. Then I do the same to the second one.

Just in case anybody might ever be tempted to pity-fuck the grotesque old cripple I've made, I stab my boot into his jewels repeatedly like I'm trying to kick field goals. Once I'm on a roll, I work my way up his ribs, snapping every second one. By then, I'm so worked up, I'm ready to undo all my fine work by stomping Sarge's skull into the floorboards. Before I can turn his head into tread-marked pulp, the first of the recruits tackles me. They've seen enough. They were up for watching a beating, but most of them won't stand still for a murder. I've got three of them pinning me down a couple of seconds later and I tell them what a bunch of pussy-ass fucks they are. That helps me get it all out of my system. It doesn't make me any new friends, but it's not like I'm going to be bunking with the raw recruits ever again.

The MPs who show up a few minutes later haul my ass straight to lockup, and I expect to be sharing a cell block with a bunch of ten-year-plus convicts for a long time. At least until I start sprouting grey hairs out of my nutsack. They'll ask me if it was worth it, losing all those days I'll never get back, just to fuck up some drill sergeant who, in his own sick way, was only trying to teach me an important life lesson.

Abso-fucking-lutely. If I had it to do all over again, they wouldn't even have to draft me. I'd sign up for it, just to feel that kind of satisfaction one more time. I can't imagine how it could have felt any better. Except, maybe, if it had been my daddy.

● ● ●

I'm three days in a cell, eating mashed vegetables and meat mush off a steel tray, sleeping on a damp mattress under a handkerchief blanket, and shitting in a toilet with no seat. No one comes to see me, nobody lets me out for air. And after two weeks of ten-mile marches with fifty pounds of kit on my back, it's a goddamn vacation. Throw in a bottle of Wild Turkey and a barmaid with big tits and I've never had it so good.

But vacations don't last forever. Day four comes, and instead of my serving of pulverized leftovers, I get a guard who tells me to button up my shirt. I've got a visitor.

It's a long march down an off-green hall lined with buzzing fluorescents. The bad lighting makes the ugly colour even more stomach churning and I'm almost glad to be brought into a cramped interview room, even when I see who my visitor is. The MPs unshackle one wrist so they can run the chain through a steel eye that's screwed deep into the bench they sit me on. Then it's locked tight again, only giving me a few inches to wiggle around and readjust my butt cheeks on the hard planks. There's not enough movement to let me make trouble, but I've still got my smart mouth. It's enough to make myself a nuisance.

"Well now, if it ain't my very own state representative come to see little old me," I say. "You stumping for votes, Senator? 'Cuz there's only one ballot to be cast in this room and I didn't cast it for you last time. Don't expect to cast it for you next election cycle, neither."

The fat man in the expensive suit lets it roll off him till I've said all I'm likely to say.

"Convicts don't get to vote," he tells me.

"Then I guess your visit is an extra waste of time."

"My seat in the upper chamber is secure, so don't you worry yourself. And I'm not here as your representative—legal or state."

"To whom do I owe this honour, then?"

"From time to time, I act as a facilitator for certain parties," he says.

"What parties are these?"

"Powerful parties with positions that need filling. Special work for men with certain qualities."

I shake my head and I'm not shy about laughing in the career politician's face.

"You have the wrong fella. My daddy used to tell me I wasn't a quality person. All the times he told me that, and I guess it sunk in."

"I've been told you have potential."

"Who said that?"

"Earl Billings."

"I don't know who that is."

"He was your drill sergeant."

I never knew him by any other name than "Sarge." On our first day, he told us to call him Sarge but think of him as God Almighty.

"Nice of him, considering."

"Oh, he hasn't said anything since your altercation. You beat him into a coma. But two days before that, I read his report on the new recruits. You were singled out."

"Thought highly of me, did he?"

"No. He thought you were a no-good hood. A lowlife punk. Dangerous, undisciplined. A grenade with the pin out."

"And then I went off right in his face," I smile, remembering the fun I'd had. "Who knew Sarge was such a good judge of character?"

"He was a talented man with a lot to offer this great nation, until he met you."

"Well he sure bled like a real trooper."

"The man was a war hero. Silver Star, Medal of Honor."

"I guess he should have retired while he was ahead."

"Billings killed a lot of soldiers in the last big dust-up. But he saved a lot more. In the war, and after the war. Especially after the war."

"What'd he do?" I wonder aloud. "Rescue them out of a burning building?"

"No wise-ass, he trained them. He made them hard. Hard enough to survive combat and come home. That's what he was trying to do for you until you made a vegetable out of him."

"My daddy always told me to eat my vegetables. He said they'd make me big and strong. But I don't like vegetables. I'd chew them up and spit them out when he wasn't looking. Just like that green bean, Sergeant Billings."

"You should have listened to your daddy a lot more."

"I listened. Just like I'm listening now. Don't mean any of it sinks in."

The senator takes a slow deep breath and then lets his fat cheeks push it out. I can feel the hot wind clear across the table.

"I was hoping the army would straighten you out," he says. "It didn't."

"Special-Ops, then," he replies, raising his bulk out of the groaning chair that's glad to be rid of him. "The wetworks division. You pull this kind of crap with them, they'll put you down like a rabid dog. And they'll do it with my blessing. This is the best I can do for you. Unless you'd prefer Leavenworth."

"No I would not."

"What's that?" he asks, leaning his ear in, fishing for that magic word of token respect he'd whupped into me when I was half my current size and age.

"No I would not, sir."

A sharp knock on the door summons the MP in the hall to let him out.

"Your mother says hello," he tells me as he leaves. "I'll let her know you're doing well."

• • •

Afghanistan is where Special-Ops puts me nearly a year later. There's not much to see. A lot of beige land filled with beige rocks and beige targets blending in with their beige clothes. Most of it I see through a scope, half a klick or more away, while I wait for my spotter to tell me what current conditions I need to adjust for, and when we've been cleared to take the shot.

Another head comes off. At this distance, you can barely see the impact. What you see, they call "pink mist." It's the puff of blood and brain matter that blows out the exit wound in a head shot. Red blood cells and red meat, pulled apart, diffused by the light, appearing pink for that split moment after impact, and then gone forever, like the life you just ended. Every time I see it, I feel a sense of accomplishment. A great satisfaction. One more enemy of the homeland down, only a billion more to go.

Maybe that makes me a patriot. Or a psychopath. But I see that spray of mist, like a flag at a carnival shooting gallery, popping up to tell me my aim was true, and I feel like I know my place in this world. And when the target tips over and eats the dirt, I couldn't be any happier.

Except, maybe, if it had been my daddy.

Dig Two Graves

STEFANO HADN'T EXPECTED to hit clay so soon.

He'd only been digging for fifteen minutes, tops. Maybe it was thanks to him being so efficient. He'd brought the right tools, after all. Everyone always thinks *shovel* when they have to dig a hole. Few people are forward-thinking enough to go *pick-axe* as well. Shovels are essential for moving the earth, but pickaxes are a lifesaver when it comes to loosening up the soil.

Efficient or not, Stefano couldn't have been more than three feet down in the deepest spot before the grey clay prom-ised to make progress a lot slower. He briefly considered starting over again in another spot, but there could just as well be a layer of clay anywhere he chose to dig, for a mile in all directions. It was already too late to choose another location, and another false start could drag this job on till morning. Best to knuckle down and invest all his effort in the hole he'd al-ready started. Once this was done, he could take a nice hot bath, clean up, give his sore muscles some TLC, and then sleep away the day. At least he could look forward to walking away from this task. He was the only one there who could boast that.

Stefano switched back to the pickaxe and hacked at the clay. Every chunk fought him, but piece by piece it began to break up, and another few shovelfuls could be excavated.

"Untie me and I'll help you."

Stefano didn't even look up from his work as he took another swing.

"Nice try, asshole."

Royce had been cooperative, it had to be said. Not helpful per se, but cooperative given the circumstances. How could he help, with his hands duct taped behind his back, and his legs mummy-wrapped up to his knees? He couldn't even stand, let alone hold up his end with the shovel or the pickaxe. It was a two-man job, and there were two men present, but all the heavy lifting fell to just one of them. Royce had the easy part.

He watched Stefano grunt his way through the next six inches before offering anything else.

"What's that thing they say," wondered Royce aloud, "about seeking revenge?"

"What thing?"

"Something like: when you go after revenge, dig two graves."

"I'm not mad at two people," said Stefano. "Just you."

"I think the idea is that the second grave is for yourself."

"That's dumb."

"It's a thing they say," said Royce. "It's supposed to be profound."

"It's dumb. Only one of us is going in the hole. It might have been me if you saw me coming, got the drop on me. But it didn't pan out that way. I got the drop on you, so this hole is all yours."

"Maybe it's something about the cost of revenge. You might get it, but you're going to end up just as dead as your enemy."

"I'm not digging two fucking holes!" snapped Stefano. "One of these is plenty. It's just got to be deep. Good and deep."

"Don't knock yourself out on my account," said Royce. "When they talk about unmarked graves, they're usually shallow unmarked graves."

"That's just it," said Stefano. "Shallow unmarked graves get found. That's why they get talked about. Nobody ever says anything about deep unmarked graves, because nobody ever finds them. Like nobody is ever going to find you."

Stefano took another swing, aiming deep. The impact was hard. The tip of the pickaxe had probably struck a stone, and it sent a painful vibration up the handle that made him let go of the wood. It might not have hurt so much, but Stefano was already sprouting blisters across his palms. They'd be in full blossom before he was another foot down, and burst by the time he was done.

"Fuck!" spat Stefano, looking at the state of his filthy hands. He'd have to rub a lot of disinfectant into his seeping blisters once he got home.

"Problem?" asked Royce.

"Nothing that concerns you."

"The only thing that concerns me right now is that hole you're digging."

Stefano shook out his hands and took a fresh grip on his tool.

"You should have brought some work gloves," Royce observed. "I've done enough gardening to know."

"I'm not planting flowers, I'm planting you."

"Same difference."

"I'll remember if there's ever a next time."

Stefano was certain there would never be a next time. It had taken a long while and a concerted effort for Royce to push him this far. He doubted anyone would ever get that deep under his skin again.

"Cut me loose and I'll go buy you a pair. I know a hardware store that's open late."

"Shut up!"

"I'm just making an offer. A nice offer. Real friendly. You should take advantage."

Stefano hammered the pickaxe spike deep into the clay and left it there while he strode over to where Royce lay in the clearing. He pointed his most blistered finger in his face and warned him, "Don't mouth off!"

Putting his finger away, he hoped Royce didn't get a good look at the bad shape it was in.

"You got two choices here," he said. "You can go in the hole dead, or you can go in the hole alive. Either way, you get buried. Nobody wants to get buried alive, so shut your face!"

Royce thought about it and then decided it was worth mouthing off some more.

"You bring a gun?"

"No, I didn't bring a goddamn gun," said Stefano, on his way back to the hole.

"So how are you going to finish me off before I go in the hole?"

Stefano looked to the night sky for patience. He didn't find any up there. Just a lot of stars and distant worlds that didn't give two shits for his problems down here on earth.

"I'll smash your head in with the shovel or something before I start dumping dirt on you," he suggested. "You know. For mercy's sake."

"That doesn't sound so merciful to me," Royce muttered.

"Would you rather be buried alive? Smothered to death under all that mud? Keep talking and I'll make it happen."

"I think you want to bury me alive. I think that was your plan all along. I'd be dead already if that wasn't your intention from the start."

Every word out of Royce's face reminded Stefano why killing him was such a good idea. Mostly he just wanted the son of a bitch gone, but being cruel about it was sounding like a better idea all the time. Making him watch his grave get dug was nasty on purpose, but Royce's bullshit was keeping the cruelty option on the table.

The final foot down was the hardest. Clay and rocks, rocks and clay. By the time he was done, Stefano had calmed down enough to return to a more merciful state of mind. Royce had been silent long enough to earn some small consideration. He'd wait until he had him in the hole before caving his head in with the shovel. Or the pickaxe. Stefano hadn't decided which tool would be best. The important thing was to keep all the spilled blood and brains in the hole.

It was autumn, and the leaves had been coming down for a couple of weeks now. There were enough scattered around that they could be spread over a freshly filled hole to hide the fact that the soil had recently been disturbed. But a puddle of blood splashed across the surface wouldn't be so easy to hide. It might be spotted by someone on a nature walk—at least until the next rainfall came and washed away the evidence. Best to keep the murder itself contained to the tight space he'd cleared, where all the evidence could be buried.

That decided it. Pickaxe. He'd put the pickaxe through Royce's head, and then leave it behind in the hole. He wouldn't need it to fill in the pit again. That job was all shovel.

"Are we done?" Royce asked, when Stefano set his tools down and returned to where he was lying.

"You are," he confirmed.

Stefano grabbed Royce by the ankles and shuffled backwards, dragging him towards the pit. The blanket of dead leaves rustled under Royce's ass as he slid across them, unable to slow his progress towards the grave now deemed finished enough to receive him.

Stretching his legs wide, Stefano straddled the outer edges of the trench he'd dug, and pulled Royce down the middle of the furrow until he dropped heavily to the muddy base, settling into the frame of excavated earth that was just big enough to accommodate the entire length of his body.

"Good fit," Royce commented, looking at the walls of solid soil that surrounded him on all sides. "You didn't even have to measure. It's like you've done this a dozen times before."

"Once is enough," grunted Stefano. "First time. Last time."

Sweat was still pouring off his face, dripping off his chin. Now that the hard part was done, it was like all the effort was catching up with him at once. Stefano felt overheated and lightheaded. The aches and pains, lying in wait to torment him tomorrow, seemed to gang up a good ten hours early. They hit hardest down his left side. And even though he was standing upright, it felt as though he were lying on his back, with somebody piling weights on his chest, one after the other.

"You okay?" asked Royce, seriously enough for it to sound like genuine concern.

Stefano wasn't. Not in the least. By the time he began to consider that he might be in some very real medical distress, he no longer was. He was instantly past all that.

Some heart attacks are so severe, they kill their victim before he can even hit the ground. In Stefano's case, tipping forward into the grave that had finished him off, there was no ground to catch him. Just Royce, who got the full force of Stefano's body as it fell several feet past the surface and landed on top of him. That extra moment of travel to the bottom of the pit only served to make sure he was extra dead by the time he settled.

Royce had the wind knocked out of him by the impact, and it took him a few minutes to collect his senses and realize Stefano wasn't messing around. Wasn't fucking with him. Wasn't anything anymore.

Royce considered a smartass comment or two he could make about the trick fate had pulled on Stefano, but decided it wasn't worth the effort. There was no more audience to hear him. And fate might yet make him a victim of Stefano's plot, even if his killer wouldn't be around to enjoy his triumph. They were deep in the woods, far from any road or trail, and the likelihood that anyone would discover Royce at the bottom of his deep unmarked grave, even lying conspicuously unfilled, was as remote as the location Stefano had picked to have his revenge.

He struggled under the corpse for an hour, trying to worm his way free. But between the tight quarters of the grave and the dead weight on top of him, Royce utterly failed to improve his situation. Even without the earth piled on top of him, he was buried alive under two hundred pounds of flesh and bone. After so long a night and so hard a struggle, Royce finally gave in to exhaustion and fell into a deep slumber. His last conscious thought was that he would sleep like the dead—literally so if he couldn't figure a way out of his predicament when he woke up again.

● ● ●

When morning came to the clearing, Royce got the early rays of sunshine straight in his face. The brightness shone red through his eyelids, and when he opened them, he realized the sides of the grave could not shelter him from the light because he was no longer in the hole.

"Where the hell...?" Royce began to ask, but figured it out himself in the same moment.

The hole—his grave—was only a few feet away. Still open, unfilled, with Stefano likely lying at the bottom.

Royce had not walked out of it in his sleep. His arms and legs remained duct taped together. Someone, out here in the middle of nowhere, had to have helped.

"Hello?" he said to no one in particular.

"Oh, hi," answered a voice. "You're awake. I figured you were just sleeping, and I was right!"

There was some sort of wooden construct standing on end at the edge of the clearing. Royce's vision remained hazy against the rising sun, but he could see a figure walking out from behind whatever it was that was being built. As he came closer, Royce could see it was a boy, no more than twelve or thirteen years old. And he was carrying just about the biggest knife he'd ever seen.

"Did you pull me out of that hole?" Royce asked, his attention mostly focused on the blade, and the sunlight that was glinting off its razor-sharp edge.

"Sure did," said the boy. "I tried to wake you up, but you were down for the count. As for your friend..."

He tapered off, not sure how to break the news to Royce.

"Well, I hate to be the one to tell you, but he didn't make it."

"That's okay," Royce assured him. "We weren't really pals or anything."

"There's a lot of ways to get killed out in the woods," said the boy wisely. "Not a mark on him, but your friend seems to have found a way just the same. At least a bear didn't get him. You don't want a bear to get you. Awful way to go."

As Royce's eyes got used to the light, he could see the construct the boy was working on. Two fairly hefty branches, long and straight, stripped of offshoot twigs and leaves, stood on end. Lashed between them were two panels of textiles, bracketed by smaller branches that were tied to the bigger ones at ninety degree angles, forming a frame.

"What are you making?" Royce asked.

"It's a jacket stretcher," the boy announced proudly. "I also know how to make a rope stretcher, and the usual kind you make out of a tarp. Oh, and I can do a duct-tape stretcher, too. But I don't have any of that stuff."

"I've got plenty of duct tape here," said Royce of the strips that still bound him, "but I don't think there's enough to make a stretcher."

"At least there were jackets. One belongs to your dead friend. The other is mine. You only need a couple to make a stretcher. His shoe laces gave me just enough rope to finish the job."

Royce looked at the jackets that were neatly folded to form a surface. The two stripped branches ran up through them and out their inverted sleeves. It was a clever configuration that looked sturdy. He recognized the leather one on the bottom. Stefano had been wearing it the previous night. The top one was bright green and had a collection of fabric badges of varying designs sewn into it.

"You're a Boy Scout," Royce concluded.

"Yup," the boy confirmed.

"That's a lot of badges."

"I'm almost an Eagle Scout."

"Well," said Royce, who had never been much of a joiner, "congratulations."

"I'm not there yet," said the boy. "Only four percent of Boy Scouts ever make it to Eagle Scout, but I'm going to be one of the few who do."

Since he'd become a Boy Scout a year and a half earlier, the boy had dreamed of joining the ranks of the select few great Americans to have earned this momentous achievement. Luminaries such as President Gerald Ford, astronaut Neil Armstrong, cult leader L. Ron Hubbard, crack-smoking mayor Marion Barry, and darknet felon Ross Ulbricht ranked among the group of elites. In over a hundred years, only two million scouts had qualified for the rank of Eagle Scout. A tiny number compared to the many tens of millions who had worn the uniform, but failed to rise to become the cream of the crop.

The boy walked back to his jacket stretcher to put on the finishing touches.

"You see that spot?" he said, pointing at one of the scarce bits of vacant real estate on the back of his jacket. "That's where I'm putting my Emergency Preparedness badge."

"Oh yeah?" said Royce. "How do you get one of those?"

"You're going to get it for me."

"How do I do that?" Royce asked, already certain he wouldn't like the answer.

The boy removed a folded booklet from his back pocket and looked for a specific page.

"There are nine requirements," he said. "This one's number five."

Finding the correct subsection, he marked the spot with his finger.

"With another person," he read, and added as an aside, "That's you."

The boy returned his eyes to the booklet and continued.

"Show a good way to transport an injured person out of a remote and/or rugged area, conserving the energy of rescuers while ensuring the well-being and protection of the injured person."

Refolding the booklet and stuffing it back into his pocket, he mentioned, "That's also you."

The boy picked at a few stubborn nubs on the arms of his stretcher, making sure there would be no splinters forthcoming, either for rescuer or the rescued.

"Lucky for you I came along when I did. And lucky for me you were in such a predicament. Now I get to save you. And that's one more badge down."

"And you think you're going to drag me out of here on the back of that contraption?"

"It's not too far," said the boy. "Maybe a mile, mile and a half. It's flat land most of the way, then there's a trail, and it'll be smooth sailing from there."

That sounded about right. Royce remembered the forced march in the dark. Stefano only used the last of his duct-tape roll to bind his legs once they had arrived at the clearing.

"Maybe that's not such a super idea," said Royce, who didn't look forward to the reception that would be waiting for him on the other side of this operation.

There would be a lot of questions about his and Stefano's nocturnal activities. Technically, he was the victim of an attempted murder who had done no wrong that night. But the inquiry would inevitably get into why that murder had been attempted at all. And therein lay a whole mess of reasons that would point to a long list of crimes. Stefano had been pissed off with good reason. And if the police knew the half of it, they'd be quick to bury Royce all over again—in a prison, with multiple consecutive sentences. He wasn't so old that he wouldn't end up doing every last day of his time. But by then, he'd be ripe to step out of his cell and straight into another grave. This one official, complete with a coffin and a headstone.

"If you use that big knife to cut me loose," Royce suggested, "I can just walk back."

The boy considered that option carefully, then rejected it.

"That doesn't work for me," he said. "I need to rescue you. No rescue, no badge. No badge, no Eagle Scout. My hands are tied."

"It's my hands that are tied," Royce pointed out. "They don't have to be. It's still a rescue without you dragging me all the way back to civilization."

"Earning merit badges isn't easy," explained the boy. "It's hard. And that's the point. They wouldn't be worth a thing if they were easy."

Setting the stretcher next to Royce, the boy rolled him onto it, and made sure he was in a comfortable position before lifting the front end off the ground and beginning the long trek. The back end of the stretcher dug twin ruts into the ground as they made their way into the woods, and began the twisting, circuitous route that would return them to the outskirts of town.

There was no talking sense to the boy, so Royce concentrated on freeing himself. Despite his best efforts to carve smooth arms for the stretcher, a few rough spots remained, and Royce was able to catch the end of his duct-taped wrists on a sharp edge of wood. Ten minutes of constant friction finally got the tape to tear. Once his hands were free, Royce leaned forward, picked at the edge of the tape around his shins, and began unwinding the long strip that held them together.

"Hey, what do you think you're..." the boy began, when he felt the load of his burden shifting too much. But by then, Royce was already free and off the stretcher.

Running from the ambitious would-be Eagle Scout seemed to be the best option. Royce certainly didn't want to get into an altercation with a child over his unwillingness to submit to rescue—especially when that child came armed with a big-ass bowie knife. His hope was to lose him in the trees and then double back to the path in his own time.

As Royce ran, he could hear the rustle of leaves behind him as the boy gave chase. The boy was shouting at him, demanding he return to the stretcher and resume his role as a badge-earning victim of wilderness misadventure. Royce ignored him and continued to zigzag his way through the woods.

Dodging trees was exhausting, and Royce kept hoping to find a straightaway that would allow his long legs to put some distance between him and the boy. At last he stumbled upon a clearing. With one last glance over his shoulder to see how near his pursuer was, Royce burst into a full sprint.

And only made it another twenty feet.

Before he could see it coming, he'd lunged straight into the grave Stefano had dug for him hours ago. It was still there, still yawning open, waiting for him. And this time it would not be denied.

As one leg plunged into the hole, the other was left behind to trip over the edge. Royce fell forward hard, his chin catching the opposite edge of the ditch. The full weight of his body pitched down, pulling his head back sharply, and snapping his neck right at the base of his skull.

Like Stefano before him, Royce was dead before his body settled at the bottom of the pit.

"Darn it!" yelled the boy, as he stood at the edge of the hole and peered down to see what had happened. The Emergency Preparedness badge, so tantalizingly within his grasp, had just been yanked away. When would he ever see another opportunity like this?

With no rescue in the forecast for today, the boy decided it would be best to cover the bodies over before scavenging animals found the dead men and helped themselves. Stefano's shovel lay among the leaves by the hole, so the boy took it and began returning the soil to the spot where the mound had been dug up. As he worked, a thought occurred to him that brightened his foul mood.

He'd have to check with his Scout Master when he returned home. But provided he could lead people back to the correct spot and unearth the bodies, he was certain this act would qualify as partial requirements for at least three other merit badges. Surely the Geocaching, Geology, and Orienteering badges would be put within reach.

None of these merits were among the essential Eagle Scout badges, but every bit helped, and they all counted towards the required grand total. Even with this unfortunate setback, he would still be that much closer to his ultimate goal.

Sometimes, the boy thought, patting the earth down with the flat of the shovel, people get what's coming to them.

Pinch Hitter

MURDER IS AN UGLY THING. Don't believe the hype. Most people make a mess of it. That's because most people are amateurs.

It isn't any prettier when the professionals do it. Maybe it's done with a little more skill, a little less mess, a touch of flair. But it's still a nasty, ugly thing—unglamorous, unromantic, visceral and grotesque.

I suppose murder is a lot like sex that way.

I don't fuck professionally, but I do kill professionally. Truth be told, I'd rather have this job than the other. I'm better with guns. There's no performance issues with a gun. It's always good to go. Squeeze the trigger and the action happens. You only have to aim your weapon and be on target.

Another way murder is a lot like sex.

Being a hitman isn't exciting. I provide a service. The exchange is purely functional. A set sum of money buys you one murder. The amount of money and the number of dead it pays for are standard, immovable. Sometimes I'm provided a photo of the target, often it's just a name. A name is all I need.

Typically I'll walk right up to the target and ask them if they're so-and-so. I like to be sure. Not once has anyone ever said to me, "Who wants to know?" They never answer my honest query with another question. They simply confirm that I've found who I'm looking for. And then I shoot them. They never see it coming. Usually they assume I'm a delivery man, not a hitman, and they never suspect that the only package I have for them is a jacketed soft-point.

A headshot is good. Two headshots are better. Time permitting, I'll put a few more in their chest and shut down some more vital organs. Five shots max. I use a .38 revolver so I don't have to worry about jams. Simple, reliable. I hold back one in case somebody was counting shots. If they're smart enough to count shots, they're smart enough to let me leave in peace, because they'll know I have one more round that could be fired in their direction if they try anything funny.

Few bystanders ever count shots. Most run—or hide until I'm gone.

I have never been in a gunfight. If you're a hitman and you get in a gunfight, you're doing it wrong. No one has ever fired a shot back at me, and if they did, I wouldn't stick around to trade more bullets.

I don't worry about targets having security to deal with. Those aren't the kind of jobs I do. If the target is high-profile enough to be surrounded by muscle or hired guns, they don't get a hitman. They get a hitsquad. Ex-military types with semi-automatic rifles and body armour usually. They sweep in, unload on security first, confirm and kill the real target second. It happens so fast, the other side rarely gets to do any shooting before they're wiped out.

Rarely. But it happens.

I've never been on one of those squads, never seen one in action. I wouldn't want to if I had the chance. I like to keep things simple, safe. There's not as much money to be made my way, but there are much better odds of living to spend it.

Ten grand a hit. That's the standard. Non-negotiable. Which, unfortunately, means I can't hold out for more. That price has been set in stone for years. No accounting for inflation. So I have to do at least three or four hits a year just to scrape by. Some years there's an upper-management shuffle, or a territorial dispute, and I make out well. Other years there's peace, and I'm lucky to pick up a couple of jobs knocking off cheating spouses, would-be blackmailers, or somebody's coworker who's competing for a promotion.

You take what you can get when you can get it. It's feast or famine in this line of work. Lately, it's been a famine. There's always somebody who needs to get dead, but contracts have been scarce. Not just for me, but for all the shooters in the business. That's why I was surprised when my handler, Jerzy Staszko, told me Milo Finch turned down a job.

"Milo's out," he said. "You're in."

It was the first thing out of his mouth once he came up to my apartment to give me the news and reassign the contract.

"What's with Milo?"

"He's too sick to work."

"What do you mean he's sick? Like cancer or something?"

"Nah, he has a bad cold."

"He's missing out over a sniffle?"

"He has a fever, runny nose. Sounds like shit on the phone. What if he sneezes in the middle of the job?"

"So take a pill and power through. There's over-the-counter stuff that can suppress symptoms for a few hours."

"What about side effects? Don't that all say 'Do not operate heavy equipment'?"

"A handgun isn't heavy equipment."

"The job is heavy though, wouldn't you say?" said Jerzy. "You don't want to do it drowsy, hopped up on cold medicine. Anyway, what's it to you? Don't you want to earn?"

"I could use a payday."

"Then quit your bitching and be glad Milo caught that bug that's going around."

Jerzy Staszko isn't what you'd expect from someone who books murders, pairing hitters and marks. He looks like an accountant, and I guess that's what he is. A little man with glasses and more hair on his face than his head, you'd never pick him for a guy who's orchestrated more death than the most prolific serial killer they have locked up in your local supermax. Years ago, he used to pull a trigger now and then. These days, he matches marks with his modest stable of shooters he knows he can rely on.

Milo was reliable. Right up until he flaked out over a head cold. I'd never heard such a shit excuse in my life.

"Aren't you forgetting something?" I asked Jerzy, as he let himself out.

"Like what?"

"You got a name for me? Or am I supposed to randomly pick people out of the phone book until I get the right mark?"

"No name, no photo. I don't know who the mark is. For that you're going to have to see The Man Upstairs."

Even handlers have handlers. I always knew Jerzy was on a leash. I even knew who held it. But face time with that level of player is not for the likes of me.

"Since when does he give hitters the personal touch?"

"Since never."

The Man Upstairs actually took his meetings in a custodian staff room at the lowest level of a parking garage, deep underground. Nevertheless, he was The Man Upstairs. You don't get any higher than him in the syndicate. I knew of the meeting place, but had never been down there myself. I wasn't high enough on the ladder. Hell, I wasn't even on the bottom rung of the ladder. I was down in the dirt with the rest of the street-level scum, which is how I preferred things. It's easy to keep your head down when you're already so low.

"Tell me now, Jerzy, what's the job I'm walking into here? He doesn't want me to shoot the President or something, does he?"

"This is on a need-to-know basis, and I don't need to know. I only know a time. And that's one hour from now, so you better get going."

"I'm rethinking this."

"Rethink it on the drive over. You don't want to be late. And if you end up with second thoughts before you get there, rethink those too, because you don't want to disappoint The Man Upstairs."

● ● ●

The whole way to the meet I thought about taking a U-turn and heading out of town on a long vacation. If jobs hadn't been in famine mode for so long, I might have had enough cash to make myself scarce for a good long stretch. But my pockets were empty, my options few. I wondered if it was too late to come down with a fake head cold, too. Probably. Jerzy would have already told the syndicate council I was on my way, and if the council expected you, you'd better show up.

There was a dipped driveway waiting for me off a side street that linked up to the main drag half a block away. I pulled in next to the ticket machine, punched a button for my numbered slip of paper, and waited for the automatic door to rise. A booth was situated at the bottom of the ramp, but the gate was up with no attendant on duty. If a syndicate meeting was in session, it meant no civilians were on the premises, and parking for the attendees was free and undocumented.

The parking garage lay deep beneath a downtown shopping mall. After hours, there wasn't a single car left inside except for the ones belonging to the council. They were all clustered together at the very bottom, across from an unmarked blue door that led to a staff room no staff was ever permitted to enter. Even the janitors didn't have a key. The syndicate had their own cleaners. They weren't there to scrub the place down for coffee cups and candy wrappers and scuff marks on the linoleum. They had a different approach to sanitizing the room and keeping it bug free.

Three of those cleaners were standing guard outside the door. All eyes were on me as I pulled into a vacant spot several spaces removed from the rest of the cars. I wanted to make sure they could see my approach and had all due opportunity to determine I was who they were expecting and posed no threat. I'd brought my gun along, but kept it in my coat pocket where it would be instantly discovered, removed, and kept for me until I came back out of the room beyond the blue door.

Once they were satisfied the .38 was all I had on me, I was given clearance to approach the door and knock. It may have looked plain and utilitarian, but it was steel-plated and could probably stop an RPG without scratching the paint. I could feel the hard reinforced surface under my knuckles, and the metal absorbed the chill air of the sub-basement like an extra layer of armour.

I was let in without a word by a man who was too old and fat to be muscle. Everyone in the room was a council member, high enough in the syndicate to be authorized to hear every word that was said within that inner sanctum.

There were six folding chairs—uncomfortable and plastic —arranged around three folding card tables set end-to-end. The place was sterile. Not for surgical procedures, but for other matters of life and death. Anything that entered that room came in by unanimous approval, and there was no place to hide contraband if, by some miracle, you got it past the guards. They'd frisked me so thoroughly, I had expected rubber gloves to come out for a cavity search at any moment.

"Hello," I said, to the blank stare that greeted me, "I'm..."

"We know who you are," said the man who sat at the head of the table.

I thought better of offering my hand for anybody to shake. No one seemed interested in socializing. The councilman who had let me in returned to his vacant seat without even acknowledging he'd let me into the room.

"You asked to see me," I said. There was no point phrasing it as a question.

The head of the table—The Man Upstairs—ignored my statement and turned to his colleagues.

"Gentlemen, I propose a brief adjournment. We have much more to discuss this evening, and hours ahead of us. Five minutes for coffee and refreshments, and we'll pick up where we left off."

There was a coffee machine in the corner. Sandwiches were piled on a covered tray. It was a Spartan spread, but enough to fuel them as the council discussed whatever pressing business they had to attend to at the monthly summit.

The men rose from their seats and stretched their legs. Some lit cigarettes, though there was little ventilation to cope with smoke in the stuffy room. Air ducts would have been a potential security risk.

"Walk with me," the chairman of the council said, clapping a hand on my shoulder. The Man Upstairs didn't take walks with just anybody. A walk meant a private conversation, and that level of privacy was only necessary if there was something extra-important that needed to get said, one-on-one.

I was led back out the blue door a moment later, and guided away from the three guards who remained at their post outside the staff room.

Everyone knew the parking garage was where decisions were made and fates were decided. Even the cops. But surveillance, with or without a warrant, was an impossible nut to crack. They'd love to know what the syndicate talked about in that staff room, but there was no way in. Far underground, they couldn't drill deep enough to feed a wire. Even if they were able to get someone inside, it was a sparse concrete cubbyhole that was swept regularly. The tiniest mic on the market would have been spotted in an instant.

Although that shoebox was the most secure spot in the city, and had kept every secret discussed inside for many years, the rest of the garage was just as impenetrable.

Walking the levels, strolling the columns, it was a layout that gave the detective techies nightmares. After hours, with no other people or vehicles about, every word spoken bounced around, both echoed and muffled at once. You could have wired the whole place and never picked up more than a tantalizing snippet as a juicy conversation passed by. A hint of incrimination, a single choice word, and then it would be gone. Inadmissible.

This is where The Man Upstairs took people to say things that weren't even fit for the ears of his fellow syndicate councilmen.

"Jerzy Staszko speaks highly of you."

"We've worked together for years," I said.

"Closely," he said. "For many jobs."

"Yes," I agreed.

"But not this job," I was told. "This job is more specialized. The council is in agreement, and you're the man for it. You report to me directly."

"And the rate?" I asked, hoping for a pay bump accordingly.

"Is the same as it's always been."

I wasn't surprised, but my unfulfilled expectations were noted.

"Ten large isn't buying me talent," I was informed. "It takes no particular skill to point a weapon at point-blank range and pull the trigger. A child with a pop-gun can do as much. What the money buys is moral flexibility. Most people—most normal people—won't commit murder for ten thousand dollars. Some of them wouldn't at any price. Or at least they think they wouldn't. Ask them to kill a stranger for a million dollars, and suddenly they waver. Many of them will think, *maybe just this once*. It is, after all, a life-changing sum. But at a ten-thousand-dollar price point, it's a wage. Oh, it's a good chunk of change for a small amount of effort and a short amount of time. But you can't retire on it. You know you'll have to do it again to keep the flow going. That's where economics and moral flexibility meet. The amount I'm willing to pay, the amount you're willing to accept, and the willingness to do some dirty business we can both live with."

"Milo isn't sick, is he?"

"He isn't well. Oh, he has the bug that's going around, to be sure. Not the flu bug. This one is much more detrimental to our business. Milo Finch has come down with a bad case of regret. He's sick in his soul. The work got to him and now he's developed a conscience. It's growing inside of him like a malignant tumour, getting bigger every day, festering, spreading."

"Are you telling me Milo is the mark?" I said.

"Friend of yours?"

"We've socialized. Went to a few ball games together. Talked shop."

"He ever mention this crisis he's been having?"

"He's expressed some doubts."

"You didn't think to say something?"

"Everybody has doubts about their life choices, no matter what they do for a living. It's normal."

"So you two are close?"

"You could say that, yeah."

"Good. He'll let you get close enough to put two in his head."

"I suppose he will."

"Then the only question that remains is: how morally flexible are you?"

"I'll need more money for this one."

"The fee is ten grand, like always."

"No wiggle room?"

"None."

I dropped the attempt to negotiate and accepted. Times were lean, and somebody was going to collect the fee on Milo. I decided it might as well be me.

• • •

Before I'd even driven all the way off the lot, I was on the phone with Jerzy. For whatever reason, he'd been kept out of the loop. If I was going to do this thing, I wanted him in, regardless of the syndicate's wishes. They would never have to know about a personal conversation between old work buddies.

"I'm sorry to hear Milo won't be recovering from his illness," Jerzy said, once I sketched out the situation for him.

Personal conversation or not, it was still over the phone, and you never know for sure who might be listening. We kept things non-incriminating, just to be sure, but the topic at hand was clear enough to us both.

"Why do you think the council didn't want you to know about it?"

"We're taking care of one of our own, here," Jerzy said. "Milo's provided a valuable service for years. He deserves a bit of discretion. Only one person needs to know about it, and that's whoever's bringing him the cure for what ails."

There was more to it than that, and it didn't need to get said. If word got out that Milo was hit for no greater crime than turning down work, company morale would suffer. You want your hitters doing their job out of greed, not fear. They're supposed to kill for cash, not because they might be next if they ever say no.

"They could have sent you to pay him a visit," I suggested.

"You know I haven't had to play doctor in years," said Jerzy.

"You stop by his place, you give him his flu shot, and you go before you catch any germs. It's not brain surgery."

"Well, it kind of is."

I suppose a round or two through the skull was brain surgery of a sort. But it went beyond any mere lobotomy. It made scrambled eggs of a man's mind.

"You know what I mean," I said, tired of speaking in metaphors for any eavesdropping third parties.

"They asked for you," said Jerzy. "That's all I know. At least, that's all I knew, until you decided to tell me more than I ever needed to hear."

"I thought you might appreciate knowing what's up, and what's about to go down."

"At my age, I've learned not knowing some things is a gift."

"Okay, Jerzy, have it your way. I'll tell you when it's done."

"I don't even want to know that much," he told me and disconnected.

● ● ●

I let myself into Milo's building unannounced. It only took five minutes of waiting around out front before someone leaving let the door swing shut slow enough for me to catch it. Once I was on Milo's floor, I went to his apartment door at the end of the hall and knocked, trying to make my knuckles sound casual. It must have sounded non-threatening, because Milo opened up a moment later, not even bothering to ask who it was.

His face froze when he saw me standing in his doorway, and before I could say a word in greeting, he practically shouted, "Oh, shit!"

Milo shoved right past me like he was rushing to catch a train. I turned and saw it was no departing express he was looking to hop aboard, it was the elevator. After it let me out, no one had summoned it to be elsewhere, so it had lingered on the floor. Only now were the doors sliding shut as it sought to return to its default setting on the lobby level.

Even at a full sprint, Milo missed the doors by an inch. When he couldn't slip his fingers between the narrowing slit, he pounded on the call button, arguing with the car that it wasn't too late to pick up a passenger.

He was still playing bongos on the elevator button when I caught up to him. I could have put a round through the back of his head and taken the stairs before anyone knew there was an intruder in the building, but my curiosity got the better of me.

"You run fast for a man who's supposed to be at death's door," I commented.

Milo spun around, cornered against the sealed elevator that had decided to ignore his plea.

"I'm running because death has come knocking."

"Can't a guy come over and visit a sick friend?"

"Not tonight he can't," said Milo. "I know why you're here, so don't bullshit me."

"You want to talk about this someplace more private?" I suggested.

"I step behind a closed door with you, you'll start blasting," said Milo.

"I could do that right here, right now. Nobody's watching."

"You trying to prolong my suffering?"

"I'm trying to understand the lay of the land before I do anything rash."

The idea of isolating himself from the rest of the world, with just me and my gun, held no appeal to Milo until I suggested we could have a drink together. He had a bottle of gin in his fridge. He also had a gun of his own stashed somewhere inside, so I made sure I had mine out, in plain sight, ready to use, in case he reached for it. Once I'd made the talk-or-shoot options clear enough to him, Milo poured us a couple of stiff ones without incident.

"How many shooters is Jerzy running these days?" he asked me, handing me my glass.

"You mean other than you and me?"

"Exactly."

"I don't know," I said. "This isn't a sewing circle. You're the only one I've ever really hung out with."

"Go down the list with me."

I had to think about the other names and faces of men in our line of work. I was aware of a handful of players I'd heard of or met once or twice.

"There's Ben Brenner," I said.

"Dead," replied Milo.

"No shit? He seemed like a good sort. What happened to him?"

"He died. What do you want, an autopsy?"

"Gino Trieste," I said, pulling another name out of the hat.

"Dead."

"Gabe Strauch?" I asked, figuring I already knew the answer.

"Dead," confirmed Milo. "And so's Felix Wrebb, Johnny Doller, and Mitch Lemos."

I didn't know those names, but I took Milo's word for it.

"People die for all sorts of reasons," I said.

"Don't you get it, man?" said Milo, exasperated with me. "They're closing the circle."

"What do you mean?"

"This job you're on. The one to take me out. That wasn't the same hit I turned down. Obviously. The syndicate isn't going to hire me to kill myself, are they?"

"So who was your target supposed to be? Jerzy didn't know."

"Jerzy didn't know because Jerzy was it. That's why I said no. And me saying no put my head on the block."

"Did you tell Jerzy any of this?"

"I told him some bullshit about being sick. I don't want to kill the guy, I don't want to see him dead, but I'm not going against the syndicate to tip him off."

"And now?" I asked.

"Looks like I'm done even after I kept my mouth shut. Just me knowing about their intentions towards Jerzy is too much information."

"And now you've gone and shared it with me."

"They'd have you hit him next."

"Probably."

"And after that, someone would come for you."

"Maybe."

"Definitely," said Milo.

"Why take any of us out?" I said, feeling slighted, unappreciated. "We do quality work. No one's turned snitch. And we come cheap. I asked for a raise for this one job and basically got told to go fuck myself."

"You wanted more money to do me?" Milo asked.

"I figured they should sweeten the deal on account of us knowing each other. A few extra Gs for remorse didn't seem unreasonable."

"Considerate of you," he said, and meant it.

"It's those fucking hitsquad assholes," I decided. "The council wants to dump the freelancers and go with the goons they already have on the payroll."

The hitsquads worked on retainer. They pulled a regular salary to be ready to go at a moment's notice, when there was work that needed to get done fast, or a turf war that needed to get settled before it dragged out and started to eat profits. The syndicate probably figured, since they already had these guys good to go as a team, they might as well make use of them individually—as shooters for the more mundane hits that were our bread and butter. It was a business decision. And we'd fallen off the bottom line.

"Well now that we're all burned, I guess someone better tell Jerzy," said Milo.

"He said he didn't want to know what was going on."

"And if not knowing ends up getting him killed?"

"Yeah," I considered. "That, he'll probably want to know about."

I got my phone out and put in the call.

"Jerzy, I need you to get your ass over to Milo's place right now," I said when the other end picked up.

He probably figured I'd made a mess of things and needed help scrubbing evidence.

"Milo's here with me now," I told him, once he'd finished with his initial barrage.

"No, he has not passed," I said in answer to Jerzy's next question. "In fact he's recovering nicely."

I held out the phone to Milo so he could add his two cents.

"Come join the party, Jerzy," he said at the speaker.

Given his tone, Jerzy didn't sound like he was in a party mood.

● ● ●

By the time Jerzy arrived at the door half an hour later, Milo and I had polished off the better part of the bottle of gin. We quit there because we knew there was work that needed to be done before the night was out. Shoring up our courage was a reasonable thing to do, but we didn't want to get sloppy drunk.

"What the fuck?" was Jerzy's sole question when he saw the two of us in Milo's apartment, alive and well and free of any bullet holes.

We sat Jerzy down, handed him what was left of the gin, and told him exactly what the fuck. Even before he was done with his first shot, he knew we were screwed. He needed a second shot right after that to cope. Once he'd tossed back his

third, Jerzy was angry enough to want to do something about
it.

"Is the council still in session?" he asked.

"Should be," I said. "It's only been an hour or so since I
was there. Two since you came up to my place to send me on
this fool's errand."

"They can do five or six hours at a stretch," said Jerzy.
"There's a lot of business to discuss and they won't meet again
for at least a month."

"We're not going to last a month if they want us gone,"
said Milo. "We have to do it now."

"Do what now?" asked Jerzy, like he wasn't already on the
same page.

"You know," I said. And he did.

Milo had multiple handguns and accessories in his stash. I
accepted a spare sidearm, and Jerzy, who hadn't carried a piece
in years, helped himself to one Colt, and one Smith and Wesson.

"I just realized something," said Milo, opening a fresh box
of ammo for his guests.

"What's that?" I wondered.

"There's three of us."

"I can count that high."

"Three hitters, all on the same job," said Milo. "What does
that make us?"

And I knew: a hitsquad.

"Fuck, you're right," I said.

"I always hated dealing with those assholes," Jerzy said
absently, loading his Smith and Wesson. He'd been the syndicate's talent scout since they first formed the squad years ago.

"You'll never have to again after tonight," I observed.

"No, I guess not."

"Do I have time to go buy a pair of urban camos?" said
Milo.

And we all laughed.

"Fucking clowns," Jerzy chuckled.

"I wouldn't mind having one or two of their AR's right now," lamented Milo. "You can stick the night-vision and flashbangs up your ass, but some heavier firepower than these pop guns would make a hell of a difference."

I had to admit, I didn't like our chances.

"The whole council is going to be packing," Jerzy said. And we knew he was right. "They might be a bunch of old farts like us, but they're old school. They've exchanged bullets before. They've probably caught a few in their day. If this turns into a gunfight, we're outnumbered and outclassed."

Not one of us had been in a gunfight before. It didn't seem like a good time to start.

"Maybe bullets aren't the answer," I suggested.

"You think you can talk your way out of this?" said Milo, with zero confidence such a thing was remotely possible.

"Yeah," I said, pondering my next move, "I think I can."

● ● ●

I spiralled down the parking garage levels twenty minutes later and found the collection of cars still occupying the same spots they'd been in when I was assigned the hit on Milo. At the very least, The Man Upstairs would have been waiting around for my report on how things went, eager to assign me the Jerzy job next for another ten grand. But, as expected, the whole council was still in session, and the cleaners remained on high alert at the door.

Pulling into the same spot I'd parked in before, I got out of my car and made another slow approach, my arms spread apart for them to see my hands were nowhere near my piece. The blue door waited several paces behind them. All I needed was a few words with the council and I was sure I could sort everything out between us.

I stopped my approach directly in front of the middle guard and let him dig into my pocket for the .38—exactly where he found it on offer last time. Drawing my weapon, he was about to give me my second frisk of the night when something caught his attention. Or, more to the point, the lack of something. A distinct smell was notable in its absence.

He might not have known the specifics of my assignment, but he knew I'd been dispatched on a special hit for the council. Raising my revolver to his face, he sniffed at it like a hound dog, and lines of suspicion cut deep furrows in his face.

"This weapon hasn't been fired," he announced, noting the lack of gunpowder residue offending his nose.

Busted.

"No," I admitted. "It hasn't. And it won't be."

I reached into another pocket, this one inside my coat, and found the grip of the backup Milo had supplied me with. This one was an automatic, which I still had a strong bias against, but Milo's choices had been limited. Automatics don't often jam, but they can. And when they do, it's always at the worst possible moment.

I stuck the barrel in the middle guard's face and said, "But this one will."

The automatic didn't jam. A single bullet fired out the end, close enough to the guard's face to scorch his entire forehead black. The slug took to the air for all of three inches before burrowing through his skull and bursting the back of his head like an exploding melon.

The two other guards reached for their weapons and never got more than two fingers on them before they were on the receiving end of their own headshots.

Expected to return and report, no one was expecting me to bring company. I looked back and saw Milo and Jerzy both in their shooting positions behind the two rear doors of my car. They'd practically been lying on top of each other in the back seat. Once I'd executed the middle guard, they'd been on target with the flanking pair no more than two seconds later. Even at range, in a quick aim-and-shoot situation, my trust in their marksmanship had not been misplaced. Milo was an excellent shot, and Jerzy wasn't so rusty after all.

We didn't offer the three guards a double tap. We didn't want to make any more noise than necessary. It didn't matter. All three shots were spot on target and none of the guards were going to get any deader than they already were.

We were fortunate Milo kept a few suppressors in his apartment armoury. They didn't silence the shots, but they kept them from being deafening as the reports echoed through the vacant parking garage. With luck, the steel door on the staff room was thick enough to further muffle the sudden noise outside and keep the council ignorant of the fact that they'd just lost their entire cleaning staff.

That still left it to me to talk things out with them. I approached the blue door and gave it a knock as Milo and Jerzy dragged the three corpses we'd made out of the line of sight.

If my play went wrong and this turned into a firefight, the council could send a lot of lead flying out that open doorway. And if things went even a little bad for them on their end, they could lock the door and wait for help to arrive. There wouldn't be a damn thing we could do to force our way into that pillbox.

A pillbox. That's how Jerzy had described the council's chambers. Like the German bunkers our boys storming the beaches of Normandy had to face. Those concrete pillboxes were damn near impenetrable defence points. You were never going to shoot your way in, and even artillery would fail to crack them open. There was only one way to deal with armed men dug in like that.

I waited for the door to open, hoping no one was wise to what had just gone down. At last it did, but not by much. I wasn't being invited inside.

That was fine. I only wanted to talk.

"Is it done?" The Man Upstairs asked me.

"It's done," I told him.

And just like that, I'd talked us out of the jam we were in. Five words was all it took. Three from The Man Upstairs, two from me. The important thing was that he'd cracked the door to have this exchange.

Milo handed me the Molotov cocktail. Jerzy lit the gasoline-soaked wick. I was the one who threw it into the room, right over The Man's Upstairs' head, hard enough to break it on the back wall.

A split second later, both Milo and Jerzy put their boots to the door, kicking it shut. Guns weren't the only tools we'd brought on our hitsquad mission. We also had wooden wedges and hammers. Bashing those wedges into every joint and edge around the door, we could barely hear all the shots being fired at us as the steel plating dimpled from the inside. But that blue door held them all in, and probably sent a few ricocheting around the interior of the staff room.

Yeah, there was only one sure way to deal with armed men hunkered down inside an impregnable pillbox. You burn them out.

Sparse as the contents of the room were, there was enough flammable material to fuel a fire. Those plastic lawn chairs would ignite, and they'd put a lot of toxic fumes in the air. The card tables would go up like kindling. Clothes would burst into flame as well—and the flesh underneath would burn. It wouldn't be an inferno, but with no ventilation to speak of, the oxygen in the room would get eaten up in seconds, and anyone who didn't fry would choke to death long before help showed up to pry that blue coffin lid off of the council's tomb.

The bullets pounding against the back of the door ceased, replaced with the sound of fists banging on the plating, begging to be let out. The wedges held, sealing the room and the council's fate. The thumps didn't last long, stopping before the first thin wafts of black smoke could be seen on our side, leaking out the narrow fissures of the door frame. The fire was probably already extinguished, and the room was now a gas chamber—a vacuum of unbreathable atmosphere, a vacuum of power left behind by the dead men who littered the floor.

We lingered long enough to be sure of our success, but things needed to wrap up fast. Long-held speculation that there were wires hidden throughout the parking garage were borne out by the distant sound of sirens. Our friends in the police department never had a lick of hope of capturing any discernable conversation on tape, but they were always listening just the same, hoping they would luck out one day. Hoping The Man Upstairs would pause by a wired column long enough to say something legally actionable.

They never got more than two consecutive words they could understand. But gunfire? They understood what that meant clear enough. Suppressors or not, they had heard the shots, even if the council inside their bunker had failed to. It gave them all the excuse they needed to roll in.

The three of us were back on street level and around the corner from the shopping mall before the first cops arrived on site. We drove the legal limit, like three friends out for a late-night cruise, as squad cars lined up along the boulevard, and a cluster of officers opened the automatic ramp door, guns out, cautiously breeching the scene of the suspected shooting.

"You think we're back in business?" Milo, in the backseat, dared hope.

"There are always people who need to make somebody dead," said Jerzy. "I'll ask around. Things might be lean for a while, but it'll pick up once I get word out."

"On the bright side, there's only three of us left looking for work."

"More contracts to go around that way," I agreed.

With the syndicate council dead, their groomed hitsquad was out in the cold. Routine killings don't require paramilitary types. Suddenly, mundane work-a-day murders were back on the table. Our business model for freelance hires was the only viable service out there. Give it a few weeks, maybe a few months on the outside for things to settle, and the famine would break at last.

And then we would feast.

Platinum

THE TIP ABOUT THE FORTUNE in platinum was gold. All I needed was an in. That's where the plumbing cover-business came in. Everybody needs a plumber from time to time. And if they don't need one in a timely fashion, there are ways to contrive a clogged drain.

Ernesto Leyva was a breeder. He had no wife, no kids, but spoke fondly of his children—felines all. Three hypoallergenics patrolled the house. They were of a variety hotly in demand by kitty lovers whose own bodies betrayed them when in proximity to cat dander. Leyva suffered itching eyes and congestion all his life, even as he longed for a furry companion—or three. It was an old pal from school, reunited after years apart, who pointed him towards certain breeds that would not provoke allergic reactions. Once he learned of Ernesto's plight, he was quick to hook him up with a friend of a cousin of a spouse of an associate's brother who arranged for the sale of exotic breeds of common pets.

Before long, Ernesto Leyva was so enamoured with his Devon Rexes, he took to breeding more of them himself, selling freshly weaned kittens to other allergy-laden cat-enthusiasts for serious dollars. It wasn't the main thrust of his business—he'd already earned his fortune in the oil and mining industries—but, like so many rich men, even his hobbies made the kind of money the rest of us working stiffs could only ever dream of earning.

And I, of course, was interested in slicing off a piece of that wealth for myself.

Like I said, the plumbing business was just a front. It served as both a way to infiltrate the homes of the wealthy and powerful, and as a means of laundering the money I made from robbing them—several weeks after fixing their pipes, once I was a distant memory.

Most jobs I was offered got subcontracted to other plumbers, who would pay a small commission for the work I passed on to them. But anything that came in from a high-tax-bracket end of town got the personal touch. I'd go there myself, assess the job, appraise the contents of the house, and get to work. By the time I fixed their toilet, hooked up their washing machine, or replaced a leaking pipe, I'd know the layout. What windows were routinely left unlocked; which rooms were rigged with motion detectors; where spare keys or pass cards were kept; and what the best valuables were. Given enough time to snoop, I could get my own keys cut, or find where security codes and safe combinations had been written down. Once I'd finished my sweep and wrapped up the plumbing contract, I'd wait. Six weeks was about average. Even paranoid rich people don't change their alarm codes that often—if ever. All the holes in their security systems I'd spotted when I was on site were likely to still be there when I came back one night, usually when the property owners were out of town, and let myself in. When the theft was discovered and police summoned, no one would suspect the lowly plumber who had snaked their drain weeks earlier. I wouldn't be worth so much as a mention in the report if anyone remembered I had ever been there at all.

The Ernesto Leyva home was a different sort of heist. Word had been passed around the criminal circuit that somewhere in that house, Ernesto had a fortune in platinum tucked away for a rainy day. Most bullion hoarders will go with gold or silver rounds, government-issued bars or coins. But platinum and palladium are right up there with the other precious metals, and just as easily fenced for cash at pawn shops, auction houses, and currency-exchange storefronts. As the rumour spread, the likelihood of someone knocking the place over increased, and I wanted to make sure I was that someone.

Waiting around for Leyva to develop a pipe problem was out of the question, and hoping my front would get randomly selected from the list of potential plumbers was a chance not worth taking. In situations like this, I had to invest some of my own cash to make things happen.

In a big enough estate, there was always someone among the hired help I could turn to. An underpaid maid, a dissatisfied gardener, a bitter butler—just one person on staff willing to take a bribe was all I needed. Once accepted, I'd give them specific instructions on how to sabotage a toilet, back up a waste-water line, or burst the underground irrigation system that watered the vast lawn. Once that was done, all they had to do was make sure my name and number came up as the first and best option for a quick and reliable fix.

As far as these backstabbing staffers were concerned, I was just some crooked plumber looking to soak their boss at an inflated hourly rate for a bunch of work that didn't need to get done. No biggie. They could afford it, and the extra cash the maid put in her pocket was considered compensation for any past slights or insults she had endured throughout her years of mopping the floors and making the beds of people who considered themselves above such mundane housework.

My in at the Leyva house had gone smoothly. The mess made of the plumbing took two days to undo once I got the call, and in that time I was able to scout the place thoroughly.

The hard part was waiting the next few weeks for Ernesto to leave on a business trip and give most of his staff some time off. I was paranoid that some other enterprising burglar would hit the place before my window of opportunity, but my luck held, and the criminal element remained hesitant, still trying to gather intelligence about where that bounty of platinum could be found.

I was sure I already knew.

I'd discovered the safe hidden behind a hinged bookcase in Ernesto Leyva's office within an hour of me stepping foot on the property. Finding the combination took nearly all the rest of my two-day stint. Every minute I wasn't working on the sabotaged pipes, I was hunting through drawers and notebooks and files, careful to leave everything exactly as I found it so no one would know I'd been snooping. All the typical hiding spots came up empty. There was nothing taped underneath desk drawers, no notes tucked behind framed photos, not a single slip of numbered paper between the pages of some old tome, wedged in there like a forgotten bookmark.

I finally lucked out when I peeled up one corner of an eight-by-ten rug and found a tiny envelope stuck to the back of the fabric, between the rug and the non-slip rubber pad beneath. Inside was a thin square of paper with four handwritten consecutive numbers between one and a hundred. I knew what they had to be for. Once I'd copied them to my notebook, I replaced the paper, the envelope, and the rug exactly where I'd found them and hustled to complete the rest of my expedition.

The combination was only half the battle. The safe also needed a key to unlock a plunger that blocked the mechanism before any numbers could be dialled in. I'm no master safe-cracker, but I can pick a simple lock. Unfortunately, this was a safe lock that required a non-standard round-headed key. Those things aren't your usual pick-and-pin combo. There are specialists who can handle a circular keyhole with a dedicated tubular pick or, failing that, a drill, but I'm not one of them. And I wasn't looking to share my take in order to hire outside help for so simple a task. What I needed to get the job done was the actual key.

The combination number had taken so long to find, there was no time left to hunt for a key. I was nearly resigned to missing out on my one chance when I was lucky enough to spot the key hiding in plain sight.

Ernesto kept a large aquarium in his office, set into a heavy counter base not far from his desk, where he could watch a lone white fish, only a few inches long, make the rounds through its habitat of water plants, submerged drift wood, and fancy rocks. It was a lot of gallons for one measly fish. But it turned out the big tank of filtered water had another occupant of note. In the midst of such a tastefully constructed ecosystem, there was a single piece of pet-store kitsch that stuck out. Sitting on the sandy bottom was a plastic pirate treasure chest. A tube fed down to its base, slowly pushing air inside, until it reached critical mass and the lid popped up to release the accumulated bubbles. Then it would snap shut again and the process would repeat. The treasure chest only blew its load once every five minutes or so. I happened to be looking right at it one time when it popped, and in that moment, as it yawned open, I saw the key resting inside on top of the fake booty of painted doubloons.

I left it where it was, sure it would be waiting for me in several weeks' time, on the night I would return and empty the safe.

● ● ●

When the long-anticipated evening of the robbery finally rolls around, everything is waiting as I'd left it. The locked window that was earmarked to be my access point still has the few inches of fishing line I'd left hanging outside, behind a row of bushes, out of sight of any casual observers. I had tied it to the interior latch when I had access to the house, fed it through the base, and resealed the box-frame window. With an autumn chill in the air, no one attempted to open the window since my visit, and the line remains unmolested. Pulling the latch aside from the exterior of the house, I'm able to push the window up and open and climb in. I'm careful to remove and pocket the line before locking the window behind me. The window isn't part of my escape plan. When I leave again, I'll do so by the front door. It will probably trigger an alarm, but I'll be long gone before anyone responds. My initial point of entry will go undiscovered, and the apparent rapidity of my break-in and robbery will keep the timeline of the crime mysterious once police detectives look into it.

The first thing I do once I'm in is remove my shoes and stuff them into my duffel bag. Muddy footprints tracked around the house is not a clue I'm going to leave behind for the cops.

As I make my way to Ernesto's office, I nearly trip over one of his cats. They swarm around me, underfoot, starved for attention while their master is away. Whoever is looking in on them during the day, refilling food and water dishes and emptying litter boxes, isn't offering them enough of a human-companionship fix to satisfy their needs. I pause long enough to give them all a pat and let them rub up against my pant legs. Then it's back to work.

The office is at the back of the house, so I risk turning on a single desk lamp so I can see what I'm doing. The filter system of the aquarium hums away as I tilt back the feeding hatch, pull up my sleeve, and stick my whole arm into the tank, reaching for the pirate chest. The water is deep and, despite my best efforts to stay dry, I end up dipping my sleeve as I pick at the lid of the chest with my fingernails.

The bubble-blowing bit of kitsch turns out to be a higher-end piece of fishbowl decor than I'd given it credit for. It's firmly attached to the bottom and made of a sturdy plastic. With my arm overextended, it proves hard to pry it open, and I have to wait around for the expanding air pocket inside to trigger the mechanism and open it for me.

The wait feels like forever as I let my arm soak, not wanting to miss my chance to snatch the key. While I stand there, the lone fish nibbles at my arm hairs, checking to see if I might be tasty or not. When I prove to be an unappetizing snack, it lazily drifts away and looks for something else to occupy its rice-grain-sized mind.

Finally, the tiny treasure chest exhales, and two of my fingers slip in and pinch the safe key between them. But before I can claim my prize, the lid snaps shut again, right on my knuckles, and holds my fingers in a surprising tight grip. I find myself at a bad angle to extract them—not without losing hold of the key. After a minute or two of awkward struggle, I realize I'm going to have to wait for the next lid-opening cycle if I'm going to retrieve the key as well as my fingers.

The sleeve of my sweater continues to soak up more and more water. Before long, I can feel the wetness spread to my shoulder and run down my side. The water saturates the fabric bunched at my hip and starts to drip onto my stocking feet, pooling underfoot, forming a puddle.

I try to count the minutes as my feet get wet and the puddle expands. Surely it's been longer than the usual five-minute cycle. When I finally get up on my tippy toes and look over the top edge of the tank and down into the water, I see the half-open pirate chest is leaking a steady stream of bubbles, and isn't filling with enough air to trigger the next lid pop. I remain trapped, with the key clamped between my fingers. I could force my fingers free easily enough, but then I'd lose the key and have to try all over again. I'm determined there must be a better solution.

Beside the desk there's a power bar filled with plugs. Most of the cords feeding into it are for the aquarium, powering the filter, heater, and lid light. I track one of them that can only belong to the tchotchke that has me in its grip. Cutting the juice might set me free, and I figure it's worth a try.

The plug is out of reach, so I grab the wire instead and pull, trying to work the prongs out of the socket. My hand slips higher up the cord and I feel a stretch that's rough, frayed. Cats can be as bad as teething puppies. They'll chew on a soft rubbery wire for fun if they're in the mood.

Ernesto ought to keep an eye on those furballs, is the last thought that occurs to me. I wouldn't want the little guys to electro—

●　●　●

I wake up on the floor, staring at the ceiling, lying moist in a shallow film of aquarium water. I'm pretty sure it's only been moments since I went down, moments since my heart made a narrow decision whether to resume beating or not.

There's a cat on my chest, sitting inches from my face, staring. She looks sympathetic. Or is that pity?

The cat gets off me as I slowly rise to my elbows. I stay propped up like that for a few minutes before attempting to sit. Taking my time, I run through an inventory of my body parts and injuries. The worst pain is in one of my feet. The electrical shock grounded itself through the sole of one foot, burning a hole in my sock. A close second is the hand that found the exposed copper wires that had given me the jolt. My fingers are swollen and blistered and I can't make a fist as the flesh balloons. For some reason, my other hand hurts as well. I open it and find the safe key. The charge had caused my hand to contract and hold onto it in such a tight death grip, there's a distinct image of it pressed into my palm. The impression is so well defined, I could probably take it to a locksmith and get a copy made that would be a perfect fit for the keyhole.

No need for a copy—the original will serve its purpose just fine.

The edge of the desk helps me get to my feet. I'm in such rough shape, it feels like a long walk to the bookcase where the safe is hidden.

The key fits, the plunger pops out, and I'm free to dial in the code. I use my flashlight to see by because the desk lamp is off. My misadventure with the electrical cord blew a fuse somewhere, and now power in the office is out, maybe even the whole house.

I go slow and make sure I get the numbers right. I'm in no condition to sit around and make multiple attempts with a finicky combination lock. When I pull the safe's arm down, it gives, and there's a slight hiss as the tight seal swaps air between the interior and exterior. As the door swings open, I shine my light into the cavity to see what my labours have won me.

There's no bullion inside. Not a single coin, round, or bar.

Other than the usual sort of personal papers and legal documents that are no good to me, there's a ledger. I take that, hoping it will tell me the score. And it does. As soon as I lay it out on the desk and start flipping pages, looking into Ernesto Leyva's business dealings, I get the picture I've been missing all along. The numbers say it all.

Hypoallergenic felines aren't the main thrust of his animal-breeding entrepreneurial enterprise. It's a sideline, a dalliance, compared to the real breeding program. The cat sniffing at my soggy feet isn't so rare a creature that she or her sisters can account for the figures I'm seeing in the ledger. Much as he loves his kitties, Ernesto's real passion is fish. Specifically: The Platinum Arowana.

A quality specimen can run as high as mid-six figures. The platinum-white tone is the result of an extremely rare genetic mutation that sets it apart from the more common arowana colours. Even with many lesser shades to choose from, trade between collectors around the world amounts to hundreds of millions of dollars per year. The platinum variety is the Rolls-

Royce of the arowanas, making it the undisputed king of pet fish.

According to Ernesto's records, he keeps his latest cherished moneymaker in a climate-controlled, pH-balanced, micro-filtered tank in his office where he can admire it and keep a close eye on his investment. An aggressive, solitary fish, the arowana needs a lot of space and alone time, accounting for the huge aquarium for one immature fish that is still a foot or two away from growing to its full potential.

I swing my light to the tank and find the fish I'd never looked at twice floating on its side at the surface of the water.

I ignore my pain and residual heart palpitations as I hurry to the tank, scoop out the fish, and set it down on the rug so I can try to revive it. Blowing into its gills proves futile, and my one-finger heart massage fails to provoke even a single flip of its fins. That fish was the most expensive piece of sashimi in the world, and I cooked it. Lightly broiled, you might as well put it on a cracker and call it an hors d'oeuvres.

On my feet again, I hold up the fish by its tail, dangling, dripping. Alive it was worth more than any haul I'd ever made. Maybe more than all my best hauls combined. Dead, it's hardly worth the effort to throw it back into the water as a fish unworthy of being called the catch of the day.

The Devon Rex that has most closely dogged my steps since I broke into the house sits expectantly in front of me, looking up at my worthless bounty. Worthless to me, but of great value to her.

I toss my inadvertent murder victim to the hungry cat. She immediately sets to pulling it apart and eating it in greedy gulps. Her sisters sense there's a treat in the offing and run to join the feeding frenzy, making sure they get their fair share. Before a single minute has passed, the body is gone, and any residual evidence is getting licked out of the carpet fibers by rough feline tongues probing for the last hints of flavour.

On the front stoop, I shut the door behind me and put my shoes back on. As I walk away from the house with my war wounds and my empty bag, I contemplate the life-changing score that slipped through my fingers and down a cat's gullet. Like I had any idea where I could have fenced a fish so valuable that it came with its own implanted micro ID chip. What was I going to do? Drive it around town in a bucket, hitting up my contacts to see if anyone was in the market for a rare pet worth hundreds of thousands of dollars?

No, the job was a bust right from the moment I first decided to pursue a rumour nobody had thought to double check. A fortune in platinum. I can't say it was a lie, but it was never destined to be mine.

Even so, I'll always think of it as the one that got away.

Mercy

THE DECISION TO MURDER HIS WIFE of thirty-seven years came quite easily to Herman Schwinn when, at last, he arrived at it. Loretta had been ill—deathly so—for the last eleven years of their marriage. The doctors had stopped bothering to visit in person, having always noted her condition as "unchanged."

Whenever the Schwinns received an infrequent phone call from the hospital, Loretta was usually asleep or too weak to speak for herself, and it fell to Herman to report that she remained "unchanged." For years, this state of affairs continued, and even the token phone calls had ceased. It was assumed, perhaps too easily, that Herman Schwinn would check in himself when his wife's condition switched from "unchanged" to "passed."

As the years crawled by, Herman Schwinn went about his duties of bathing and dressing his wife; feeding her the mush that constituted nourishment, and the pills that amounted to life.

And, with power-of-attorney, he cashed her cheques.

Between his pension and her disability pay, Herman was well off, and stood to enjoy the rest of his life—if only there were any joy to be had. He possessed no great desire to travel the world or live high on the hog, but the constant burden of dealing with a terminally ill woman who lingered without end took a terrible toll.

The closest thing to recreation Herman had was his nightly shot of brandy he took to help put himself down for the night. He usually fell asleep in his armchair in front of the eleven o'clock news. When the rising sun woke him up again in the morning, the new day promised to be a rerun of all the previous days of tedious caregiving. The only thing that ever seemed to change were the sports scores and headlines of that late-night broadcast, and even they had begun to blend together into one long indistinct dream.

Murder had always been a notion playing around at the back of Herman's mind, toyed with but never taken seriously. It was a fantasy, a phantom. But eleven years is a long time. Long enough for a phantom to solidify, and for a fantasy to demand it be pulled into reality.

No one would miss Loretta. She was already forgotten about in most quarters, and Loretta herself wouldn't miss her miserable sickly life once the last flicker of it had been snuffed out. By the time anyone ever got around to wondering what might have become of her, Herman Schwinn would be in a grave of his own, unanswerable to anyone for how he chose to spend the final years of his life as an undeclared widower.

The plan was simple to the point of being only one more drab chore in a decade-plus of petty tasks.

As per schedule—a routine performed thousands of times in a row—Herman would make his rounds before lights out. He would check in on his wife, make sure she had eaten enough to sustain her for one more day, ask if she needed anything else before bed, and then tuck her in.

"I love you," they would say to each other; words that had lost all meaning and were spoken more as a superstitious ritual.

That's when, instead of switching off the lamp next to the bed, Herman would put the pillow over Loretta's face and press down hard. With any luck, she would be too feeble, too lethargic, to even understand what was happening. And if she did, well, there was no fight left in her anyway.

Afterwards, it would be a simple matter to carry her emaciated remains up to the attic, where a trunk awaited. The air was cool and dry, and the body would likely mummify over the coming months and years. Loretta was halfway there already.

Once the horrible thing was done, Herman would go and have his nightly belt of brandy. And perhaps, for the first time in ages, he would enjoy his drink.

Shoring up his courage, he climbed the stairs to attend to his wife one final time. Although there were many selfish reasons for this act, there were perfectly pragmatic ones as well, and Herman felt no guilt.

It would, he was certain, be a mercy.

• • •

The decision to murder her husband of thirty-seven years came quite easily to Loretta Schwinn when, at last, she came to it. He had been a good husband, as husbands went, dutiful and conscientious in his daily chores to keep her alive despite her own body's best attempts to end itself. No one could have reasonably asked for more. But as the years faded from one to the next, duty was all that remained. The love that had once been there had withered, the compassion was only habit.

As she lay down in bed, following the colossal effort to get back up the stairs, she set her empty prescription-pill bottle on the end table next to what was now, most certainly, her deathbed.

"Not to be taken with alcohol," was the warning on the label, more prominent than the name of the medication, the pharmacy it came from, her patient-identification number, or the remaining refills that were no longer necessary.

It had consumed all of Loretta's remaining strength and stamina to get out of bed and make her way down to her husband's study. Six pills would have handily killed a horse. She dissolved a dozen in the remaining quarter bottle on the beverage cart. Herman would never drink the whole amount, but she'd left the brandy imbued with enough opiate to get the job done several times over. Her husband was not a sipper. He took his shots straight, and would find himself on the floor in a fatal coma before he even noticed the brandy tasted off.

Herman deserved better than the depressing thing his existence had become. Loretta knew he couldn't live without her, but he had no life with her either. She had become his purpose, his curse, and he stubbornly refused to just let her slip away naturally. When the inevitable finally did come to pass, he would truly be lost, the poor dear man. She preferred not to think of her final act as murder. It was a gift—both to him, and herself.

With Herman gone, she would live out the last hours of her life in bed, slipping in and out of consciousness rather than sleeping, as was her lot. With no one to wake her or tend to her, one of those black stretches would last forever. She would drift away, content that her husband, at least, would not have to contend with the terrible grief, the mourning and memorial service, or the few final lonely years that would have seen him waste away to nothing.

It would, she was certain, be a mercy.

Keeping the Piece

I'D BEEN ON THE SHOW for three weeks, contracts signed, ink dry on the page, when Ryan Monahan, my producer, called me up and said we were going on safari.

There was no script. Word one hadn't been written yet. It was all vague notions and spitballing—the results of overpaid executives justifying their expense accounts and pretending they were creative people in the arts instead of paper-pushing accountants. One of them had a vague notion about doing a gangster story. Because that hasn't been done to death.

The show was called *Mobbed Up*, which we all agreed was a stupid title that needed to be changed before we went on air. It was a title we also agreed we were probably stuck with because the broadcaster already had a mountain of paperwork with *"Mobbed Up"* printed on the corner of every page.

Compiling notes, reading books, watching documentaries, getting a feel for the subject, I hadn't even run an update patch for my screenwriting software before Ryan interrupted my process. Calls had been made, friends of friends had been contacted, a few favours owed got repaid, and he was determined we should all go on safari to meet one of the wild animals.

The arranged meet-and-greet was to happen in a swanky restaurant in Old Town. A nice spot with stone walls and low ceilings, it had probably once been a miserable factory sweat-shop and had since been gentrified into a trendy dining spot for the rich, powerful, or influential. If you were one of these things, you could get a reservation. If you were two of these things, you could get a choice table. If you were all three, you could walk in without a reservation and sit wherever you want-ed. We were just a bunch of film-industry assholes, so we had to make a reservation a week early. Maybe we could have shortened the wait if we told them we were bringing a celebri-ty. But our guy wasn't the right kind of celebrity. He wasn't a movie star, but he'd been name-checked in more than a few headlines, and featured in dozens of articles. The newspapers loved to run his mug shot. It wouldn't surprise me to know he kept a scrapbook of all his clippings, going back to his first arrest as a juvenile offender in the police-beat petty-crimes fea-turette of a suburban giveaway rag.

His name was Gerard "Glassy" Conroy, and if you didn't know which one of the five Conroy brothers he was, it didn't matter. One of the middle ones. What was important was that he was one of *those* Conroys. The infamous ones. He'd agreed to meet with us, and share some insights into his line of work, because the youngest Conroy brother, Jack, had it in his head that he didn't want to join the family business, running num-bers, pushing junk, and loaning out money to simps no bank would touch. Baby Conroy thought he might like to be an ac-tor, and he had the looks for it. His headshot was promising. Whether he could string two words together and make it con-vincing was another matter, but his audition—pre-open-call—was a lock. That was the trade. Some face time with Glassy, and his brother would be considered for a role in *Mobbed Up*. No guarantees. Nobody was going to get their legs broken if it didn't work out. But for a couple of hours, a free meal, and a taste of the showbiz circus, Glassy was willing to have a conversation.

"Why do they call him 'Glassy'?" was my first question, before I even agreed to attend.

"He's a gangster," I was told. "They all have to have stupid nicknames."

We were early the night of our agreed-upon rendezvous, careful to make sure our reserved table was ready for our guest, with each of us in place. Glassy was the last to arrive, an hour late. It built suspense. Very show business. The meeting hadn't even started, and already he had a feel for how to play it. We were three appetizers and full bottle of wine in when he was shown to our table.

The man looked like he was on his way to a Halloween party dressed as a Martin Scorsese film. I don't know if gangster movies accurately represent how real gangsters dress, or if their fashion sense is dictated by how they're portrayed on the screen. I suspect there's some sort of unhealthy feedback loop going on that results in a lot of black suits and gold chains. I was at least gratified to see he hadn't come to dinner in a track suit.

His hair was slicked back with enough gel to withstand gale-force winds that would have had better luck bending a steel bulkhead in half. He was freshly shaved and smelled of half-a-dozen additional products that had helped his whiskers stand erect, his pores to relax, his razor to glide smoothly, and his skin to stay silky-soft after so much abuse. It was clear he was very image-conscious, unlike the film-industry schlubs sitting at the table. There were few of us residing behind the camera who cared much about how presentable we made ourselves. The only image that mattered was what got put in front of an audience. They're the ones who paid for tickets, bought DVDs, and subscribed to cable channels. We served at their pleasure. And if it was polished, image-savvy gangsters they wanted to watch on their gigantic widescreen televisions, that's exactly what we were going to give them.

The introductions were short and to the point, and I don't think Glassy took stock of a single name at the table. Our faces however, those he scrutinized and analyzed and made conclusions about. A name might tell you a thing or two about a man's family, his ethnicity, how casually he cared to be treated. A Richard who preferred to be called Rick, or Rich, or Dick was saying something about himself. But not as much as his face, his eyes. Glassy read people for a living. Sometimes it kept him alive.

By the time he took his seat, he'd read everyone at the table and had already decided who was a pushover, who might be a threat, who liked him at first sight, who held him in contempt, and who feared him. If we thought we had our poker faces on, Glassy had just peered through the backs of all the cards in our hands.

Satisfied none of us were out to screw him, he slowly opened up by the time our orders arrived. Even so, he spoke in non-incriminating metaphors and imprecisions.

Things were said, he'd tell of one implied criminal exchange. *Things were done*, he'd say of another. He let our imaginations fill in the blanks. And none of us doubted that we wouldn't care to have such things said to us, and would especially never want such things done to us.

He hinted at the basic business model his family worked under, without ever getting into numbers or specifics. Money-lending was the key component. People starting clubs or restaurants on shaky ground were welcome with open arms. If their fledgling business succeeded, good on them. They'd pay back their loan and the fat wad of interest and everyone would move on with their lives. But if they floundered, the Conroys would move in and take over in every way that mattered, short of having their name on the paperwork. From that moment forward, the failing business would become a highly profitable one as it was used to launder money from the family's more overtly criminal activities. Perpetually empty mom-and-pop eateries would report massive income to the government every year, punishing taxes would be paid enthusiastically, and the remaining newly legit proceeds would get paid out to all manner of "employees" within the Conroy organization.

It all seemed like a fairly harmless game. Play by the tax man's rules and everybody gets rich. But behind the scenes, one or two levels down, the game got rough. There were rival gangs, vying for the same sources of illegitimate money that would need to get laundered on Main Street in front of everybody. This was the hidden end of the business. Hidden until a body count made the papers, or there was a mass arrest by a police task force that had been dispatched when some politician's bribe didn't show up in a timely fashion.

Glassy let us read between the lines and figure out what he was getting at on our own. We were a bunch of clever college grads after all, and we'd seen the sorts of shows our peers produced. Not all of it was bullshit. The screenwriters and the directors and the producers who had come before us had done their fair share of research. Just like we were doing now. He didn't need to spell it out for us—except when he did, just to watch our reaction.

"The only thing that works better than violence," Glassy told us at one point, sharing a pearl of wisdom he'd learned after a lifetime in the business, "is extreme violence."

That pearl felt oft-repeated, staged, said for effect. But the effect was real. We all felt it. None of us at the table had thrown a punch in anger since we were children on the playground. But Glassy knew violence. Real violence. An older brother of his was currently in jail, awaiting trial on two counts of forcible confinement and one of second-degree murder. Or was it two murders and one confinement? Either way, he was innocent, Glassy assured us. And he didn't literally wink when he said it, but his voice sure did.

It was during a lull between courses and imprecise anecdotes about unspecified persons, when Glassy was taking a bathroom break, that Howard Kellen, a dipshit in development, took the opportunity to take me to task.

"For Chrissake, quit it, would you?" he hissed at me, as soon as he was certain our guest was well out of range.

"Quit what?" I asked, in genuine ignorance.

"What you're doing."

"What am I doing?"

"You're intimidating him."

"*I'm* intimidating *him?*" I scoffed.

"You're freaking him out."

"How am I doing that?" I asked.

"All that not-talking you're doing. You're just staring at him, like he's an exhibit in a museum or something."

"I'm listening," I said. "That's how I learn things. I shut up and listen. You might want to try it."

Howard had been talking Glassy's ear off half the night, filling in any gaps in the conversation with his own insights about growing up on the mean streets of white-bread suburbia—trying to bond, trying to talk tough, trying to win the respect of a real mobster with his take on the morality of loan-sharking, pimping, or a personal favourite of his: drug-dealing.

A particular gem had been voiced when he told Glassy, "I don't begrudge anybody a puff of pot or a line of coke, but if you sell my kid heroin, I will fucking kill you."

It wasn't an accusation. The drug dealer in question was hypothetical. But there was a certain implication that crossed the line. I thought Glassy Conroy might laugh in his face at his impotent posturing. Or break his jaw with the third as-yet uncorked bottle of wine that had just arrived at the table. Instead, Glassy, who had kids of his own, nodded knowingly. I was sure his family had a hand in selling heroin to a lot of parents' kids, but he could well anticipate his own reaction to someone dealing smack to one of his own.

"Some things you don't abide, don't forgive," he agreed. "And things like that, they're worth killing for."

Howard toned it down after that. His call to violence had been an empty one. If someone sold smack to his kid, I'd be surprised if he could muster the nerve to politely ask the dealer to spare the child. Glassy, on the other hand, probably *would* kill the guy. And worse.

It was an informative meal, and I came away from it with some worthwhile insights, a bit of flavour to add to my script, and a stack of notes to jot down when I got back home. Once we said our goodbyes and thank-yous, I went outside to look for a convenient cab I could flag. With none in evidence, I made a call and was told one would be there in ten minutes.

"Hey, Hemingway," I heard a voice call at me from the restaurant parking lot.

I turned and saw Glassy standing in the dark patch of asphalt, a couple of dozen yards away. I might not have recognized him, but enough illumination was cast by the streetlight to glint off the gold chain hanging over his black, tailored clothes.

The rest of the production crew was long gone, off in their own rides, one by one or two by two, with various borough destinations in mind. Living so close to the city core, I never saw much value in getting my own car. Most of my commutes for work happened online, through email or streamed conference calls.

"Don't you got a ride?" Glassy asked.

"Cab," I called back.

"C'mon," he said, and pressed his key fob. I heard an engine start, and a pair of headlights lit up in one of the customer-only spaces. "I'll give you a lift."

It was a kind offer. And how do you say no to a man like Glassy Conroy? You best not.

The film industry can be touch and go. There's an ebb and flow to most careers. Some years you make out like a bandit, others you wonder if you're going to end up on a breadline. I'd been doing okay lately. Not great, but a few episodes of television in the last quarter had balanced my books and made for a successful year. Even so, one look at Glassy's car and I knew it was worth more than my last few years combined.

I strapped myself in and shut the door. Before we took the first corner, I was trying to decide which was more overpowering—the new-car smell, or Glassy's aftershave. Both were expensive, seductive. Combined they made for a rich scent, even if the money that had paid for them was rotten.

Over dinner I'd been mostly silent, only interjecting with the occasional comment or question. And that was with half a dozen men at the table. Now, alone with Glassy, I was wondering how to make small talk. He didn't wait around for the silence to get awkward. Glassy had an agenda.

"This guy the movie's about..."

"TV miniseries," I corrected him, and then wondered if correcting Glassy about anything was such a good idea.

"Miniseries, sure sure," he said. "The guy it's about..."

"Robbie."

"Robbie," he nodded knowingly, like he was intimately acquainted with the man who was, as yet, a rough sketch of a fictional character. "Robbie's a guy a lot like me, yeah?"

"Yeah, I suppose," I said. "I mean, he's like a lot of guys in your line of work. Sort of a composite character. Not based on anybody specific."

That last part I was quick to add, hoping to stem any legal action that might be brewing somewhere down the road. My contract was clear about me being on the hook right along with my producers should any libel lawsuits crop up because of something I wrote.

"You think my brother would be right for the part?"

I thought his brother would be lucky to land a bit part with more than two lines, but I didn't want to dash Glassy's hopes. Or worse, renege on what he might have assumed was a fair exchange, a done deal. His time and company for a leg up to his kid brother.

"I don't know," I said as honestly as I dared. "I haven't seen his sizzle reel. Just the headshot. He looks the part. Beyond that, though..."

I trailed off, hoping that would satisfy him. It didn't.

"You'll put in a word for him though, right?"

He phrased it like a question, but it didn't sound like a question.

"I'm just the writer," I said. "They don't care what I think about things like that. They barely care what I have to say about the story."

I tried to make light of this hard truth of screenwriting. Glassy wouldn't let me laugh it off.

"And you're okay with that?"

"It's the business," I shrugged. "That's how it works."

"I would not be okay with that," he said coldly, staring dead ahead at the road like he wasn't driving on it so much as running it over.

I was dreading how much more awkward our conversation might become when it was interrupted for another. Glassy's phone, cradled in the cup holder, vibrated and flashed on. Glassy left it where it was, but swiped right and let the speaker do the talking.

"Yeah?" answered Glassy.

The call display said "Shenanigans" which I knew was a pub the Conroys owned. Not one of their laundering fronts, but a legit family business that served as a profitable hobby and hangout. A woman's voice came on with a tone that was both familiar and demanding. It could only be the sister. She never made the papers and stayed clean, if only to have someone in the family who wouldn't be doing time and could always be relied upon to handle logistics, like defence lawyers and bail.

"We got a guy here making trouble," she said.

"What sort of trouble?"

"He's just being a loud prick. Grabby with the new girl. I cut him off, but he still wants another pint and says he won't leave till he gets one."

"Hand him the phone, Maureen. Lemme talk to this guy."

There was a lengthy pause in the conversation, during which I heard a muffled exchange on the other end as Glassy's sister convinced her belligerent customer to take the phone, informing him who he was about to speak to. As soon as an unfamiliar voice trepidatiously said, "Hello?" Glassy got to the point.

"You listen to me, you piece of fuck. I'm on my way there right now. If you're still in my place when I get there, you're leaving without a tooth in your head, you hear me? Now pass me back to my sister."

There was another pause, this one much briefer.

"Is he leaving?"

"Just grabbing his coat now," I heard the woman say through the speaker.

"Okay then," stated Glassy. "Love you, Maureen."

"Yeah yeah," she said, before he punched the red hang-up button.

I'd seen doormen bounce misbehaving customers out of clubs before. I'd never seen somebody do it with a few words from across town. Usually there was a bit of physicality to it. Not necessarily a fight, but a firm hand on a shoulder, a guiding push towards the door. Often it would take two bouncers, one on either side of the man being ejected, to make sure things didn't get ugly, and that full cooperation would be forthcoming. Glassy had kicked somebody out without stepping foot on the premises.

"We still going to the pub?" I asked after two blocks of silence.

"No need," said Glassy. "It's been handled, and we got better places to be."

I knew then that this wasn't a convenient lift home. I hadn't given my address, or even mentioned what neighbourhood I lived in, and Glassy hadn't asked. He knew where we were headed, even before I agreed to get in his car.

Edging down a service lane behind a row of dilapidated buildings in the red-light district, Glassy stuck his car into a space opposite a loading bay that was reserved for trucks. Or the cars of gangsters who parked where they damn well pleased.

Without a word of explanation, he led me down a narrow alley to a side street off the boulevard. I looked up and saw the neon sign high above that advertised "Massage." Below that, was a qualifying "XXX," suggesting there was more to the massage than firm hands working out knots in your back. There was a doorman Glassy didn't even acknowledge, though the doorman made sure to offer him a respectful nod as he passed. I was likewise permitted hassle-free entry in his wake.

"Is this one of your businesses?" I inquired as we climbed the stairs.

"We own a piece of it," Glassy confirmed.

"So..." I began, unable to contain my suspense any longer, "what are we doing here?"

"Me?" he said. "I'm making the rounds. Which is what I do most nights, looking into our interests, making sure things are flowing nice and smooth."

He stopped in the stairwell and turned to face me, several steps below him.

"You, though? What you're doing here is up to you now, isn't it?"

"Research I guess. For the show."

"Research?" said Glassy, turning his lip up and contemplating my stated task. "If you say so."

"That's the whole point of tonight, isn't it? I'm a researcher."

"You're a tourist," Glassy decided. "Like some white-collar on vacation who wants to walk on a beach and dip his toes in the surf. Maybe take a picture with the catch of the day, the big fish. But you don't want to go swimming because it'll fuck up all that sunscreen you just put on."

Glassy seemed satisfied with the allegory he'd painted. I wasn't as certain what he was getting at. But, of course, writing for television, I'd long had my taste for metaphor or symbolism beaten out of me. It didn't play to target demographics.

"C'mon," he said, when I saw me thinking too hard about it. "Come and get your feet wet."

And he led me the rest of the way up the stairs to the parlour on the third floor.

"Glassy," greeted the old woman behind the counter that was set up to accept your choice of payment.

"What's new?" he asked, though the question wasn't directed at the cashier so much as the three-ring binder that was sitting on the counter top, tethered on the end of a chain that made sure no customers would walk off with it.

Glassy flipped through the pages of the book, each of them an eight-by-ten full-body shot tucked into a clear plastic sleeve. They were all glamour shots of girls. The outfits were revealing or, just as often, not there at all. The photos were professionally done, and there was a real effort to make them erotic rather than pornographic, but their intended purpose was to push product.

The old woman stopped Glassy on one page before he could flip past, sticking her finger down like a gnarled bookmark, tapping her long nail over the head of one of the options on the menu.

"That's Tiffany," she said. "We got her in on Tuesday. Nice Ukrainian girl."

"They're all nice Ukrainian girls these days," groused Glassy. "What happened to the Filipinos?"

"It's been slow from that end. Maybe the economy improved. Or maybe they need a war to get things moving again."

"Anybody else coming in this week?"

"Tiffany is it. We got a couple more on the way for next week."

"More Ukies?"

"Probably."

Glassy sighed. He wasn't happy, but he'd make do.

"I like to give the new girls a try," he told me, "while they're still relatively fresh. Y'know, before they've taken a ride on ten miles of cock."

"Tiffany is in number three. She's free," Glassy was informed.

"Amuse yourself," Glassy instructed me, and walked away down the hall without another word. He let himself into Room Three and shut the door behind him.

Left alone with the massage parlour's manager, I gave her an awkward friendly smile that was not returned. Finding a couch in the waiting room, I sat down, hoping it wasn't too filthy, careful not to touch it with my bare hands. A television in the corner kept the old woman entertained as she clocked her hours. Nobody else came in, and I couldn't hear any activity from the other rooms in the place.

"Business is slow?" I asked, after the first five minutes had passed.

"It's early," said the manager. "The bars haven't let out yet."

Her eyes never left the sitcom she was watching. I recognized it as a show I'd pitched for once. It was a gig I had failed to land. My jokes weren't funny enough. The ones that made it to air weren't any funnier, but the laugh track seemed to think they were hilarious.

Twenty minutes after we'd first arrived, Glassy came out of Room Three looking as trim and perfect as he had when he'd met us at the fancy restaurant. Not a hair was out of place, not a single crease or wrinkle was to be found on his clothes. However long his tryst had been, he must have spent at least half the time de-mussing himself.

He was surprised to see me sitting on the couch, demurely awaiting his return.

"Didn't you pick yourself out a girl?"

"I'm not carrying much cash," I said, but way of excuse.

"They take credit cards," Glassy informed me, like I should know better.

Even if the business name on the statement was low-key, safely generic, I still had a wife who would ask what the charge was.

"It's okay," I said. "I'm good."

But Glassy was nothing if not a generous host.

"You want a piece of this?" he said, jerking his thumb over his shoulder at the room he had just vacated. I could see the girl through the open door, putting her bra back on.

Without waiting for my response, he stuck his head back in the room and said to the girl, "It's okay if my friend here gives you shot, right honey? Sure it is."

"Go on," he told me. "My treat."

It was a kind offer. And how do you say no to a man like Glassy Conroy? You best not.

"Tiffany" put every bit of enthusiasm into her perfor-mance as you might expect from a prostitute who had been stuck with a two-for-one gig she couldn't refuse, from a man who would not be denied. I felt bad for her, and did my best to finish as quickly and efficiently as possible while she lay be-neath me, counting the passing minutes and the dollars she wasn't earning. Just when I was considering faking an orgasm to get the exchange over and done with, I caught a wave and rode it to a moderately satisfying climax. I flushed the compli-mentary condom, wiped off, tidied up, and left with a "Thanks" that I'm sure sounded ashamed. I never caught the girl's real name and barely heard the slight grunt of acknowledgement she gave me as I left her behind to await the next client. One who would pay for her, once the bars let out for the night.

"Well, it's been fun," I said leadingly, like it was time to call it a night.

"Sometimes the work is fun," agreed Glassy. "And sometimes it's real work. Hard work you gotta put your back into."

"I'm sure," I agreed.

"Like now, for instance. I got a stop to make. It's not far and it won't take long."

It wasn't an invite. It was a statement of where the evening was going, and I was along for the ride.

"Not far" to Glassy meant still within the city limits, but miles away. We skipped from one neighbourhood to the next, cutting through several districts before we landed in an end of town I'd been warned to stay out of since I was a boy. If you didn't bring your own ride, there was hardly any way in or out of the area. No bus lines passed through, and there was only one subway stop, which was closed at that time of night. You could walk it, but nobody walked much of anywhere in that dozen-block stretch after dark.

As soon as we crossed the freight tracks that officially marked the northern boundary of the area locally referred to as The Manx, Glassy slowed the car to a crawl. Named for a guy called Mankiewicz who used to own a bunch of shops along the riverfront back when the streets were cobbled and full of horses, the place was now an economic dead zone of boarded windows and foreclosed homes. There wasn't much to see, but the snail's pace we'd adopted made sure we wouldn't miss any of it. Glassy was looking for something, and any movement that wasn't us, or any noise above the soft roll of the tires, was primed to draw his keen attention.

"Looking for something in particular?" I asked, the first words I'd spoken since we pulled out of the spot behind the massage parlour.

Short of a stray dog or rat ripping through one of the trash bags that had failed to be collected for at least a month, each street we passed was deserted.

"I wasn't twiddling my thumbs while you were getting your rocks off," Glassy said. "I've been texting back and forth with Sean."

Sean was one of the Conroy brothers. Older or younger, I couldn't keep track.

"There's a guy we've been keeping an eye out for. He needs a talking to, and someone spotted him down The Manx. We're closest, so this one's on us."

"You make us sound like officers responding to dispatch," I commented.

"You want me to turn the flashers on?"

Glassy held up his fist and rotated it on the end of his wrist, howling like a siren. And he laughed, like a little boy playing policeman. I smiled back at him, playing along.

"We going to arrest the perp?" I joked.

"No, we're going to kick the shit out of this prick. He owes us money."

Just as quickly, Glassy was back to dead serious.

"How much?" I asked.

"Doesn't matter. It's the principle of the thing. We've carried him for long enough and now he's avoiding us. That cannot stand. A man has to face up to the debts he owes and the people he is indebted to."

Finally, after combing up and down the same few streets over and over again, scrutinizing the last-known whereabouts of the man who had provoked the ire of the Conroy brothers, there was movement: one lone pedestrian. The only one we'd seen since we bumped our way over the tangle of train tracks ten blocks back.

"That's him. That's Iggy Sloane, the miserable cocksucker," said Glassy.

"How do we handle this?" I asked too late. Glassy was already handling it. He rolled down his window and repeated his last thought. Only this time he shouted it at full volume out into the night.

"Iggy Sloane, you miserable cocksucker!"

And Iggy, unsurprisingly, bolted.

Glassy gunned the engine and raced down the street, keeping pace with his fleeing mark. The whole strip, there was nothing but wall-to-wall row houses, with not a single nook or passage to slip away. Iggy was trying to make it all the way to the next block at a full sprint. Only at the intersection would he have options, and a chance to lose the Conroy brother who had tracked him down. He was never going to be permitted to make it that far.

Glassy jerked the wheel hard and stuck the nose of his car straight in Iggy's path. Iggy barely had time to stop, slapping his hands down on the hood to keep his momentum from carrying him right over the top and off the opposite side.

In the same moment, Glassy popped out of the driver's side and observed the palm prints on the bodywork of his ride. There was no dent, only twin impressions fogging the finish, quickly fading in the cool night air.

"Did you just touch my car?" Glassy demanded. "Did you just fucking touch my car?"

"I'm sorry, Glassy! I'm so sorry! I didn't mean to..."

Glassy put Iggy on the ground with an open-hand slap across the face that sounded like a starter's pistol going off. It made me jump in my seat.

"You poked your head up for a fucking craps game, you degenerate piece of shit? You think we wouldn't hear about it?"

Iggy curled into a ball as Glassy jabbed him repeatedly with his steel-toed loafer.

"On your feet, fucker!" he demanded. "Let's do this thing! Or do you want me to curb-stomp you like the fucking cockroach you are?"

There was no fight in Iggy, only the desire to minimize the pain and damage by going into turtle mode. If Glassy wanted to throw any punches, he'd have to get down on his knees to do it, and the pants he was wearing were too expensive for that. So he satisfied himself with making his position concerning Iggy Sloane's fiscal irresponsibility clear with his feet alone. When his toes weren't stabbing hard into soft crevasses, his heel made for an effective cudgel against exposed extremities. It might have looked like he was doing a Riverdance revival with an unwilling partner if there had been music playing, and it lasted about as long as a jaunty Irish jig.

Glassy was winded once he was done. It had been a short but intense bit of cardio.

"Like I said, it's real work. Fun of a sort, but work just the same."

He looked down at Iggy Sloane and judged that maybe his lesson in economics needed to be topped up.

"You want a piece of this?" Glassy asked me, stepping back so I could have my space to add to the hurt. "Go on, you know you want to. Guy like you has to have a lot of pent-up rage. Get it out of your system."

"Who's he?" Iggy grunted, an ounce of prideful spite still left in him. "Your new butt-boy?"

"Shut up, asshole!" I shouted. "Haven't you had enough?"

"You see what I have to deal with?" Glassy said to me. "I'm a nice guy, I don't break anything, I don't cripple them, and still they get mouthy."

"I wasn't sayin' nothin' against you, Glassy," Iggy was quick to clarify. "I was talking about the faggot riding bitch with you."

Curled on the pavement, doubled over on his side, Iggy made a tempting target. I don't know what came over me, why his words riled me so, but I took a run at him and hammered my foot into the tight fold between his legs. Iggy hollered like a gutshot deer, but he didn't try to say anything smart after that. I don't think my blow left him capable of speech at all.

"Whoa! Right in the balls! You savage motherfucker!"

Glassy was laughing.

"I like to spare them a shot in the balls unless it's personal. You just made it personal. He's not gonna forget you!"

"What, like he's going to come after me for revenge?" I asked in a low voice, wondering how far I'd stepped over the line and what the ramifications might be.

"Iggy here? Nah, he's not the revenge sort. You put the fear of God in him, is all. You ever see Iggy on the street again one day, you don't look away. You stare him down and remind him he's your bitch. He'll remember you, sure enough."

Message sent and received, Glassy could cross Iggy Sloane off his to-do list—at least until he missed his next payment. I was hardly aware I'd gotten back in the car with him until we were several blocks north. Rolling over the train tracks again shook me out of my haze.

"What's our next stop?" I asked, as my senses returned.

"I was going to take you home."

I must have looked crestfallen. It wasn't that I was particularly enjoying myself. But I felt engaged, plugged into a world I always knew was there, just below the surface of civility. Movies and television exploited it, but always kept their distance. This was real, and it felt like the revelation of a secret everyone knew but only a select few understood.

"You mad-lad," Glassy grinned. "You want more, don't you?"

"This is research," I reiterated.

"We've gone past a ride-along for research purposes. You're now an accessory to assault and battery. Hell, I think you fucked up Iggy worse than I did. Congratulations, you're a criminal."

"I'm going to be writing about this world for the next eight weeks. And I learned more about what it's like in the last five minutes than I have in my whole life."

"What, you didn't get all you needed out of my bit of dinner theatre tonight?"

Glassy wasn't offended. He knew he'd been talking a lot of shit, all of it nebulous.

"You didn't want to say anything specific—anything incriminating—over dinner."

"And now you have incriminating things you won't want to get specific about the next time you're out for drinks with your work buddies."

"Exactly," I said. "I'm in it now. Or, at least, I've broken the surface. I want to know what's next."

But Glassy turned me down cold, shaking his head, trying to be the responsible adult.

"I have to let you off," he said. "There's something else that needs to get done tonight, and that's a bit of family business you want no part of."

"Show me," I countered, emboldened.

"The thing with Iggy was nothing. That was only collecting on a debt. Money owed, with all parties in agreement. This one... This is a settling of accounts and that's a whole other animal."

"You sound like you're going to go kill somebody," I said, suddenly not so eager after all. There was a limit to what I was willing to be an accessory to.

"No," Glassy was quick to say, but sounded unconvinced. "Nothing like that. I'm just saying things could get rough. Things might not go so well."

"Things got rough with Iggy."

"That? That was just some tough love. I set him straight like I would a dog that shat on a rug."

"So what is this, if not a hit?"

"A hit!" Glassy snorted. "Listen to you—a fuckin' hit!"

He had his laugh, but it was short lived. His final task of the evening was weighing on him, just beneath the good humour.

"There's a guy," he explained. "Someone else in the business, not part of our end. And there's a disagreement over a piece of property. He thinks it belongs to him and we know it belongs to us. We set a time to meet and work it out. Just the two of us. Which is why I was thinking about bringing along some backup."

"Doesn't that kind of violate the terms of a one-on-one meeting?" I said.

"Of course it does," said Glassy, like his reasoning was obvious. "That's why you do it. So it's two-on-one if things don't go so well."

I nodded like I agree or understood, and did neither.

"Normally, this would be a job for our first-born Conroy. I'd be the wingman, watching his back while he took the lead. But he has his time to do in the joint, and nobody else is available for this type of work. Maybe Maureen—and believe me, she's tougher than some of my other brothers—but she's our designated civilian and I can't get her mixed up in this kind of shit."

"I wouldn't be any use to you if it turns into a fight or worse," I said.

"This is true," Glassy agreed. "But the whole point of bringing an extra guy is so it doesn't come to that. Once he sees it'll be two-on-one if he starts something, he won't start anything at all. We can have our conversation, and everybody leaves healthy."

"What would I have to do?" I asked, hesitantly.

"Nothing at all," Glassy said firmly. "If you want to do this with me, you do it best by doing absolutely nothing. Remember, he doesn't know you. You're an unknown element. So you just stand there, like you're a mean son of a bitch who can handle himself, and he'll have to assume you're not to be fucked with."

Glassy's version of nothing sounded like a tall order.

"I'm a writer, not an actor," I protested.

"You write for actors, don't you?"

"Well, yeah."

"You act all their parts in your head when you're writing them down, don't you?"

"Kind of, I guess."

"You're an actor," he declared. "Just don't make up any dialogue. You let me do the talking."

"What are you going to say to him?" I asked.

"Not a damn thing," said Glassy. "I'm going to imply. I'll be implying my ass off."

"Implying what?" I said, afraid of the answer.

"Consequences."

"So a threat."

"The threat will work," he assured me. "I'm good with the threats."

Glassy slowed the car to a halt at a stop sign and waited too long. There was no traffic to challenge us, but he left the car idling. After a few moments of consideration, he reached for something tucked under his belt, in the small of his back, hidden by his suit jacket.

"But just in case..." he added, and withdrew a snub-nose revolver.

"Of course you have a gun," I said, fidgeting in the passenger seat and averting my eyes from the weapon.

"No shit I have a gun," said Glassy. "But this isn't my gun. This is your gun."

He held it out for me to take and I made no move to do so.

"You've shot a gun, right?" he asked me as an afterthought.

"Sure," I said. "In video games."

Glassy looked sickened.

"Jesus H. Motherfuck. What are you, ten years old? You never handled a piece before?"

"A toy gun maybe, when I was a kid. Never had a real one in my hand."

"Fucking Hollywood liberals, man."

"I've never worked in Hollywood. Most of my jobs are out of Toronto."

My feeble defence didn't impress Glassy.

"Even worse," he said. "Here, grow a pair and grab hold of this."

He held out the snub-nose for me so insistently, I was compelled to take it.

"Is it loaded?" I asked, looking down at the hunk of metal in my hand, feeling its heft.

"It's a paperweight if it isn't loaded. Of course it's loaded."

Glassy shut off the car engine and got out, leaving it parked in the middle of the road. There was nobody around to be inconvenienced by its position. I opened my door and followed his lead, knowing better than to ask what he had in mind. He'd let me know soon enough.

"Over there," he said, jutting his chin at an empty lot behind a vacant garage.

Glassy walked across the road to the kitty-corner and checked out the rusted corrugated-steel fence that had failed to keep anybody off the property. Topped off with barbed wire, there was no need to climb it. Several panels of the fence were missing, and it was easy enough to duck under and squeeze through.

The lot behind the garage was a collection of car parts uncommon enough to have once been worth setting aside. The years and weather had not been kind to them, and everything was too corroded to be of any use to anyone outside of a scrap-metal dealer interested in their melt value.

"Let's pop that cherry," said Glassy. "Aim it and squeeze one off."

The revolver hung at my side. My grip was loose, and my finger was consciously far from the trigger.

"Aim it at what?" I asked stupidly.

"At something you'd like to shoot."

"What if somebody hears the shot and calls the police?"

"Who gives a fuck? We'll be long gone by the time any uniforms respond."

If this was a training session, at least it would be a short one.

There was an empty oil drum across the lot from me. There were already a lot of holes in it. Adding one more wouldn't harm anything. Plus I thought it was a big enough target I might actually hit it. A man-sized target.

No sooner did I have the gun levelled than I lowered it again and turned to Glassy.

"Shouldn't we be wearing protective gear?" I asked, think-ing of all the shooting-range footage I'd ever seen, real or fictional. "Like goggles or noise-cancelling headphones?"

"We should," Glassy nodded sagely, and made no move whatsoever to magically summon these items into existence. He only kept staring at me until I felt ashamed and unmanly for even bringing it up.

I raised the gun again and supported my wrist with my other hand like I'd seen TV cops do countless times. If my form was wrong, Glassy offered no suggestions or criticism.

Remembering to squeeze, not pull, I slowly applied pres-sure to the trigger. I ignored the hammer as it drew back, keeping focus on the front sight at the end of the short barrel instead. Just when I thought nothing was going to happen, the hammer snapped back and the gun went off with a sharp crack. A new hole appeared in the side of the oil drum a dozen paces away, sounding a single discordant note that echoed out of the empty cavity.

"Oh shit!" I exclaimed in surprise.

"Feels good, right?" Glassy smiled.

"Yeah," I agreed.

"Pop off a couple more."

Emboldened, I took aim at the drum and plugged it twice more. I wouldn't claim my shot grouping was tight, but I was on target, which seemed promising for a novice.

"Jesse Fuckin' James," Glassy approved. "You *were* aiming at the drum, right?"

"What can I say? It looked at me funny."

"Then I guess he had it coming."

I took aim like I might start blasting away again, but Glassy stopped me before I got too trigger happy.

"Okay, that's enough. Think you got a feel for it now?"

"I guess."

"You better. You've got three more shots to see you through. I didn't bring any extra cartridges, so if you have to blow your load, make them count."

"I'm not shooting a gun at anybody."

"Of course not," agreed Glassy. "But if you do, you get three chances to be on target. After that..."

Glassy shrugged, considering my limited options.

"Fuckin' run, I guess."

"What if you need to reload?" I asked as we headed back to the car. I figured Glassy must have a box of ammo in the glove compartment, or hidden away in the trunk.

"You think I get into gunfights every day? Outside of target practice, I've never had to fire more than one shot at a time. And that was usually a warning shot to get somebody's attention. This isn't the wild west. This is business."

"Business with guns," I pointed out.

"Same as a security guard," said Glassy. "Same as a cop. Only we do less shooting than those murderous fucks because the law isn't on our side when we start throwing lead around."

Any hope I had that the meeting between Glassy and his territorial rival would happen in a public place, like a coffee shop or a mid-town square always full of people regardless of the hour, were dashed when the next leg of our drive took us to an empty warehouse wedged between the highway and an industrial park in the north end. There was no night watchman patrolling the grounds—no sign of life at all. When he pulled over to the curb, Glassy did so half a block away and on the opposite side of the street. We sat in silence, observing the dark building for several long minutes, like we were on a stakeout.

Glassy checked his watch. It was meet time. Keeping a bunch of film-industry peons waiting was one thing, but gangsters don't appreciate other gangsters being fashionably late. We needed make a move, but I could feel Glassy's reticence.

"This part is no fun at all," he said. "Not unless you're hired muscle with a mean streak. The ones who are always looking for a fight, always ready to put the hurt on, always looking to provoke something into happening—even if it doesn't need to. I don't like to keep those guys on the payroll. You never know what fucked-up shit they're going to do next, to escalate things, to get their fix. This sort of situation is best settled with family, friends. They know what needs to get done and how far to take it."

"You think this might get...well, you know."

"I sure as shit hope not," he said. "You remember when I told you the only thing that works better than violence is extreme violence?"

I nodded. How could I forget?

"There's one thing that works better than extreme violence."

"What's that?" I said, afraid to ask.

"The threat of extreme violence," said Glassy. "It still gets you what you want, but nobody gets hurt, nobody gets dead, and nobody has to go to prison forever."

"This is the thing you're going to imply?" I confirmed.

"That's Plan A."

"And if it doesn't work?"

"Then there's going to be violence, and we all hope it doesn't have to get extreme."

My heart was pounding out of my chest as we approached the warehouse and let ourselves in through a service entrance that had been left unlocked. Down a drab corridor, featuring one door to an office and another to a break room, we came out onto the stock floor that was currently stocked with nothing at all. Only a man.

The man was big. Not huge, but solid, like he not only kept himself fit, but actively sought to bulk up. The muscles he'd sculpted were tightly tucked into a tailored suit that advertised the fact that he was successful as well as in shape. The tie around his neck was almost as shiny as the gold chain around Glassy's. He restricted his garish jewellery to one hand, which sported a Rolex and three different gold rings. I didn't doubt they were all genuine. This guy was the real deal, in both the image he projected and the danger he presented to Glassy's interests.

He heard us come in, but didn't feel threatened enough by our presence to even turn around. Instead he kept admiring the wide open space he'd been inspecting—the point of contention between him, whoever he represented, and the Conroy brothers.

"It's a sweet spot," he declared. "A well-positioned asset."

He looked beyond the plain industrial walls of the warehouse to the possibilities that lay beyond, to the north and south, and the money that was to be made.

"Trucks leave the plants over there, hit the on-ramp to the highway a stone's throw away there. And in between, all this nice empty space to fill with the skim. The trucks barely have to slow down as they pass through on their way from manufacturing to market."

"I know it," agreed Glassy. "That's why we took it."

"You took it all right," said the man in the brilliant tie. "You took it from me. And I'm taking it back."

Glassy opened his mouth to counter that point and was interrupted before he could speak. Not a sign of respect.

"That's not an ask," the man cautioned. "Not a request. It's a statement of fact. So you and your brothers can go look for another property, away from me and my skim. And then we'll have no problems, you and I. It's as simple as that."

He sounded like he was making a magnanimous offer, but Glassy wasn't having any of it.

"Zane Russet defaulted on his loan," he said. "That's money owed us. And if there's no money forthcoming, then the property he bought with that money belongs to us."

"We loaned money to that piece of shit on our end, too," countered the man. "More money than you. And that gives us a controlling interest. You want a buyout? Maybe we can throw a few bucks your way so there's no hard feelings."

"I'm here to negotiate in good faith," Glassy said. "But what's a bit of money when this place is a licence to print it? A buyout doesn't amount to shit."

"Ah, so you're here to negotiate in good faith?" said the man. "That why you came alone like we agreed?"

I bristled at the mention of my presence but tried not to react. Until that moment, I'd felt invisible—present but unacknowledged and unimportant. I stood still, as instructed, like I belonged there and could handle myself. The gun must have made for a distinct bulge in my jacket pocket, and I was acutely aware of it dragging me down. It felt like fifty extra pounds that would have me on the floor if my knees gave out. They were already shaking under my pant legs, threatening to turn noodle on me.

"Who the fuck's he?" demanded the man. "Another one of your brothers? I can never keep them all straight, there's so goddamn many of them."

"He's not a brother," said Glassy coldly.

"Half-brother then? Did Daddy Conroy go spilling his Irish cream ale around town? Or maybe the postman had it in for your mom."

Only schoolyard kids get upset by that kind of yo-momma bullshit insult. Anyone much past puberty outgrows it, ignores it, laughs it off as the immature, idiotic attempt to push buttons it is. Nobody else takes that kind of thing seriously.

Only schoolyard kids. And gangsters.

Glassy closed the space between him and his rival in seconds. He didn't have a gun out, only a finger, but he wielded it like it was just as deadly. Jabbing it into the man's chest, squarely into his expensive tie, he was about to let loose with all those threatening implications he had at the ready. The promises of violence, extreme or otherwise. Before he could rattle off a single one, the man's hand struck like a coiled snake. Glassy's poked, point-making finger was gripped tightly in his fist in an instant. Once he'd twisted it back sharply, Glassy was forced to fall to his knees to keep it from breaking. The man's other hand shot out and had him around the throat a second later.

Any point he wanted to make to counter Glassy's was purely physical. He had a message to send. This wouldn't be to Glassy himself. This would be to his brothers. And the message would be Glassy's body, with the life squeezed out of it.

There had been a miscalculation somewhere along the way. Maybe bringing backup was interpreted as a sign of weakness. Or maybe my feeble tough-guy impression had been transparent to an actual tough guy. Either way, I was ignored as utterly inconsequential as the man struggled with Glassy.

The fight was all one-sided. Glassy got off the floor and kicked at the man's shins like he was trying to chop down a mighty oak, but there was no perceivable effect. Even his best shots failed to elicit so much as a wince.

An attempt to worm his way out of his adversary's iron grip went badly for Glassy. He managed to twist around so his throat was no longer in a choke hold but, presenting the back of his neck, the choke was easily resumed when the man took hold of Glassy's necklace and yanked it back hard, digging the links into his flesh. A quality piece of bling, a well-made chain, it didn't break. Up to this moment, it had been an expensive fashion accessory. Now it was a garrote, strangling its owner.

Unable to get his fingers under the chain to relieve the pressure, give himself some slack, Glassy used his last bit of breath to bark a raspy order at me.

"Use it! Fucking use it!"

And, to my credit, I didn't freeze.

Getting the gun out of my pocket was an arduous affair that took an extra few seconds that felt like an hour. Once it was clear though, I didn't hesitate. My arm shot straight up, and so did the bullet I launched from the barrel. It was a warning shot, fired into the ceiling.

I thought it would be a prudent opening move. I didn't want to escalate things, only slow them down, and maybe get the two gangsters caught in a life-or-death struggle to resume more civil negotiations.

If either of them even heard the shot, they didn't act like they had. Their determination to kill each other continued unabated. And Glassy was coming out at the bottom of the dispute—decisively so.

There's something in conflict that binds men together beyond simple camaraderie. It's a bond that forms naturally, instinctually. Cultivated by eons of evolution, such bonds have made men with nothing in common into effective fighting units since the beginning of time. In short order, it could make them fight for each other and die for each other. From the days of pitching spears at woolly mammoths in hunting parties, to the years of facing the meat grinder of trench warfare as soldiers, they did so together.

I'd known Glassy for a single evening. He was a criminal who probably deserved what he was getting. And he'd said it himself: I wasn't his brother. We weren't friends. It would be a stretch to even call us acquaintances. But in a few short hours, we'd been through a strange sort of adversity, a string of encounters and misdeeds so far out of my normal realm of experience, the night had felt like a month-long ordeal. And, so help me, I felt the bond.

Was it enough to kill for him? In that moment, the most primitive instincts in the least evolved parts of my brain said yes.

The next shot I took was aimed squarely at the man who was murdering my acquaintance, my friend, my brother, Glassy Conroy.

And I missed. By a lot. So did the next shot. It wasn't the same as gunning down an oil drum. Not at all.

I'd pulled the trigger on the next three spent chambers by the time I realized I was empty. But even out of ammunition, I was still armed with a weapon. It was an all-but-useless hunk of metal with no bullets, but sometimes you just have to go with what you have.

I crossed that empty warehouse floor like I was floating. I never felt myself take a single step. My tunnel vision shut everything out of my line of sight except for my target: the back of that big gangster's head.

I didn't hit him with the grip of the revolver—I smashed the whole gun fame into his skull, making a sizable dent where the cylinder landed. He released his grip on Glassy's chain at once as the shock of the blow rippled through his whole body. Glassy scrambled out from under him like an animal released from a trap, wheezing and sputtering as he found the oxygen his body had been longing for.

The man remained hunched over, but didn't go down right away, so I let him have another. That one put him on the floor. Terrified he might get up and try to do to me what he'd been doing to Glassy throughout their last minute of combat, I put my knees into his back and brought the gun down yet again, as hard as I could.

As I wound up for a fourth blow, my hand came away wet. I didn't let it distract me and redoubled the force behind my final swing. That one satisfied me, and I left him face down on the concrete. His muscles twitched and spasmed, but there seemed to be no coordination behind it. He wasn't getting up or moving in any meaningful way.

I backed off, staring at my handiwork, until I'd put half the length of the floor space between us.

By then, Glassy had recovered enough to inspect my work. He was coughing, trying to clear his throat, but other than the red gouge around his neck, he seemed to be fine.

"Is he dead?" I asked.

"He ain't well," said Glassy.

He leaned down for a closer look. There were no more twitches forthcoming.

"Yeah, that'll do him," concluded Glassy. "I think you put bits of skull through his brain."

I took a deep, quivering breath and let it out slowly. A couple more and my head started to clear.

"I seen guys get capped before," said Glassy. "And I seen guys get pistol whipped. I have not seen anyone get killed with blunt force trauma from a goddamn handgun. That was some crazy shit."

I looked at the gory hunk of metal I held in my open palm. And the blood all over my hand, dripping. Strands of matted hair were stuck in the mechanism of the revolver and twisted around my fingers.

"I knew you were a stand-up guy," said Glassy. "First day on the job and you made your bones. You know how long it took me to make my bones? It wasn't day one, that's for fuckin' sure. It wasn't even year one. And when I did, you know what happened? I puked my goddamn guts out."

Being sick sounded like a good idea. But I held it in. I didn't want Glassy to see me lose it.

"Who was he?" I asked.

"Competition," said Glassy.

"I mean, what was his name?"

"What's it matter now?"

"I want to know."

"You engraving his tombstone?"

"I want to know who I killed."

"No you don't. You don't need to put a name to your bad memories."

"Maybe it won't be such a bad memory."

I was still high on adrenaline. There was no guilt or remorse. Not yet at least. I wondered when those emotions would hit me, and how long the thrill would last. I felt invigorated, even elated. Glassy could see it.

"You really are a savage motherfucker," he said.

"What do we do now?" I asked, as the edges of reality started to seep back in.

"We leave. The property's burned. It was an asset, now it's a crime scene. We don't own it, we have no connection to it, we never even heard of it."

"What about the body? Do we, you know, dispose of it or something?"

"You're not putting that disgusting mess in my car," Glassy said. "No, the body stays here for the police to find."

"The police?" I practically shouted. "They'll comb the whole place for evidence! What happens if they trace this back to me?"

My elation was vanishing quickly, replaced with dread and creeping panic.

"The cops aren't going to trace shit," Glassy said. His tone was confident, dismissive. "Did you touch anything? No. Did you scatter a bunch of clues and personal belongings around? No."

"But there's always fibres, DNA..."

"They're not gonna find any of that shit, are you kidding me? Do you even have a record, with your prints and DNA on file somewhere?"

I considered the handful of parking tickets I got when I used to drive and thought better of mentioning those petty infractions to Glassy.

"But..." I protested, "I've got blood all over me."

"That washes off."

"And my clothes," I added, looking at the spatter that had soaked in up one sleeve. There were probably more droplets—on my shirt, my pants, my shoes—I had yet to spot.

"Run them through a couple of cycles. If the stains don't come out, throw them away. Do not," he added firmly, "take any of that shit to a dry cleaner."

"I don't know, Glassy," I said, thinking about all the different ways this could go wrong for me. "I think I'm fucked."

"Look," he said, explaining things slowly, calmly, from experience, "this is how it'll play out. The cops are going to come in here, take some pictures, identify the body, and find out who turned up dead. And their reaction to that will be: good! Another dirtbag they'll never have to arrest and process again. 'The victim was known to police,' is what the papers will say, somewhere around page eight, and they'll never mention it again. The cops will want to talk to a dozen different guys in the know who might have had something against this asshole. I might be on that list. If I get the call, I'll go down to the cop shop one day to tell them I don't know nothin'. My lawyer will be there to tell them to fuck off if they try probing any deeper than that. And then it's over."

"They keep murder files open for a hundred years," I said, remembering past readings on the subject.

"Sure they do. But nobody gives a shit after a week."

"I'll give a shit."

"And that's something you'll have to live with for the rest of your life."

I must have looked glum at that notion.

"Living with it is easy," Glassy said. "You just have remind yourself from time to time that it was you or him."

"But it wasn't, was it?" I said. "It was *you* or him."

"Well thanks for choosing right. But do you really think he would have let you walk out of here after you watched him kill me? Not a chance in hell."

I still wasn't feeling the guilt I thought I should be feeling. But paranoia—there was plenty of that. It would stick to me for years, and keep me looking over my shoulder for a long time.

Now that I was done with the revolver, I tried to return it to Glassy.

"I do not want that back," he said, observing the soiled weapon. "That's a keeper for you. You tuck that away someplace safe. I'd recommend the bottom of the river."

On our way out, Glassy gave the door handle a thorough wipe with the sleeve of his jacket, making sure to smear any fingerprints we may have left on it beyond recognition.

"So whereabouts do you live?" he asked, as we walked back to the car.

"Up near Grosvenor Park," I said.

"That's a long walk, but you should make it by sun up."

"You're making me walk home?"

"I can't have you back in my car," Glassy apologized. "DNA."

"I thought you said DNA didn't matter."

"DNA all over *you* doesn't matter. But I'll be a person of interest. If the cops get lucky with a judge, they might land a warrant that'll let them snoop through my ride with a black-light, a microscope, and a fucking sniffer dog."

Glassy let himself into the car on the driver's side. He left the passenger door locked, but rolled down the window opposite him so he could lean over and talk to me.

"So, Hemingway, you'll put in a good word on Jack's behalf, right?" he said. "You'll do that for me. For your pal, Glassy."

"Sure Glassy," I said, standing alone in the middle of the road. "I'll put in a word."

"Okay then. We good? No more questions about things that were said or things that were done tonight?"

I did have a question. But it was personal, unrelated.

"Why do they call you 'Glassy'?"

For all the specifics he didn't want to get into over dinner, this seemed like a particularly taboo subject, not for the ears of an outsider. It gave him pause. And then he told me anyway.

"My oldest brother, William—the one in the can right now—he always said he could see right through me. Like a piece of glass."

"Okay," I said. That was acknowledgement enough.

Glassy started the engine.

"You gonna write about me in your show?" was a parting afterthought.

"I'll be drawing on you for inspiration when it comes to certain characters," I said.

"Do me good."

"I'll be fair."

"Am I gonna be a bad guy?"

"You'll be layered. Complex."

"Nah," he said, considering the likely outcome, "I think I'll be a bad guy. The TV don't like guys like me to get away with nothin'."

"Well, any resemblance to people living or dead is purely coincidental."

"What's that bullshit?"

"Just some legalese ass-covering we say in the business."

"Sure, sure," Glassy said. "But be careful my ass gets covered, too. Like if you ever feel a compulsion to write about anything that went down tonight..."

"I won't," I said firmly.

"But if you do," said Glassy, "make sure I'm dead first."

The passenger-side window rose back into the empty space and reflected my haggard, tired face back at me. I spent the next few minutes watching Glassy's car recede, far down the straightaway service road that ran next to the highway, before he made a sharp left turn and was gone from my sight.

Then I attempted the long walk home, in shoes that were all wrong for that kind of a hike, afraid to call a cab or take a night bus for fear that someone might notice the blood stains. My heels were a blistered shredded mess by the time I walked up the path to my house. The sun was coming up, but it was too early for any witnesses other than paperboys and crack-of-dawn joggers to spot me. None of them looked at me twice, and my wife wouldn't be up for work for another hour.

I didn't try to wash any of the clothes I'd been wearing that night. Everything went straight into a garbage bag that went out with the next trash pickup. The gun was another matter. That I washed off in the sink, scrubbing out every crevasse until the nickel plating shone, and it looked new enough to have just come off the factory assembly line.

I thought many times about taking it for a walk out to the middle of our city's lone suspension bridge and tossing it over the side. Instead, I kept it on my desk, next to my computer, for the next six weeks, as I worked on the first draft of the miniseries. And the two weeks after that, while I was rereading and editing. The only thing I disposed of were the empty casings of the six rounds I'd fired off. They were tossed down a sewer a good thirty blocks away from home while I was out at a meeting for another TV show that was supposed to be a go in the spring.

At the back end of my eight-week deadline, I went down to the production office of *Mobbed Up* to hear the first round of notes and to weigh in on certain development decisions, like my opinion actually mattered to anybody. Casting was the main topic of discussion, and the conference table was littered with headshots of every available Irish actor, as well as every Jewish or Italian actor who could pass for Irish. My input on this process, I knew from experience, was only welcome if I was backing up the position of one of the producers, debating the merits of one actor over another with his partners. Forwarding my own suggestions as the writer would be politely tolerated at best, then ignored.

Nevertheless, when the focus switched from supporting cast to who should be our lead, I was compelled to interject.

"It has to be Baby Conroy," I said suddenly.

"Jack," said my story editor, once he consulted the audition sheet before him. "Jack Conroy?"

"He's our guy," I repeated with conviction.

"You sound awfully sure," said Ryan Monahan, like I was overstepping my bounds. Which I was. And we all knew it.

"I saw his tape."

"A toothpaste ad and two one-liners. The most screen time he's had was playing a corpse on an autopsy table in one of those cookie-cutter police procedurals."

"The Miami one?" asked one of the lackeys from the broadcaster who was sitting in, keeping an eye on the investment.

"Phoenix, I think," posited an office minion.

"Nah, it was the Detroit one," interjected the director, who had been signed only a week earlier. "You could tell because everything was tinted blue. Blue is the tint for the Detroit one."

"Whatever," said Ryan. "He was a convincing corpse, sure. Really solid with the not-breathing part. But other than that..."

"Look," I said, "he knows this life. He grew up around it and he knows these guys like his own family. Some of them *are* family. He was nearly our Robbie for real. He can play this part, I know it. He'll play it and he'll nail it like nobody else can."

The film and television industry is filled with people who second-guess themselves all day long. Nobody knows for sure what's going to work, and mostly they're all terrified of making a wrong decision that will cost them their jobs. When they run up against someone with conviction, they stop and wonder if they actually know what they're talking about. Conviction puts doubt in their heads and fear in their hearts. Conviction can win arguments, even when there's nothing to back it up, and it comes from a place of little or no power.

"There's a part for half a page in the second act," Ryan said after a few moments of consideration, when I didn't back down or waver. He flipped through the first dozen pages of the script in front of him randomly. "Who was it now? Colin the Shitkicker. A few lines of dialogue, a bit of physicality. I like him for that."

"We can do better," I said, staring him in the eye.

"He can't be Robbie," said Ryan, as conviction butted heads with practical reality. "He's nobody. We need a name for Robbie."

"How about Robbie's best friend?" I compromised. "I think he'd be a perfect Quinn."

"Yeah. Yeah, I can see him as Quinn," Ryan said, picturing the on-screen dynamic. "It's a few scenes. Nothing too taxing. A car bombing at the top of episode two and we've already shot him out."

"Quinn goes up in a blaze of glory and a star is born," agreed the broadcaster rep. "He'll get more work out of that role."

"It'll certainly add some sizzle to his sizzle reel," noted the casting director.

"Especially when Robbie takes a look inside that body bag," the story editor weighed in. "Love that scene, by the way."

Everybody loved that scene. So much so, maybe I wouldn't have to rewrite it death.

"Yeah, I think this will work," said Ryan, and immediately moved to make it happen, instructing the casting director. "Put a call in to Jack Conroy's agent and say we want him for the Quinn part. Offer scale. Do not go higher than plus twenty percent. This is a big break for him. Remind the mouthpiece he wants us more than we want him."

"But we're going to get him, right?" I made sure to confirm.

"Of course. But we'll get him on the cheap. That's half his appeal."

Before the month was out, the cast was signed and locked—Jack Conroy included. That's when the news came to me in a roundabout way.

"Did you hear about the hit?" Howard Kellen asked me, after cornering me at one of those industry gatherings everyone wants to be seen at and nobody ever actually wants to go to.

I thought he was crowing about the animated children's movie that had premiered at a festival the week before. His name was on it somewhere, and it had been picked up for foreign and domestic distribution by one of the big players in L.A. That didn't mean it was going to be a hit, or even a moderate box-office success, but it was always fair game to brag about your movie in that narrow window of opportunity, before it came out and had a chance to bomb. Before it got swept under the résumé rug and forgotten.

"Which hit is this?" I said, playing dumb, not wanting to give Howard any credit for his pending possible success. Turns out I really was dumb. I'd missed the story entirely, but Howard was happy to tell it to me with a certain strange glee that came with being the bearer of dark tidings.

I had to dig the details out of a recycling bin once I was back home. It wasn't page-one news, but it was in the A-section. The headline called him Gerard, but it was Glassy all right. His mug shot had made the papers one last time. The family would probably choose a better photo of him to run with the obituary. Details about what had happened were sparse, but it had been a hit all right. Automatic gunfire, sprayed across his property, had woken up Glassy's neighbours late one night. If they hadn't known or suspected what he and his brothers did for a living, there was no doubt now that he was dead. The police were still picking through the grass of his front lawn, looking for shell casings that would probably never lead to an arrest.

The imprecise copy hit the usual clichéd terminology you always see in such articles. The victim was "known to police," the incident was a "settling of affairs," the murder was "likely gang related." Only one detail was clear. The gunmen had shot Glassy so full of holes, you could see right through him.

I followed the story closely after that, making sure to pick through the daily crime-report featurette carefully before stuffing any old news into the green box. There wasn't much to see beyond the notification of a funeral and memorial I didn't attend. If the Conroy brothers had enacted any retribution for the slaying of one of their kin, no bodies turned up.

Last I heard, Glassy's widow had filed for financial compensation under the Victims-of-Violence Act. Her husband had, after all, been a victim of violent crime. You should have heard the talk-radio lines light up about that one. The outrage that beamed off the broadcast tower will float out into infinity. Maybe one day the signal will get picked up by some space aliens, long after the human race is extinct. They won't understand a word of it, but it will make their ears bleed.

It was six more months, eight more drafts, and three more polishes before principal photography on *Mobbed Up* began. I visited the set on the first day because writers are welcome to do that much before making themselves scarce for the rest of the shoot.

As I wandered down the row of white trailers that took up every parking space that had been reserved along a busy city street for the next few days of location shooting, I spotted a familiar face. I didn't recognize Jack Conroy from his head-shot. He was the spitting image of Glassy—what Glassy might have looked like ten years ago, before his business started to make him hard. At any rate, he was certainly a Conroy. I went over to introduce myself.

"I knew your brother," I told him, after handshakes and a few polite words that didn't mean much.

The familiar snicker of Howard Kellen somewhere behind me made my skin crawl. He probably thought I was bragging, building myself up, and maybe I was. As far as Howard knew, my entire interaction with Glassy Conroy had been over a meal and had ended with the after-dinner mints. He knew nothing of the lift home, and he never would.

"You're the writer, aren't you?" Jack stated more than asked. It felt like he already knew me. Actors are good at making you feel like that. At least the talented ones with a future are.

"Yeah, all those pages came off of these fingers," I admitted.

By then the script had been turned into a rainbow of pink, blue, yellow, orange, and green pages, each colour signifying a new draft with new changes that were only there to justify somebody's job. So many people got to weigh in with notes that needed to be addressed with in-name-only fixes, the story had become unfamiliar to me. The words on the page no longer felt like my own. I doubted I'd ever bother to watch the show when it aired.

"Oh yeah," Jack said, "the screenplay. Sure sure, nice work. It's a great part. Thanks so much."

It was the usual thing you'll hear from an actor. Always insincere. The dialogue you wrote for them, the character you built, is only ever just a thin skeleton. They're the ones who will put meat on the bones. The final rewrite.

"But that's not what I meant," Jack continued. "You're the writer who was with Glassy. That night."

"The night things were said," I echoed from an old conversation.

"Said and done," Jack nodded.

"He mentioned me?"

"He said you were a stand-up guy."

I didn't know how much Jack, the one civilian brother, knew. And I didn't want to.

"I was glad to be there for him," I said, steering wide of anything more specific. "I was sorry to hear what happened."

"It's the life he lived," Jack said sadly. "The life he chose. He got a few more months of it, thanks to you. But it was only a matter of time. It catches up with all of them in the end. That's why I chose different."

"I hope this role does well for you," I said sincerely.

"My agent has been getting calls. He says there's buzz."

"I'm glad."

I asked after his sister, and as many other Conroys as I could remember by name. There wasn't much else that needed saying, and before we could run out of pleasantries, Jack was called to set for the next take.

"Look at you, cozying up to Al Capone Junior," Howard said, once Jack was gone and there was no one else to hear his snide remarks. "It's like you're a regular friend of the family."

"Hey Howard," I said pleasantly, like a close industry associate, a work friend, an office buddy. "Could you do me a super-big favour?"

"Yeah, sure, I guess," he said.

"Could you go fuck yourself?"

"What?" Howard asked, like he hadn't heard me. Or like he heard me, but was having trouble deciphering the meaning of the words in that sentence.

I turned around and locked eyes with him, invading his space, challenging his understanding of the world and how things worked. The glare I gave him was so intense, he winced.

"Go. Fuck. Yourself," I repeated in a tone that made it clear I would not be repeating myself again. It sounded like an order. A command that was to be obeyed. And Howard shrunk like a whipped dog. A bitch. *My* bitch.

Whatever he said next was muttered, stammered. Something about him being needed urgently elsewhere. That somewhere else seemed to be the space between the makeup and wardrobe trailers, where he could hide and I wouldn't see him. I let him crawl away, glad to be rid of him.

That night I went home and turned on my computer to do some writing for the first time since I'd handed in my final draft. The revolver Glassy had given me lay resting next to the monitor, still shiny under the desk lamp. A weapon once, a paperweight now. I didn't click on the icon for my screenwriting software. Instead I loaded up a regular old word processor. Nothing fancy, just a workhorse for text, for prose. For literature.

My fingers caressed the keyboard. Words appeared on the screen. They flowed out of me naturally, without worry, without consideration, without hesitation or inhibition.

And I wrote whatever the hell I wanted to write.

Acknowledgements

The author wishes to thank Michael Brodie, Ellie Presner, and Alex Ruaux for not calling the police when they first read the stories contained herein. Due to their judicious restraint, I remain at large and ready to reoffend.

About the Author

Shane Simmons is an award-winning screenwriter and graphic novelist whose work has appeared in international film festivals, museums, and lectures about design and structure. His art has been discussed in multiple books and academic journals about sequential storytelling, and his short stories have been printed in critically praised anthologies of history, crime, and horror. He was born in Lachine, a suburb of Montreal best known for being massacred in 1689 and having a joke name.

Also by Shane Simmons

Novels

Necropolis
Epitaph
Sex Tape
Filmography

Collections

Raw and Other Stories

Booklets

Carrion Luggage
Choke the Chicken
Hot Pennies
The Red Baron: An Ace for the Ages

Graphic Novels

The Long and Unlearned Life of Roland Gethers
The Failed Promise of Bradley Gethers
The Inauspicious Adventures of Filson Gethers

Author's Note

Small-press publishers rely on reviews from readers like you to help get the word out about their books. Whether it's a simple star rating or a written critique, every bit of feedback helps convince the impersonal computer algorithms of Amazon, and other literary outlets, that the book you just read has merit and deserves more exposure. Please support independent authors, editors, and publishers by taking a few moments to share your thoughts and opinions with other potential readers who may be sitting on the fence about trying an intriguing novel or collection. Your suggestions or comments can make all the difference when it comes to helping them find a new writer they'll like, or matching a struggling author with the readership he or she deserves. Thank you.